GEMINI TWINS

Jonathan P. Brazee

Semper Fi Press

A Semper Fi Press Book

ISBN-13 978-1-945743-38-2 (Semper Fi Press)
ISBN-10: 1-945743-38-7

Printed in the United States of America
January 22, 2020

Acknowledgements:
I want to thank all those who took the time to pre-read this book, catching my mistakes in both content and typing. I want to thank Kelly O'Donnell, James Caplan, Micky Cocker, Audrey Rich, and Allison Rich. Any remaining typos and inaccuracies are solely my fault.

Original Cover Art by Almaz Sharipov

Dedicated on their first birthday to my own "Aires" twins, Danika Dawn and Darika Marie.
You bring sunshine into my life.

North Las Vegas, Nevada
January 22, 2020

GEMINI TWINS

Chapter 1
Nika

It was a warm and sunny morning the day the twin's world fell apart.

"Race you!" Rika shouted, breaking into a sprint.

"No fair," her twin, Nika yelled with a laugh as she chased her down the worn trail to the pool in Morales Creek.

With school in its mid-summer break, Rika and Nika Ingersoll had gotten up early, packed a lunch, and jogged down the path to join the rest of the Young Guns Pack down on the creek. This was their world—no adults allowed. Not that many adults would tramp around the Morales farm and fight the thickets and scrub-thorns to get to the worn bare dirt between the rocks and above the deep pool in the creek. But over the last few years, it had given the group of now mostly high school seniors a feeling of control to have the place to themselves.

Their last summer vacation would soon be over, and then the group would break up to start their senior year, go to uni, tech school, get a job, or enlist in the military, their lives captured by the adult world. That made it imperative that they grasp every last opportunity to enjoy their youth like this.

The twins made sure that they did, cajoling, threatening, and begging so that they all held onto their childhood just a little bit longer. Adulthood would come soon enough. Already a few of them had drifted off. Lonnie and Nick, for two, already in the deep throes of love and too "mature," as they put it, to gather with the rest by the creek.

Not that Nika never thought of romance. Take Fel. Cute and funny, he had possibilities, but there would be time for that later. There were a lot of people in the Regency, and Nika wasn't going to settle on one of their small group just because he was handy. Still, it wouldn't hurt to get a little practice in before she went out into the galaxy.

The twins were the first ones there, dropping their packs in unison on the shelf, bent over to catch their breath from the sprint.

1

Neither one of them had won the race, coming in at the same time. Which was par for the course. The twins were evenly matched, and they did everything together.

Tall trees leaned over them, giving shelter from the rising sun. Over the pool, however, the sun's rays already reached into the clear water. Nika loved the place with all her heart—Rika, not as much. For Rika, the day was being with the rest of their crew. Nika would be happy just to spend the day alone at the quiet creek.

Alone meant without the others, not without Rika. The twins were inseparable, and Nika couldn't imagine being without her sister.

Their much-loved Grandma Dellie dabbled in the ancient astrological signs, and she insisted that since the two were Geminis, they were "double twins," closer than most. Nika didn't know about that. She just knew how she and Rika felt about each other.

"I'm going to miss this," Rika said.

"We'll be back for semester break," Nika reminded her.

"But not with everyone, not like this. An era is passing."

"And into a new era. You and me, uni students together."

"Together forever. But for now, if this is our last hoorah with the gang, let's make it an epic day," Rika said.

Leaving their packs where they fell, they both stepped up to the edge of the shelf, two meters above the water. Morales Creek wasn't that big, and in most places, it ranged from ankle to knee-deep as its crystal waters coursed down from the hills. At this bend, however, the rocks formed a pool about twenty meters long and almost three meters deep in the middle.

The water looked inviting, cool and clear. A little too cool now, maybe, but as the sun warmed up, it would feel good.

"It's so peaceful here," Nika said, just soaking in the view.

There was a rush from behind them. The twins started to wheel around, but before Nika could complete the turn, strong arms grabbed her, cutting off her shriek of alarm and lifting her off the ground.

"No, no!" she screamed, kicking back with her heels. They connected but didn't do much. At only seventy-seven pounds, she didn't have much force behind them.

Beside her, Rika was in full attack mode, flailing away at her captor, but just as ineffectively.

"Let me go!" Nika shouted, trying to free her arms. "Let me go!"

It was no use. Whoever had her was much bigger and much stronger, and anger filled Nika. She was sick and tired of being so small, of being weaker than everyone else. And now, she was paying the price.

Her captor moved to the edge of the ledge, dangling her over the water below.

"Don't you—"

She might as well have saved her breath. Her captor threw her out over the pool, cutting her off mid-threat. Nika managed to twist around, jackknifing her body so that she hit head first, cutting through the water.

After their hike to the pool, the water was like a cold blast of winter, shocking her body. She turned around and shot for the surface, breaking into the air just in time to see Fel, leaning over the edge and laughing, then the rocket that was her twin bullrush him, hitting him in the ass. Rika might have the same mass as she did, but this time, it was enough.

Fel flailed his arms, trying to regain his balance, but with a look of surprised horror on his face, he went over. Only, where he'd tossed Nika clear of the rocks and into the deep water, he went in too close, smacking the rock wall and tumbling around like a broken doll before hitting the water hard.

With three powerful strokes, Nika reached where Fel had gone under and started to dive for him, but he popped up, sputtering.

"Are you OK?" Nika asked.

His panic faded as he tread water, replaced with a look of chagrin. He raised his left arm, and blood was streaming from his elbow, dripping into the pool.

"Yeah, I'm OK," he said. "Just a bump."

"Fel?" Rika shouted down, leaning over with Gren, Fel's sister, both looking frightened.

Nika kicked back away from the rock face so they could see her better and yelled, "He's fine. You didn't do a good enough job at killing him."

Relief flowed over the two girls' faces, and Rika said, "I'll do better next time."

"You're a jerk," Nika told Fel before swimming over to the shelf on the far side of the pool.

There were two places to climb out of the water: on the downstream side, where there was a tiny beach and a way back up to the ledge, and on the shelf, where a flat section of rock jutted out, sometimes underwater, sometimes dry depending on the creek level. Today, most of the shelf was under two or three inches of water, only the last bit next to the rock wall dry.

Nika pulled herself onto the shelf and stood, water streaming from her. With a sigh, she stripped off her jeans and bubble-top, getting down to the bright pink styroweave unitard she wore for swimming. She shivered in the still-morning air and threw her wet clothes up where she could get them later, then sat back down on the shelf, her legs in the water.

Fel pulled himself out of the water beside her, his elbow still bleeding, the rivulets of blood mixing with the water as it dripped off of him.

"Jerk," Nika said again, wanting to make double-sure he knew what she thought of him.

"You're the one who wanted all of us to go swimming. I just wanted to help you get started. You know you always take too long to get into the water."

Which was true, not that she was going to give him the satisfaction of admitting it. Nika was more of the walk-down-the-path-to-the-downstream-side-of-the-pool-then-slowly-ease-her-way-into-the-water-type girl.

As small as she was, there wasn't much fat on her to keep her warm, and she and Rika always suffered in the cold. She preferred things on the warmer side.

At least the sun's rays had reached the shelf, and it would warm up soon. She ignored Fel as he stood, stripping off his outer clothes. Or at least she acted like she was ignoring him. At eighteen, Fel's body was reaching adulthood, muscular and fit, and she was very aware of him as he sat down beside her.

Nika hugged her knees, bringing them close to her chest. She wasn't ashamed of her body, exactly. But . . .

Rika and Nika were "cute," as everyone told them. And Nika guessed they were. But while Grandma Dellie kept assuring them they'd be "blossoming" soon, the twins had figured that at seventeen years old, this was as "blossomed" as they were ever going to get. They were still two tiny girls where the rest of their crew had already grown into their more normal-sized adult bodies. Nika looked up to the ledge where Gren and Rika were talking. Rika, as slender and petite as Nika, and Gren, who'd started to fill out when she was twelve and now, at seventeen, had generous curves that her swimsuit couldn't hide.

She was who she was, and Nika wasn't going to be body-shamed. She unclasped her arms and lay down, closing her eyes. If Fel—or anyone else—didn't find her attractive, then that was their loss. She was aware of Fel lying down beside her, and she could almost feel his body radiate heat, but she put that out of her mind.

She could hear Mark and Lim arrive, and a moment later, she heard a splash before the bow-wave washed up against her. Fel got up and dove in the water, but Nika didn't bother to look. More of their crew arrived, and their chatter filled the air.

"Nika, I've got apples!" Barb Wollermerra shouted down the from the ledge. "Got them from the Morales' place."

Which meant she'd stolen them. The Morales had an orchard on the southern part of their farm, past which Barb would have walked to get here. With it only being late summer, the apples wouldn't be ripe yet, but that wouldn't have stopped Barb from snagging a few.

Nika was just warming back up, and she didn't want to get soaked again, so without opening her eyes, she waved off her friend. She'd go back up to the ledge in a bit.

But for now, she was fine with just laying on her back in the water, head on the dry part of the shelf, while tiny fish moved in to nibble at her toes. These fish were new to Arcadia, introduced by the terraforming engineers just last year, and already, they were swarming the creek. Rika didn't like it when the fish nibbled away at her feet, saying it tickled, but Nika thought it was pleasant. If they could eat away the tiny pieces of her dead skin, then all the more power to them.

It was heaven not having anything to do: no homework, no chores around the house. Nothing. In six more days, back to the grind with uni classes starting.

Within 30 minutes, everyone had arrived, and the more aggressive started jumping off the ledge while the more timid walked down the path first. Without having to look, she knew when Rika jumped, her small body barely making the creek waters ripple. Sure enough, a handful of seconds later, Nika's twin pulled herself onto the shelf.

"You just going to lie there all day?" Rika asked, flicking water from her hand onto her sister's face.

Nika didn't flinch nor open her eyes. "Maybe. We'll lose all of this soon enough."

More of the crew were in the water, and the shrieks of youngsters who thought they were almost adults bounced off the rock walls as they dunked and splashed each other.

"All the more reason to grab all of this while we can. You can sleep when you die."

Nika smiled and relented by opening her eyes. "You can sleep when you die" was one of their father's favorite sayings, usually said when he was waking them up early in the morning for a family hike or drive. He'd missed so much time at home with them that when he was there, he seemed to go into overdrive to do as much with them as possible.

"You think he's OK?" Nika asked.

Rika didn't need to ask who. They'd been on the same wavelength since birth, astrological sign or not. "Yeah, I do. And he should be almost on his way back by now."

Colonel Franklin Ingersoll was a Regency Marine, the commanding officer of the 109th Marine Regiment. He'd been deployed for most of the twin's seventeen years, and it had only been last year that he'd come back to his native planet of Arcadia as the commander of the 109th Marines, a reserve regiment stationed in the valley. With most of his Marines and sailors "weekend warriors," he should have been able to spend more time at home with his family for once. But then the eternal war with the Krackles had flared up again, and for the last seven months, the 109th had deployed to participate in retaking Telluride. The regiment had lost many of its Marines on the planet, including Lieutenant Colonel Black, the regimental XO and a favorite of the twins, but the Telluride operation was almost over, and the Arcadian governor had gone on air to say the regiment would return soon.

"Almost over" and "over" were two different things, however, and every day, the twins and their mother kept dreading seeing an official car drive up to their house with the news they couldn't bear to hear. None of the three ever spoke of it, but the potential was always there, hanging over them.

"Sorry I couldn't keep Fel from throwing you in," Rika said.

Nika just shrugged. Rika was the "B" baby of the two, a minute younger and seven ounces lighter at birth, but between the two of them, she was the more aggressive, and she thought nothing of taking on any of the others—especially if it concerned Nika. And Fel was just being a guy, full of testosterone, but not meaning anything bad.

Nika looked across the water where he yanked on Mark's leg, pulling the smaller boy off the rocks he was attempting to scale and into the water. Mark immediately grabbed Fel's head and dunked him under. Gren, up on the ledge, waited until her brother surfaced, then she canonballed into the water right by his head. The splash was epic, reaching the twins all the way across the pool.

"Shoot! I was just dry," Nika said.

"Might as well get in, then," Rika said, kicking water at her.

The two sisters stood up at the edge of the shelf and dived in unison. They both swam down to touch the bottom, an old superstition based on nothing. As soon as they touched, they turned to look at each other, mouthing "Baba," which was what they first called each other as babies in their private twin language, then kicked for the surface.

They broke the water as one, then with clean strokes, started to close the distance to the group of five who were sitting in the shallow downstream end when a thunderclap filled the air.

"Dad's home!" the twins said together, stopping to tread water and look up, hoping to spot the Navy shuttle bringing the Marines down.

The commercial spaceport was over 100 kilometers away in Riesetown, so the only craft entering the atmosphere here would be landing at the NMRC, the Navy- Marine Corps Reserve Center at Logan.

"There they are!" Rika said, pointing to the south.

Nika had spotted the shuttle at the same moment as it flared, absorbing the immense heat on the shields, flames licking at the edges. Commercial shuttles and spacecraft came in on a much slower, shallower approach, often making full revolutions around the planet before setting down. The military liked to come in hard and fast.

Even in a cold zone, the young Navy warrant officer shuttle pilots liked to show off, or, as their dad put it, they wanted to see if they could get their Marine passengers to puke.

This pilot was pushing it even beyond that, however. The flames against the heat shielding were strong enough to just obscure the fuselage so the girls couldn't identify it. The Navy had three shuttles that were commonly used, and if this was the AS-21, which held only 60 PAX, then the debark was going to take hours, if not a full day. With the AS-53, the entire regiment could debark and be on Arcadian soil in just a couple of hours.

"Let's get home," Rika said. "Mom's going to want to get to NMRC, and I want to go with her."

The two made several strong strokes and reached the shallow end. "Is that the regiment?" Gren asked.

"Finally," Rika told her.

"Well, good for you. I know you'll be happy to see the colonel again."

None of the other Young Guns had parents in the regiment, although Lim's mother was a civilian working at NMRC. Still, they all referred to their dad as "the colonel."

"You guys can stay, but we're heading back," Rika told the rest.

As the two started scrambling up the path, Nika looked up to try and figure out how much time they had before the shuttle landed and stopped dead in her tracks.

"You gonna gawk or come with me?" Rika asked, turning back to her.

There was something wrong. The two girls had years of experience spotting returning shuttles, and they knew every type of craft in the Navy's inventory. The flames were still blocking part of her view of the shuttle, but what she could see didn't fit anything the Navy had. It could be a chartered civilian shuttle, but then it wouldn't be tearing in like a cat with its tail on fire. The shape was wrong, all angles and . . .

Holy crap!

Everybody, out of the water now! Get home!" she yelled. "The Krackles are invading!"

Chapter 2
Rika

Rika took up the rear of their little group as they hurried home. "Tail-end Charlie," their father called the last position in a patrol, responsible for making sure no one came up from behind them. Rika took the position seriously, turning every four or five steps as the seven of them made their way around the Morales farm and toward home. It would have been quicker to cut across the farm, but Matron Morales didn't suffer people tramping on her crops, and despite the emergency, old habits died hard.

It had taken the twins several minutes to convince the others that the planet was, in fact, being invaded. Things like that didn't happen here on Arcadia. They all knew about the war, of course, but those battles were all out farther along the spiral arm. Barb had thought the two were joking, trying to pull a fast one over the others, and it had taken tears—not entirely manufactured—to get the others to believe them.

Most of the others took off at a run to the south of the Morales farm toward the town where the bulk of them lived, but seven—the twins, Fel and Gren, Lemul, Hiyori, and Calder—lived in their little housing enclave at the end of Rippart Lane. Fel and Gren were leading, the twins pulling up the rear, the other three in the middle.

Rika had wanted to argue when Fel and Gren had taken charge, angry that the Grafton siblings had arbitrarily put them in the back, as if they needed more protection. The fact that Tail-end Charlie was probably the second-most important position in a formation didn't make her feel any better. *They* didn't know that. They'd just decided to put the smaller girls in the rear.

You wouldn't even know we were being invaded if it weren't for us. Well, if it weren't for Nika.

Rika knew just as much about Navy shuttles as her twin, but she hadn't bothered to put two and two together, so anxious was she to go meet their father. But leave it to her sister, thank goodness, to be so detail oriented. It sometimes drove Rika a little batty, but right now, she was grateful.

"Get down!" Calder shouted, diving for the bushes on the side of the trail.

It took the twins a moment longer, but they joined the others on their bellies.

"What's going on?" Rika asked.

Calder pointed up, and a moment later, Rika heard the whine of an approaching craft.

"Maybe it's the Navy fighters?" Hiyori asked, hopefully.

"No," Nika said.

For all Nika's smarts, she sometimes forgot that others didn't know as much as she did, and she wasn't always very communicative.

"What she means is that's not a human craft," Rika added, knowing that Hiyori needed more of an answer. "It has to be a Krackle."

As if to emphasize the point, a large craft, all angles and edges with the Krackles' distinctive gull wings, flew low directly over their heads.

"Did it see us?" Hiyori asked.

Nika pushed herself up on her arms, craning her head as she tried to see the landing craft better as it disappeared from sight. She gave Rika a short shake of her head. She knew Nika wasn't answering Hiyori's question. She also knew just what that shake meant.

"They didn't see us, or if they did, they didn't care. They're landing,"

"Where?" Fel asked, standing up and trying to catch sight of the Krackle craft.

"At the farm, probably. Or at our homes," Rika said.

Not that the two were that far apart. While the farm was pretty extensive, the farmhouse, barn, and control center were off Rippart Lane as well, just a couple of hundred meters from their homes.

"Our homes!" Fel shouted. "We've got to move it! Mace and Mom are there."

He ran a few steps down the trail, turning to urge the others on when Rika shouted, "Stop!"

"No! We have to get there before them!"

Rika pushed past the others and grabbed the bigger boy by the arm. "No! Do you hear me?

"We can't beat them to our homes. They're already landing. And if we just run like crazy people down the trail, then we might as well send up fireworks right now and tell them where we are."

Rika wanted to run home, too, to be with their mom. She was scared, more than she'd ever been in her life, so she understood Fel's rush. But the rational part of her mind knew that they had to be cautious.

"But Mace is back there with Mom. You want us to just forget our families?"

"No, of course not," Rika said, turning to look at the others before settling on Nika's eyes.

"No, we're going to go see what's happening. But quietly. We're going to recon our homes," Nika said, rescuing her.

"What's 'recon,'" Calder asked.

"Reconnaissance. Sneak in and see what's up. But not be seen. Like in the Marines. Our dad was in recon when he was a lieutenant."

The reference to their father seemed to mollify Fel a bit. Rika didn't tell him that their father had been in recon long before the twins were born, and neither of them had a clue just what recon Marines did. But she knew running home without taking any precautions was dangerous, and if she could use her father for some street cred, then their dad wouldn't mind.

"So, how do we do this?" Gren asked. "Fel's right. Mom's home now with Mace. We need to see if they're all right."

Good question. You took charge, so now what?

"We need to get off this trail. They'll be putting drones on it. We need to head closer to the creek, then up through the woods," Nika said. "Rika and I'll sneak in and take a look, then come back and tell you what we see."

"No!" Fel and Calder said in unison.

"I'll go do this recon thing," Fel said.

"What as big as you are?" Rika said derisively. "They'll spot you in a second. No, we'll be harder to see."

Not that the Krackles "saw" as humans did, but the point was still valid.

"She's right," Gren said, putting a hand on her brother's shoulder. "Let them do it."

"But . . ."

"Let them."

For once, being small has an advantage.

It wasn't that Rika was raring to go confront the Krackles. They terrified her. But frankly, she didn't trust the others not to screw it up. Fel, especially. She was worried sick about their mother, and while Krackles took human prisoners—where else did they get their zombies?—Rika didn't want anything to set them off and start a killing spree.

"I know how you two can get closer," Lemul said. "Without being seen."

Rika looked at him in surprise. Lemul Adoud was the newest member of the group, having moved to Rippart Lane just four months before. Quiet, he never talked much about himself and seemed happy just to be part of a group, any group.

"I've lived here all my life," Fel said. "I'll lead."

Lemul frowned, but he didn't argue. Rika couldn't imagine that the new boy knew something they didn't, but if he did . . .

"How can we get closer?" she asked.

Lemul seemed grateful to be taken seriously. "Around to the west, beside Fel's house. There's a draw there, covered in vines. Part of the drainage web. You two should be able to fit inside."

"Our house?" Fel asked, surprised. "There's nothing there. Just an empty field."

Lemul opened his mouth as if to say something, then closed it. He wasn't going to argue with the bigger boy. Rika didn't think he'd just make something like that up, though, and if there was a way to get in closer, then she was all for that.

And time was a-wasting. Arcadia had been invaded, and she fought back the dread that threatened to overcome her. She had to keep a level head until they knew what the situation was.

But it was hard.

"Show us," Rika told Lemul, not willing to waste more time in discussion.

Lemul gave a curt nod, then led off the trail, cutting into the trees, the twins right behind him. Fel didn't seem too happy about it, but Rika knew that could just be the stress of the situation showing through.

The ground sloped down to the creek, rocky and covered with crepe myrtle and laurel. It made for slow going, and Rika could feel the tension rise. She was afraid that Fel or Gren would break at any moment and run straight to their home. Into what, she wasn't sure, but nothing good.

"Fall back with Fel," she told Nika. "Keep him from doing anything stupid."

Nika stepped to the side and stopped, waiting for Fel.

Rika pushed ahead, grabbed Lemul by the shoulder, and said, "We need to go faster. I don't know how long Fel can hold back."

It probably wasn't a smart thing to do, but they all sped up to a jog, going around the undergrowth when they could, crashing through it when they couldn't. Within minutes, Rika's arms and face were red with welts left by branches. She didn't care. Her mind was focused on what they'd find—fear trumping hope.

A muffled explosion reached them, and all seven froze for a moment, ears straining for more.

"I'm going," Fel said, turning to cut away from the creek and directly toward their homes.

Nika grabbed his arm and whispered something, then Gren joined him. Fel was angry, ready for action, but what could he do against the Krackles? It took a precious minute, but whatever her twin was telling him sunk in, and he nodded, his face twisted and red.

Rika nudged Lemul, and they started off again. They reached the fallen log alongside the creek that they sometimes used to sit and watch the water gurgle below. Calder's house was just up the hill from that spot, but Lemul kept on, curving around another 100 yards before he slowed down and led them up the hill. Within yards, the trees became smaller. The original terraformers had heavily planted the immediate areas around the waterways, and it had taken awhile for the forest to spread out from there. The seven climbed up the slope until they reached the crest where Lemul went to his belly, Rika beside him, while the others stopped just short.

She could see the roof and upper story of Fel and Gren's house. It was intact, but the smell of smoke was evident in the air. Rika couldn't see their own house; it was on the other side of the cul de sac from their position.

Between them and the house were some small fruit trees carefully tended by Ms. Grafton. They were enough to block their line of sight, but not big or full enough to provide the twins any degree of concealment.

"So, where's this way in?" Rika whispered.

Lemul pointed to the right to the fallow field beyond the Grafton's yard, where dark green vines led away and toward the road. Rika had never noticed them before.

"Those aren't tall enough," she said, disappointed.

"Under them. There's the drainage ditch."

She looked again, then shook her head. There didn't look to be any ditch under the vines. She turned back to the others, who were anxiously waiting.

"What do you see?" Fel asked, too loud for comfort.

Rika held her upraised finger to her lips, hushing him, then half-slid, half-crawled back to them.

"Your house looks fine."

"Did you see my mom?"

"I didn't see anything. It looks quiet."

"Maybe they didn't land here," Gren offered hopefully.

13

Rika started to argue, but she hadn't seen a ship. The only indication that something was wrong was the explosion they'd heard and the smell of smoke. She and Nika had to see, and if Lemul was right, then that drainage ditch—if it was even really a ditch—was their best way in. Anything else would be a bigger risk.

They had to try it. Rika knew that they both didn't have to go, that only one had to see what was happening, but the thought of venturing closer alone was almost too much to bear. They had to do it together.

"We're going to recon and find out," she told Gren. "You all wait here. Don't try anything until we come back, OK?"

"And if you don't come back?" Fel asked.

"If we don't come back, then I don't give a hoot what you do," Rika snapped, her nerves already taught.

Fel could be such a jerk, sometimes. Rika knew Nika sort of liked the guy, but Rika had never been that impressed with him.

She gave her twin a short nod, then moved sideways, under the crest of the hill, toward where she'd seen the vines, wondering just how far they had to go before they reached them. To her surprise, the vines tumbled over the crest of the building pad. With Nika at her side, the two pushed at the vines, revealing the end of an actual ferrocrete drainage ditch.

"Never saw this before," Nika whispered.

Not that a drainage ditch was surprising. Arcadia's weather still tended to the extremes as with most newly terraformed worlds, and "whompers," (heavy, drenching rain) were the rule during the rainy season rather than the exception.

"We don't spend too much time in the Grafton's back yard."

Which was true. Ms. Grafton was protective of her garden and didn't like kids tramping around. But Lemul had known about this, and his home was next to the twins'.

"How do we . . ." Nika started, pushing the vines up. The stalks were woody, curling this way and that, with large green leaves creating a roof, of sorts, over the ditch. Fuzzy root tendrils reached to the bottom, scrabbling for purchase, ready for the flow of water. Small amounts of drying mud from light summer runoff covered the bottom—not deep, but enough for the rootlets to pull some moisture from it.

Rika pulled at one of them. It gave, but unwillingly.

"We'll just have to—"

"Pull them as we go," Nika finished for her.

Rika turned to give one last glance at the others, who were all watching them closely. She gave them a thumbs up, then scrambled up into the ditch, Nika giving her butt a push. She twisted around and offered her hand to pull her twin up with her.

There really wasn't room for the two of them, and their heads were moving the tops of the vines. They'd be easily spotted by any Krackle.

Rika lowered herself to her belly and started pushing herself forward, the ferrocrete rough on her knees. She had to detach rootlets as she moved to clear the way. Within a few meters, her hands, belly, and legs were covered in the gravelly mud.

Rika didn't think of herself as claustrophobic, but with the vines and leaves pressing down on her, and with visions of Krackle beamers frying them as they moved, she was decidedly uncomfortable. It would be so easy to back down and tell the others they hadn't seen anything. If Nika wasn't there right behind her, she might have even done that. But they owed it to the others—and themselves—to see what was happening.

Slowly, they made their way forward. The ferrocrete had been undoubtedly treated with an antivegative; otherwise, they'd have been stuck. Still, even if the water-hungry vines hadn't been able to pierce the ditch and latch on, their very presence made for difficult progress. And they couldn't simply push the mass of vines away. They had to slide under them without disturbing the tops.

"No way Fel with his big butt could get through this," Nika whispered behind her.

Rika almost laughed aloud. It wasn't that funny, so she knew it was a reaction to too much stress and worry.

Steady, girl. Just keep it steady.

She pushed forward, edging closer to the road. She didn't have a solid feel of how far they'd come, nor how far they'd have to go before they risked taking a look.

Something bit her on the leg, and she had to resist the urge to slap at it. For the millionth time in her life, she wondered why the terraformers included pests when they terraformed a world. "Building a diverse and mutually supporting ecology," was the mantra, but Rika thought that a planet would be fine without mosquitoes and other creatures that bit and stung.

She was so fixated on the bite on her leg that she didn't recognize for a moment that the ditch was turning. It was then that she realized that the ditch was just an extension of the roadside drainage web. It had been diverted away from the leveled pad on which the homes were built. And that meant . . .

"We're at the road," Nika said.

Rika shifted herself to the side, leaving room for Nika to worm herself up. It was tight, but manageable.

"So, we need to look, huh?" Rika asked.

"That's what a recon is."

"Yeah, I know."

Rika pulled her legs up under her, and then slowly started to part the vines over her head, trying to use the small breeze to hide what she was doing. Nika joined her, and together, they slid forward until they were on their knees, their heads just about to break through the foliage. To their left, Rika could already see the Grafton's house. It didn't look damaged, which was heartening.

One last twisted vine blocked most of their view. Together, they carefully inched it up so they could see out . . .

. . . they both gasped in unison and lowered the vine again, sliding back into the ditch.

Not twenty meters away, right across the road, a Krackle in full combat armor stood facing away. Rika had seen images of them, of course, but this was the first time she'd seen an actual specimen, the ancestral enemy of humankind.

The thing was easily eight feet tall and tipping the scales at three-hundred-and-fifty pounds. Vaguely humanoid-looking from the rear, the grey-skinned creature was bipedal with four arms sprouting from its massive torso. It was not related to humans, however, not in the slightest. Its shape was merely **parallel evolution**, function determining form.

Krackles were carbon-based—sort of. Their intertwined web version of DNA used arsenic instead of phosphorus as Earth-based life did, and iron oxide formed a parallel and interlocking cellular structure that still baffled the xenobiologists on how the hybrid system could have formed in the first place.

They knew what the iron-oxide did, however. It made up their sensory organs. If the Krackle would turn around—not that Rika wanted it to—they could see the difference. The thing had no eyes and didn't "see" as humans did. But that didn't mean it was blind. Krackles emitted a myriad of pulses, ranging from fast-as-light gamma waves to low-frequency sound waves, then read back the reflections. The low-frequency waves were in a 360 and gave a basic picture of what was around them. The gamma waves, which gave the greatest detail, were directional. The system shouldn't work as well as humans' sight, but it did well enough. While Krackles couldn't determine color, they could "see" things like texture and temperature, and they were unaffected by the dark of night.

"My God," Nika whispered, barely audible. "It's right there."

Rika had seen the Krackle landing craft. She knew they'd been invaded. But to see the thing just standing there on Rippart Lane, it hit home like a gutshot.

"Did you see anything else?" Rika asked.

"Just that thing."

Was that enough? Can we just go?

They'd confirmed that the Krackles had landed, and they were in their small housing development. But they hadn't seen what had happened to their families.

"We have to look again," Rika said.

"I know. I don't want to, but we do."

Rika gave her sister a long look, then both edged back up. They slowly lifted the vine once more.

The Krackle was still standing there, its body oriented away from them, thank goodness. If it was transmitting the gamma waves in their direction, Rika didn't think the vines would protect them.

Rika shifted her view to the right, and her heart dropped. Across the road, at the Morales farm, the control center was a mass of wreckage, smoke rising into the sky. The landing craft they'd seen fly overhead was in the Morales' soybean field. These were sights that she'd never expected to see, but she barely gave them a glance.

Three more Krackles in full combat gear were in the yard. Two people she didn't recognize were standing by one of the Morales' crop transporters, clad in dust-colored coveralls. It took Rika a moment to realize that they were zombies, the Krackles' human slaves.

But amidst all of that, there was one thing that had riveted her attention. Their mother was being loaded onto the transporter. She turned and gave one last worried look around, as if looking for the two of them, before one of the zombies shoved her inside the trailer.

Chapter 3
Nika

Nika stood in shocked silence while Rika argued with Fel. There was a hole in her heart, and emptiness that gnawed at her very being. She'd been afraid ever since she'd realized they were being invaded, but there had been a kernel of hope that had kept her going. Hope that the Krackles would leave their homes alone, that their mother would be there to greet them and take charge.

Lisbeth Ingersoll always knew what to do. She had to, raising the two of them in various posts around the Regency, their father off answering the call of duty. All the twins had to do was reunite with their mother, and things would be OK.

Seeing their mother being loaded into the Morales' crop transporter, however, had crushed that hope. They were on their own.

Thank God for Rika. Nika could feel the same despair in her, but where Nika wanted to curl up in a corner and withdraw, Rika was acting out, and Fel was her target of opportunity.

The other five had to have seen the shocked look on their faces when the two of them rejoined the group, and they kept asking what they'd seen, but neither girl had said a word until they'd led the others back down the hill and across the creek. When Rika had finally told them, Fel had erupted, angrily accusing the two of them of wasting time. He wanted to rush back and try and save the adults.

Rika was having none of that, asking how he expected to take on four Krackle soldiers. Slowly, her force of personality was wearing down the other boy until still seething, he finally admitted that trying to fight would only result on him being captured, or worse, as well.

"We can't just do nothing, though," Calder said, his voice choking, his eyes red and swollen with tears.

Gren put her arm around him and said, "We're not doing nothing."

"Well, just what are we doing, then?" Fel asked, eyes boring into Rika like hot knives.

Rika looked back, and the fervor evaporated, her mouth opening, but nothing coming out.

Snap out of it! Don't put all of this on her.

"They make concentration camps," she said, barely above a whisper.

Six sets of eyes swiveled to her.

She took a deep breath, forcing herself to sound confident even when that was the furthest thing from the truth at the moment.

"Concentration camps," she said, her voice growing stronger. "The Krackles put their prisoners in concentration camps. It's the first step in making them zombies. We need to find out where the camp is."

"Zombies? We're not zombies," Gren said.

"Where do you think they get their zombies?" Nika asked.

"But they've been zombies for centuries. Maybe longer," Gren said, brows furrowed in confusion.

Probably longer, Nika knew. DNA retrogression indicated that most of the Krackles' human slaves split off from the rest of humanity thousands of years ago—which meant they'd been harvested from Earth before mankind even left the planet, and that created more questions than answers.

"The ones we see. But they still kidnap us. They're making new slaves."

"We don't know that for sure," Fel said, scoffing.

"What do you think they do," Rika snapped. "Eat us?"

Calder gave a gasp and asked, "Do you think that's so?"

Jeez? How can they not know this? We've been at war with them for how long now?

"They can't eat us. We'd poison them," Nika said, waving a dismissive hand. "They don't capture us just for fun. They've got to be using humans for something, and some zombie's DNA show signs of modern humans. Maybe we work their mines or whatever dangerous jobs they have. Maybe they use us for breeding—"

"That's disgusting," Hiyori interrupted.

Nika ignored her. "Whatever they do with humans, they round us up and put us into concentration camps until they bring in the transports. If we're going to do anything, we've got to find out where that camp is. If they get our families off-planet, then we'll never see them again."

Her emotions threatened to take over, and she had to fight back the tears. What she'd said was true. There had only been one space rescue of human prisoners during the long war with the Krackles. All other rescues, even as few as there were, had been on the ground.

The others stared at her in silence as they digested what she'd just said until Rika stepped over to stand beside her. "You heard my sister. If we ever want to see our families again, we need to find this freaking concentration camp."

Chapter 4
Rika

Rika hitched up her pack—or rather, one of her father's old Marine backpacks—trying to find the thing's sweet spot. But at just over four-and-half feet tall, her six-foot-tall father's gear wasn't even close in fitting her. Instead of the pack's hip belt riding just above her hips, it hung low on her butt. And with the belt much too long to cinch tight around her, each step made the pack bang into her.

Luckily, she wasn't carrying the 400 pounds of a combat Marine, or even the 120 carried by "straight-leg," Marines—those without the augmented power harnesses. She had maybe twenty pounds of sandwiches, water, and camping rations. She'd have done better with her father's old and much smaller assault pack, but Nika had that.

Once the group had committed to trying to find out where their families were being held, Nika had kept them from charging off. None of them had food or water, and all were still in their swimsuits and shorts. They had to gather supplies. The twins had crept forward again to observe, and even after the Krackles' shuttle took off, they'd waited another agonizingly long hour before they emerged onto the street and checked out the homes to make sure the coast was clear. Only then had they returned to the others to give them the go ahead to gather supplies.

The twins had raided their father's collection of deuce gear, the various packs and harnesses he'd collected over the years. Rika had even removed his Kri-Blade from the frame on the wall, given to him by his Marines when he'd turned over his infantry company. It was a commemorative blade, bright and shiny, but it was authentic, not just a piece of art. Their father was inordinately proud of it, but Rika didn't think he'd mind her taking it, given the circumstances.

The others had been disappointed that the blade was the only weapon the two had. What did they expect, though? That their father kept beamers and missiles in the home?

Gren had a weapon, however, an old hunting rifle and ten rounds of ammunition. Not that it would do much damage to a Krackle in combat armor. One of the zombies, maybe, but not a Krackle. Gren clutched it tightly, however, as if it gave her strength.

With their military gear, even in blue jeans, hiking boots, and green "My Dad's a Marine" ballcaps, the twins had a semblance of order. Not so for the others. Lemul didn't even have a back or waistpack. He was carrying his food in a bright red and orange Woomaroo's shopping bag. Still, it was better than heading out without anything.

"We ready?" Fel asked.

He hadn't offered much in the way of suggestions, but now that they'd decided to go get eyes on the town, he'd taken charge again. Rika didn't think he was the best choice to be a leader, but she wasn't going to argue. Between Nika and her, she was pretty sure they could nudge the group one way or the other if the need arose.

With Fel in the lead, the seven crossed Rippart Lane and into the Morales' farm. Cutting across would save them time, and with the Gen4 corn shoulder-high even to Fel, they at least had some cover. It probably would have been better to go back along the creek, but all of them were anxious to know where their families were. Time was pressing on their nerves.

Rika scanned the sky before they entered the field, searching for drones. She didn't see any, but that didn't mean anything. For all she knew, they were being tracked, and a welcoming party of Krackle soldiers would be waiting for them as they emerged.

The corn might be shoulder-high to Fel, but the stalks, heavy with ears, towered over the twins. They couldn't see a thing. Couldn't hear much, either, not with the breeze rustling the stalks. Rika's imagination started to go wild, and it took a force of will and several deep breaths to pull back from the brink of panic.

"Easy, Baba," Nika said quietly from in front of her, feeling Rika's unease. "We'll find her."

And then what?

If they somehow managed to find the concentration camp, what next? Just march up to the Krackles and demand that they release the twins' mother?

Rika forced her uncertainty from her mind. First things first. Find their families, then figure out what to do.

The twins had changed into matching khaki shirts, but even with the long sleeves, the surprisingly strong and sharp corn leaves were leaving welts on their hands and faces to match the ones they'd received rushing home. Sweat was building up, stinging the welts and making them itch something fierce. With her pack banging into her butt with each step, with the welts, and with sweat running into her eyes, Rika was not a happy camper, and Krackle soldiers waiting for them or not, she couldn't wait to get out of the field.

"I'm never going to be a farmer," she muttered as she followed her sister.

"You and me both," Nika said.

She'd never given the Morales clan much thought, other than they were considered rich by their neighbors. Arcadia had very few of the corporate farms so prevalent to most other planets. Most of the farms were family affairs, started by the first wave of settlers. But if tramping around in the cornfield was any indication, farming was hard work.

"At last," Nika whispered as they emerged from the field and into the orchards.

Rika felt a weight lift off her shoulders. She could finally see more than half-a-yard, and the small breeze cooled off the sweat on her face. She knew they were far more visible to surveillance, but she didn't care at the moment. Chances were that they'd already been spotted, but the question was whether they were enough of a threat to warrant immediate attention.

From a human perspective, there was no rhyme nor reason as to what would set the Krackles off and what they'd ignore. Rika just hoped they were on the ignore list.

The group quickly made their way through the orchard, but not before snagging a few under-ripe apples into their packs or shopping bags. Rika felt guilty stealing the apples, but she thought Matron Morales would understand.

They made it to the edge of the Morales farm, right at Highway 32, the main road up and down the Lorraine Valley. A klick to the east from where they stood was the main section of Storyville, the county seat and the largest town until Riesetown some 100 klicks away. The base was located in the small town of Logan, another ten klicks down the highway. Fifteen clicks to the west was San Miguel, a smaller town of around 3,000 people.

They had another "discussion," as Gren put it, at the edge of the highway. Rika called it an argument.

Hiyori's older sister had married a year ago and moved into town where she'd given birth to a baby boy. With her parents and 13-year-old brother taken from their home, Hiyori had fixated on her sister, and nothing was going to keep her away. With Fel as an ally, she wanted use the highway to run into town.

Rika, Nika, and Lemul were adamant that they had to get off the highway and use whatever cover they could to approach. "Approach" was the operative word here, not enter the town. It wouldn't do any of them any good to get caught up in a sweep.

It took some difficult convincing to get Calder and Gren to agree with them, but the decision was made. For a moment, Rika thought Hiyori was going to leave them and take off, but she sullenly agreed to abide by their decision. They hopped the fence and pushed into the trees and shrubs alongside the highway. There would be houses and some stores, then the refueling station in their path, but they could go around those.

Within five minutes, their choice was validated when a Krackle assault vehicle, something like a cross between a Marine heavy tank and a ground effect hover, blasted up the highway. It had to be going a hundred miles per hour, pulling up road debris and dust in its wake as the seven dove for cover.

"What the hell was that?" Calder asked after the AV passed from view.

All eyes turned toward the twins.

So, just because our dad is a Marine, we're supposed to know all of this?

"It's not ours—" Rika said before Nika cut her off.

"Dagger is the code name for it. Assault vehicle with a kinetic cannon and a meson beamer. Bad news."

Rika looked at her twin in bemused shock. Nika always had her nose in a book or tablet, but how the heck had she known that? For as much alike as they were, as much as they were usually on the same wavelength, Nika sometimes surprised her.

"What Nika said. We don't want to run up against one of them," Rika said as if she'd known any of the details.

"How many of those things do they have?" Calder asked.

Rika gave Nika a glance and realized her twin wasn't going to say anything more. "Enough for us to keep our heads down."

"But we've got to keep moving," Fel said, standing up. "We'll be careful."

Rika looked over her shoulder as they started to move off again. The AV, the "Dagger," could take on a fully-meched Marine squad. It would have made mincemeat of the seven of them without even trying. A feeling of helplessness threatened to overwhelm her. What were seven kids supposed to do, even if they found where everyone was being held? This wasn't some game where they could reset and play again. This was the real thing.

She kept her thoughts to herself as they made their way closer to the town. They bypassed a couple of silent houses, unwilling to take the time to see if there was anyone inside. The BP fuel station at the edge of town was a smoking ruin. Rika gave a silent prayer for Mr. Harrison, the owner, hoping he'd gotten out before it was destroyed. She kept reminding herself that the Krackles wanted prisoners, not wholesale death.

Not on JPL-3, the thought intruded into her mind unbidden.

The corporate world had been destroyed four years before with almost a complete loss of life. Rika refused to consider that might happen to Arcadia.

"We should go to the park," Lemul said, interrupting her dark thoughts.

Lemul hadn't said much over the last hour, but he was right. Veteran's Park, on the edge of the city, rose a good 300 feet above downtown. They'd have a good view of the area from up there.

For once, no one argued. Fel grunted and cut to his left. The park was almost on the east side of the city, while they were on the west side, but none of them, except maybe Hiyori, wanted to cut through the town.

This close, sounds of activity reached them. Several Krackle aircraft, both shuttles and smaller fighters, made appearances as they hovered over downtown or flew up and down Highway 32. The occasional buzz of weapons firing reached them as Fel led the group deeper away from the center, skirting as much as possible to get the other side.

They'd left their homes around noon and made it to the edge of town in less than an hour. But now, their circuitous route took much longer, and it was close to five by the time they started climbing into the park. They'd seen nobody on their trek, which was alarming. Just below the park, in a section of nice, upscale homes, a lone mid-sized yellow dog was chained up in a yard, and it barked furiously at them as they passed by, but that was the only sign of life.

Other than the Krackles flying about, that is. As they climbed, more of them appeared, but Rika couldn't make out heads or tails of what they were doing.

It had been about nine hours since the initial invasion, which was a long time, but surely not long enough to evacuate a town of almost 15,000 people. It was almost eerie how quiet Storyville was. Scarily eerie. Rika couldn't imagine that so many people had been taken away.

The only good thing was that they'd seen no dead bodies, and with few exceptions, very little damage to property. Still, Rika's imagination was going wild on what might have happened. She thought back to the yellow dog they'd passed. She'd give anything to know what it had seen.

They cautiously entered the park, but the place was deserted. There were signs of life, but no people. A BBQ was still warm, the coals turned to ash, and remnants of what might have been steaks on the grill, now turned to blackened pieces of leather. A baby's portable playpen was beside the table, intact and undamaged. Next to it was a tan and pink teddy bear, its neck bent and blue ribbon torn as if someone had stepped on it. A parent lifting the baby out of the playpen? A Krackle? Rika shuddered at the thought.

Fel pushed abandoned plates and drinks to the side and climbed up on the table, then raised his hand to shade his eyes. "I can't see any people. Just the damned Krackles. I need to get higher, though."

He looked around, eyeing the trees. Veterans Park was fairly new, and the trees were not as robust as older plantings. He jumped off the table and walked over to the nearest, a poplar about twenty feet high. The bottom branches had been cut, leaving the first one about seven feet up. He reached to grab the lowest one and tried to pull himself up, but the branch started to crack and pull away from the trunk.

"Hell!" he shouted as he let go.

Rika had watched this silently, hoping Fel could climb the tree, but it was obvious that the soft wood and close-in branches wouldn't support his weight. It was time for her to step in. She gave Nika a glance, and her twin gave her the tiniest of nods.

"Give me a boost," she said, dropping her pack and holding her hands over her head.

This time Fel didn't argue. He grabbed Rika around her waist and hoisted her high. Rika ignored the branch he'd pulled away, taking a firm hold on the next one, and scrambled up.

"Look at that. She's like a squirrel," Calder said.

For all their small size, both twins were quite athletic, when it came down to it. It took no effort at all, and she was near the top of the tree, which swayed under even her small weight. She hooked an elbow around the trunk, wedged her leg around one of the branches, and looked down into the town. She saw nothing in the town itself that told her anything. It looked deserted. A few wisps of smoke rose into the air, but it if weren't for a Krackle shuttle drifting close to the high school, she might have been looking at a tridee still of the town.

She leaned forward, the tree bending under her weight and raising a couple of "Be carefuls!" from below. Looking to the east, her heart caught in her throat. A vast pall of smoke rose from the direction of Logan . . . and the NMRC. Of course, the Krackles would take out the region's only military base. Even with the regiment gone, Rika knew people who were still there, people who would have been working on a Wednesday morning.

"The base has been hit," she told those beneath her. "It looks bad."

"What about the concentration camp?" Gren asked. "Can you see any sign of it?"

"No, not yet."

Rika shifted her weight, scanning the areas around the town, but she couldn't make out much due to the smoke that had settled over the area. She wished she had some binos, but even they wouldn't pierce the haze.

A shuttle lifted out of the town, surprising her. Storyville's buildings were not skyscrapers, and she wouldn't have thought a shuttle that big would have been hidden from her view. She followed it as it flew low to the east out of town. It continued for about a minute before it banked to the south, then started to land. With her eyes drawn to the area, she caught movement beneath it. It took her a moment to make it out—it was a bus, moving down a road.

She tried to orient herself. If Storyville was directly down the hill from her, and both the shuttle and the bus were heading somewhere to the southeast, then . . .

It's at the old ammo depot! That's where they're taking them!

Chapter 5
Nika

Nika slowly came to, her eyes still closed as she shuddered at the dream she'd had, of a Krackle invasion, of their mother being taken—

Except it wasn't a dream. She sat up, her eyes open in the morning light. Beside her, Rika tried to snuggle closer.

With darkness falling the night before, the group had decided to stay in the park until morning. Not without some argument. Fel, no surprise, had wanted to rush off, but no one else wanted to wander around in the dark. The Krackles didn't need light to "see," and that put them at a distinct advantage at night. It wasn't just the night. They'd first noticed it when Rika pointed out that the bright blue Arcadian Cooperative Credit Union logo on their five-story regional headquarters was dark. Many of the lights were missing, and the only real explanation was that the powergrid had been cut. As more and more backup batteries became depleted, darkness would become even more prevalent.

The teens ate their sandwiches and drank from the fountain, then settled in for the night. The twins had demanded that they create a watch system, with one of them awake at all times, and Nika had taken the first watch, her nerves taut with tension, jumping at each rustle.

The Krackles hadn't attacked by the time her watch was done, and she awoke Calder to take over. She'd been tempted just to keep on as she was sure she couldn't sleep given the events of the day, but to her surprise, she'd conked out, not even waking when Rika took her shift.

But now it was time to wake. Past time. The sun had already lit the sky, albeit with an odd, orange tint from the smoke. She gave Rika a nudge. Her twin mumbled, turned over to her other side, but didn't awake.

"Get up," Nika said, nudging her harder.

"Ten more minutes," Rika mumbled.

"Now. It's morning."

Rika opened her eyes, then sat up with a start when she realized how late it was.

"Who was supposed to wake us?" Rika asked, looking at the sleeping bodies around them.

"Hiyori. She had the last watch."

They both looked around, but their companion was nowhere to be seen.

"Do you think the Krackles . . ."

"No. They took her and left us here? She left us. Probably went into town."

"Hell," Rika muttered. "You're probably right."

She extended a leg and gave Calder a shove. "Wake up." She raised her voice and said, "Everyone, wake up! It's late."

It took a moment, but the other four stirred, then sat up, rubbing their eyes.

"Where's Hiyori? Taking a pee?" Gren asked.

"I think she left us," Rika said.

"What do you mean, left us?" Fel asked, looking confused.

"I mean, we woke up, and she was gone. She was supposed to wake us up before sunrise, and now look," she said, pointing to the sun which was now over the horizon.

"Oh, crap. She went to find her sister," Calder said.

"Who isn't even there anymore," Lemul added, stating the obvious.

"Should we . . . I mean, do you think we should go after her?" Fel asked.

Nika looked down the hill toward the town. She didn't know how long of a head start Hiyori had.

"Does anyone even know where her sister lives?" she asked.

Fel automatically looked at his wristcomp to look it up, forgetting the net had been knocked out. With a rueful smile, he shook his head no.

"Then, it doesn't make any sense for us to try and search the town. She made her choice, and we don't know where she is. We do know where our families are, though. I say we keep to the plan. Hiyori knows where we're going, too, so she can join us there."

The others looked at each other for a moment before Fel said, "She's right. Hiyori made her decision. We still need to find our people."

They took just long enough to take a bite from what they'd carried and a drink from the fountain, but within ten minutes, they had their packs on and were ready to go. The plan was to leave the park, but instead of descending directly into the city, they were going to turn on McMillan as it crossed the slope, and then the dirt trail where McMillan dead-ended. It was going to add a lot of distance to their trek, but it seemed like the safer option.

With Fel in the lead once more, the group of six kids exited the park and started down to McMillan Road. Four houses down, the yellow dog from the day before rose from its belly, staring at them. Its tail wagged once or twice before it started barking at them, pulling at the chain around its neck.

"That thing better shut up," Calder said, looking around as if to spot a lurking Krackle.

"It doesn't know what's going on, poor thing," Rika said as they passed in front of the house.

"I don't care what it knows, but it's going to get us in trouble."

Nika stopped in her tracks to stare at the dog. It wasn't its fault, and chained up like that, it wasn't going to survive.

"Are you going to move?" Rika asked, nudging her from behind.

"Wait," Nika said loud enough for everyone to hear. Before she had even formed a plan, she had hopped the low ornamental fence and approached the dog, who was barking louder, and jumping forward, the chain around its neck keeping it in place.

"Nika! What are you doing?" Rika yelled.

As she got closer, the dog looked far more vicious than from the other side of the fence. It snapped yellow teeth in its excitement. Nika held out a hand, just out of reach of the dog, and said, "Easy now."

The dog jumped higher, the chain jerking it about, its hind legs whipping up as it landed hard on its head. Without thinking, Nika stepped forward and placed her hand on the dog's head before it could regain its feet. There was a gasp from her sister as the dog twisted around and lunged for her hand, a wet sloppy tongue slathering over her.

Startled, she tried to pull back, but the dog had its front paws around her hand as it tried to lick her to death.

"You're just afraid, aren't you, boy?" she asked.

Nika felt for the latch around the yellow dog's neck, which had been worn smooth from God knows how long it was chained up. The clasp was heavy, and Nika couldn't get it to budge.

She looked back at the others. Rika and Fel looked concerned, but the others were frowning.

"Come on, Nika. We've got to get moving," Calder said.

"Fel, come here," Nika said.

"What?" he asked, pointing at himself. "Me?"

"Yes, you. Come here."

He looked at the others before he shrugged and went forward, simply stepping over the low fence Nika had to hop.

The dog snuggled closer to Nika, its tail beating hard against her leg.

"What do you want me to do?"

"This clasp. It's rusted, and I can't get it open," she said, pulling the chain around so he could see.

Fel leaned over to get a better look, then reached for it. The dog barked and tried to lunge up, which made Fel jump back.

"He's not dangerous. He just wants help."

Fel looked at the dog's teeth warily, but he reached forward and tried to open the clasp. It didn't budge. Nika could see the determination come over him. Fel didn't like to lose at anything. He straddled the squirming dog, then with both hands, pressed on the clasp. He had to pull on the chain, which made the dog yelp, but with a grunt, he finally opened it enough for the chain link to fall free.

"Got it!" he said triumphantly!

Nika examined the dog's neck. It was rough, red, and weepy from where the chain had rubbed. This hadn't happened just since the invasion. The damage had been a long time building, and Nika hissed in anger.

The dog whimpered and looked up at her, licking her face.

"I'm not mad at you, boy. It's not your fault."

Rika hopped the fence and came up to them, giving the dog a pat on the head. "You freed it. Good for you. But we need to go now," she said in a gentle voice.

"I know."

Nika gave the dog a hug, then stood. She'd felt so helpless since the Krackles landed, and for the first time since then, she felt in control of something. She'd managed something good.

"You be a good boy, huh?" she said before turning, and together with Rika and Fel, started back to join the others.

The yellow dog whined, tilting his head as he watched Nika leave him. He stopped at the edge of the worn grass, his limit while he was chained. Fel helped Nika hop the fence again, and when she turned to look back at the dog, he jumped up. This time, however, the chain didn't jerk him back. Without hesitating, he ran and bounded over the fence just as Nika and the others started off again.

Nika saw him charge, a smile on her face. The dog danced around her, yipping in joy.

"Oh, great. Now look what you've done," Calder said.

"She saved a life, Cold-wad," Rika snapped, using Calder's unappreciated nickname.

"And now what? We have this thing barking all day? Why don't we just send up a freaking flare to tell the Krackles where we are?"

"OK, you win," Nika said before turning to the dog. "Stay, boy," she said without conviction.

She took a step forward, as did the dog.

"Dang. He doesn't obey," she said with a smirk.

"Well, we can't have it with us," Calder insisted.

"What do you want me to do? Kill him?" she asked facetiously.

"If you have to," Calder said. He looked at the others for support, but he didn't see any. The opposite, in fact.

"She's not killing the dog," Fel said with a menace Nika hadn't ever heard before. "And neither are you."

"But . . ." Calder started, but he could see which way the wind was blowing. "Fine, then. But if that thing starts to give us away . . ."

The six kids started moving off again, and Nika looked down at the dog that was trotting by her side.

For the first time in close to a full day, she felt happy.

Chapter 6
Rika

"You know, Baba, you can't just keep calling him 'boy,'"

The group had stopped for a break, and Nika was feeding the dog part of her last sandwich.

"I know. I just haven't thought of a name yet."

Rika didn't remind her that the dog already had a name. He had been chained in someone's yard, after all. But she liked seeing Nika preoccupied with something else at the moment. If the dog made her happy, then so be it.

Frankly, Rika was just a little bit jealous, both of her twin to have something take her mind off their terrible situation, and to have the dog sitting there loving on her. She scooted over and gave the dog a pat. It made her ridiculously pleased when the dog interrupted his love fest with Nika to give her hand a lick, too.

Rika was proud of her father. He was a Marine colonel, a leader in the Corps and respected by all. And Rika knew he was doing important things, protecting the citizens of the Regency. But being a military brat had its downside. They'd never lived in a house for more than three years, for example, and that meant always being the new kids and having to make new friends. That was one reason she'd always gone out of her way to include Lemul in their activities. She knew what it was like to move to a new place, and at least she had Nika. Lemul had no one when he'd moved in.

Almost as bad as being uprooted every few years was the fact that they'd never been able to have a pet. Planetary restrictions on the importation of pets, with quarantines that could stretch upwards of a year, meant that having a dog or cat was problematic at best. The twins had always wanted a pet, but that had always been out-of-reach.

The yellow dog was mangy and was hardly about to win any dog shows; in fact, he was downright ugly. But he was ugly in a cute way, at least until he bared his teeth. Then he looked downright vicious. But he'd already bonded with Nika.

Her twin took a final bite of her sandwich, then held the last piece above the dog's head. He sat, his eyes fixated on it, his tail wagging in the dirt like their granny sweeping up her yard.

"Not yet," Nika said.

The dog gulped, then licked his jaw.

Nika lowered the bit of sandwich and opened her hand. Like a cobra strike, the dog snapped it out of her hand, his teeth clacking while Nika laughed. Rika frowned. One little miscalculation, one little shift of her hand, and he'd have bit it. They didn't need an injury now to slow them down.

She looked up at the thought. The sun was high in the sky. Without their wristcomps working, she didn't know what time it was, but it had to be close to noon. They still had a ways to go to reach the depot.

"I think we'd better get a move on," she told the others.

"About time," Calder muttered, just loud enough for her to hear.

The guy was being a jerk, mad that the others hadn't backed him up. But Rika didn't say anything. They were all under a ton of stress, so she wanted to cut him some slack. The enemy was the Krackles, not each other.

Rika took a last swallow of water, then stepped off with the others. The pack still bounced just below her butt, but without much in it, that wasn't as bothersome as it had been. That was a reminder, however, that she wasn't outfitted for any long period of time.

Within ten minutes, the dirt road they'd been walking came to a stop along a paved road. She and Fel debated for a minute if it was Highway 32 or not. Fel thought it was, but Rika felt it wasn't large enough. Regardless, they had to cross it, which started another debate. Should they go one-at-a-time, or all at once? Rika tried to remember if her dad had ever told them what was best, but her mind was blank, and Nika wasn't helping. In the end, they all rushed over at the same time, diving for the bushes on the far side where they lay panting in fear that they'd been spotted.

No Krackles came down the road to pick them up, so with relief, they stood up and moved deeper into the trees. The section of woods wasn't extensive, though, ending at another field. And on the far side of the field were commercial buildings. Highway 32. Fel frowned, but while tempted, Rika didn't rub it in.

"Let's get away from the buildings before we cross," Fel said.

"We need to get more food," Gren told him.

"I see a Shrimp 'N Chic," Lemul said, pointing to one of the buildings a hundred meters or so away.

They were behind the buildings, and so Rika could only see the top of the sign in the front. She couldn't read it, but it sure looked like it could be a Shrimp 'N Chic. Their father hated the chain, calling it . . . well, their mother always hit him in the arm when he said it, telling him to mind his language. The twins had been around Marines long enough to know that cursing was as normal to them as breathing air, and what their father called the place *was* pretty funny.

The twins liked the place though, happy when they arrived to see that they were on Arcadia, too. Their dad may be right in that neither a real chicken nor shrimp had ever gotten near the place, but when you deep fried it, any manufactured food tasted good.

"Oh, a Shrimp 'N Chic?' Calder asked, perking up for the first time since Nika picked up the dog. "I'm up for that."

Fel looked like he wanted to argue, but just as Calder knew he was outvoted before, so did Fel now. He did convince them not to cross the soybean field but to go down to the fence line, then take that to the highway.

The six reached the back of the small strip mall and stopped to listen. The place was silent.

"Let's just go," Calder said. "Krackles won't be inside, right? They can't eat people food."

"But the zombies can," Fel said. "Right?"

He looked directly at Rika as if she was the end-all font of knowledge. But he was correct.

"Yeah, they can eat human food. They're practically human."

"Well, we can't just sit here forever, wondering if they're in there," Calder said, giving Fel a challenging stare.

"I'm going," Gren said, unslinging the old hunting rifle and holding it ready. "You all just stay here. If you hear me shout, then run."

"No, we're all going. If there's a zombie there, we need to take it out together," Fel insisted.

Rika thought Gren had it right, though. The Krackles were the big threat, and they almost assuredly had the road covered. Whether they'd do anything about six kids off on their own was debatable, but better one go out first instead of all six.

They crossed to the back of the buildings, then hugged the walls as they edged around the side and to the front. The nearest store was a small parts store, then the Shrimp 'N Chic was next.

Fel stuck his head around the corner and took a long look.

"The Shrimp 'N Chic's door looks like it's open, and I didn't see anything on the highway. I think the coast is clear."

"Then let's do it," Calder said. "I'm starving."

"I told you to bring real food, not snacks," Gren said.

"I brought what I had," he said with a shrug.

"Enough. Let's just go," Rika told them. She was done with the bickering. Getting some more food now was a good idea, but they had to find their families, first and foremost.

"You heard her," Fel said. "On three! One . . . two . . . three!"

"Don't let the zombies get you," Calder shouted as they rushed around the corner and to the restaurant.

Fel reached the door first and flung it open as they all rushed in . . . and froze. Behind the counter, a wild-looking zombie, a shrimpburger in her hand, opened her mouth and screamed bloody murder, half-eaten pieces of the burger shooting across the restaurant.

Chapter 7
Nika

"Zombie!" Calder yelled, picking up a chair by the back and holding it high like a club, while Gren pointed her old rifle at it.

The being behind the counter seemed to regain her composure as she tried to swallow what was left of her shrimpburger so she could talk.

"What are you do—"

Her eyes got wide, and she ducked behind the counter as Calder launched his chair across the floor to her, bouncing it off the counter.

"Get it!" he shouted, reaching for another chair before Nika grabbed his arm.

"Stop it, Calder!"

"It's a zombie!"

"She's a person," Nika told him, not letting go.

Calder looked confused. "Not a zombie?"

"Jeeze, you're going crazy," she said, looking at the others.

Except for Rika, the other three didn't look convinced, but at least Gren lowered the muzzle of her rifle.

Nika rolled her eyes and said, "You there, behind the counter. Are you a zombie?"

"What?" the woman's voice reached them. "Of course, I'm not a zombie. Why the hell do you think I'm one of them?"

"How do we know that?" Fel asked.

Nika gave him a frown. She'd expected more from him.

"Did you see her clothes? And her hair?"

Zombies all wore the one-piece overalls, and they shaved their heads to either bald or to a stubble. The woman behind the counter had long hair and was wearing a pink t-top and what looked to be blue jeans.

"Yeah . . ." Calder said uncertainly.

"You, behind the counter, stand up," Nika said.

"Are you going to throw a chair at me?"

"No."

"I want to hear that punk say it, not you."

Nika looked at Calder and mouthed, "Say it."

Now it was his turn to roll his eyes, but he said, "I'm not going to throw a chair at you."

"And the other one, the one with the gun. Is she gonna shoot me?"

Nika gave Gren a hard stare, and the teen reluctantly said, "I won't fire."

There was a stir, and a moment later, the woman peered over the edge of the counter. She took them in for a moment, then stood up. Skeleton thin, she looked to be in her mid-twenties or so.

"Me a zombie? I thought you were zombies. Made me lose my Double Shrimp."

Half of it was still in her hand, not that Nika corrected her.

"What's your name?" Rika asked.

"Glennis Flint. And who are you kids?"

"Flint? You related to Terry?" Gren asked.

"My brother."

"OK, she's not a zombie. I know Terry," Gren announced to the others, finally slinging the hunting rifle back onto her shoulder.

"Saint Peter's beard, I told you I'm not a zombie," she grumbled, then took a bite of her burger. "And what are you kids doing here?"

"Trying to get something to eat," Calder said.

"I mean, what are you doing out like this. The damned Krackles are everywhere."

She moved aside, though, waving a hand at the display pad. Shrimp 'N Chics did not have cooks nor serving staff, just a single "guest relations" person. Diners chose any of the dozen or so sandwiches and six sides, hit the display, and the order was reconstituted, heated, and served.

"Better get it quick, though. This place is running on backup power."

All six rushed the counter at that, quickly tapping in their orders. A small red warning triangle was flashing on the display, sign that the power would soon be cut off. Rika thought she could eat an unreconstituted and unheated shrimp or oyster if she had to, but heated sounded much better.

Within 30 seconds, their food was delivered, and six hungry kids grabbed their food and dug in while Glennis watched bemusedly.

Nika bit into her Shrimp and Bacon burger, the S-Sauce dripping down her chin. Rika reached over and wiped the sauce off Nika's face, asking, "Is it a sin that we're enjoying this so much? I mean, with Mom, you know . . ."

"Just enjoy it while you can. We're going to need the strength."

She felt a nudge on her leg, and the dog sat there, one paw on her and looking up with begging eyes. Nika pulled off a chunk of bacon and gave it to the dog, who wolfed it down.

"I'm going to get another," she told her twin.

"Now that you're getting fed, maybe you'll tell me what you're doing here?" Glennis asked again.

"We're going to find our folks," Fel said as he crammed his triple into his mouth.

"Honey, they've probably been taken. I'm surprised to see you kids running free now."

"We know they've been taken," Lemul said. "We saw it happen. We're going to the camp where they're being held."

"And do what? Break them out? Sorry, kids, but your folks are gone. All you can do now is head for the hills and hide out until the Marines come. If they come."

"Of course, the Marines are coming," Rika snapped. "My father took the regiment to take back **Telluride**, and now they're on the way home."

"I hope so, kid. But until then, you need to stay free."

"Not without my mom and Mace," Fel said.

A look of sadness swept over the older woman's eyes. "I know it sucks, but you've got to let it go. Your kin are on their way to serve the Krackles. Just be glad they're alive."

"No! We're going to find them," Fel said, pushing his face close to hers, his eyes blazing.

She put a hand on his shoulder and refused to flinch. "And then what? Get captured yourself? Become Krackle slaves?"

"If we have to, yes."

Nika was surprised at his response. She had never considered that. She really didn't know what they were going to do when they reached the camp, but that? Allow themselves to be captured? If they did that, would they even be allowed to stay together?

She looked over to her sister. She missed her mother terribly, but the thought of losing Rika, too, was something she couldn't even consider.

And what about their father? What would he do if he came back and he'd lost all three of them?

Her hand drifted down to pet the dog's head, unconsciously seeking solace. He tilted his head up and licked her fingers, either in comfort or to clean up any of the sauce on her hands.

"That won't help them. Tell you what. Why don't you, all of you, come with me. We'll head up the Silver Range, find some others. Not everyone's been captured. We'll wait until the twins' father here comes back, and hopefully, with a lot more than a regiment of reservists. We'll pull through it."

"You didn't hear me," Fel said, pushing his face closer. "We're going to find our families."

As if only now realizing how big Fel was, how menacing he looked, Glennis backed up, a look of uncertainty in her eyes. She opened her mouth to argue, but nothing came out.

"I . . . I . . ." was all she managed before she stepped back and grabbed her bright pink pack and clutched it to her chest. A child's school pack with the name Leeanne on the back. An image of a girl's face with the school ID, a blonde girl who looked like a young Glennis.

Was Leeanne her child? Was she taken, too?

Nika was suddenly sure she was right.

"You're stupid if you think you can do anything," Glennis said. "But, good luck. I can't—I won't—go with you. I'm not going to let myself become a zombie."

She hurriedly closed her pack, which had been stuffed with Shrimp 'N Chics. She gave the six of them one more look before she bolted for the door.

"What a bitch," Gren said as the door closed behind her.

"That pack? That was her kid's," Rika said.

So, you saw it, too.

"And she's going to leave her kid with the Krackles?" The scorn was dripping from Fel's voice.

"We're not all the same, Fel," Lemul said.

"Thank God for that."

"We can't do anything about her," Rika said. "But we can load up on food here. Let's do it and get on with it."

Silently, the six entered more orders.

The battery power lasted for another fifteen sandwiches before it died.

Chapter 8
Rika

The six stared at the sign from where they were hidden in the tall grass.

Main Gate
Yaakov Ammunition Depot and Armory
Regency Department of Defense
1 Mile

"So, what do we do? Walk up to the main gate and ask them to let our families go?" Calder asked.

And that was the crux of the matter, Rika knew. She had no plan. They'd been so consumed with getting the depot that it had been easy to kick whatever else had to be done down the road. But they were there now, and they had to come up with something. She didn't have anything, but she sure hoped someone else did.

"Something's coming," Lemul said.

Damn! That boy must have superhuman hearing. Rika strained, but she couldn't pick anything up. Not that she doubted him.

It took a good twenty seconds before she could hear the approach of a truck. She knew she should hug the ground, hoping not to be noticed, but she peeked as the truck reached them. She could clearly see the zombie driving it before it turned down the road to the main gate.

"I think it's got more prisoners," she said.

"We can't stay here," Nika said. "Too much traffic."

"What about back down the highway to Dwyer Road?" Gren said. "I think we can get closer to the fence over there, cutting through the woods."

"And then what?" Calder asked again. "We still don't have a plan."

Rika wished she could shut him up, but he was right.

"We recon again," Nika said.

"Like back at our houses," Rika added. "Look, until we know what's going on in there, where our families are, then we can't make any plan. We'd just be spitting in the dark."

"I think I know where you mean. There's a small strip mall—"

"With the Shrimp 'N Chic?" Fel asked. "We already came all this way, and I don't want to waste any more time."

"No, not that one. Where Dwyer Road forks off the highway. There's a small one back there with the charging station," she said, pointing down the highway.

"Yeah, that one. I think part of mainside's pretty close to it," Gren said.

Rika looked at the others. Calder was sulking, Lemul was standing there, his face expressionless, and Fel was anxious, but none of them were arguing anymore. Rika thought Fel would if he could put together a cognizant thought.

Why does Nika even like him? He's dumb as a rock.

She gave them another ten seconds.

"Then, let's get going. We can set up a little camp there while we put together our plan."

"You have a plan?" Calder asked.

"Not yet. But as soon as we get eyes on the depot, I sure the hell will."

Chapter 9
Nika

Nika stared as the Krackle transport landed on the old depot's ball field. The dog perked up in interest, and she put a restraining hand on his neck, pulling him close. Within moments, a side ramp shot out, and two zombie guards exited, followed by a handful of frightened-looking people, their hands restrained in front of them. The second person stumbled and went down, only to have one of the zombies jerk him back up.

The kids had been lying in the tall grasses outside the fence to the depot for the last twenty minutes, and it had been instantly clear that they'd been right. The depot was being used as a collection center for human prisoners. At least fifty were sitting in rows alongside one of the buildings, guarded by zombies in the tan overalls, and others could be seen being escorted back and forth.

It made perverse sense. The Yaakov Ammunition Depot and Armory had been built early on in the settlement of the area, back when raids by pirates and bandits were rare, but real concerns. Completely fenced in, there were barracks, admin buildings, supply warehouses, and of course, the armories and munitions dumps. Abandoned after the construction of the far more robust NMRS in Logan, there had been various proposals as to what to do with the facility, but nothing had ever come to fruition. Manned by a ten-person maintenance crew, it had become just part of the landscape.

"Hell, isn't that the woman, the one at the Shrimp 'N Chic?" Gren asked.

Without the binos, Nika couldn't tell, but there was a prisoner walking down the ramp with a bright pink backpack.

"Yep. Glynnis," Rika, with the binos, said. "Glad we didn't follow her."

"Damn. You've got that right," Fel said.

"I knew she was a crazy hoot," Calder muttered. "I should have beaned her with that chair. Might have saved her from getting snatched."

"Look, a Krackle," Rika said. "In the doorway."

Nika could just make out the tall shape in the transport's hatch as the human prisoners were marched across the field. She knew the Krackles couldn't actually "see," but she also knew that it was "watching" the human prisoners' progress. Maybe it didn't trust its zombie slaves to get it done.

The dozen or so prisoners were led to some old, decrepit stands where they were handed over to four more zombies, who, in turn, took them into the depot proper. The original two returned to the shuttle and followed the Krackle inside. Within thirty seconds, the hatch had closed, and the shuttle took off, flying back almost over the kids' heads. All of them froze, afraid to move a muscle.

The dog gave a frightened yip, and Calder hissed, "Keep that stupid thing quiet!"

Nika pulled the dog in closer, but she didn't raise her head again until the transport disappeared behind them. She pet the nervous dog, then shifted her attention and tried to make out more of the camp. It was no use. She held out her hand, and Rika handed over the binos.

Much better, she thought as she let the bino's tiny AIs handle the focusing.

That certainly was Glennis being led into the camp. The look of defeat was glaringly evident in her slumped shoulders and shuffling gait. Nika was sorry about that, but Glennis was not her main concern. She scanned the entire area within her field of view, looking for one specific figure.

"You see her?" Rika asked.

"No."

"There's lots more to the depot," Rika assured her.

Nika handed the binos to Fel, who eagerly took them. Rika was right. They had a very limited view of the camp. She'd seen fewer than a hundred of her fellow humans, and if most of the town was captured, much less people from the surrounding region, there had to be more than 20,000 in the camp.

So, where's mom?

She had to think of it that way. Nika didn't want to contemplate their mother not being in there. She knew their mom was not out in the hills, like Glynnis had intended. She'd seen their mom taken, so if she wasn't being held, then there was only one other possibility.

None of the kids had seen any dead bodies, but she wasn't naïve. This was war, and people do get killed, even captives valuable as slaves.

Nika pushed down her rising fear, compartmentalizing it somewhere deep inside of her. It was still there, a rumbling, festering ball that threatened to overwhelm her. She just couldn't afford to lose control now.

She glanced over at Fel. The boy's lower lip was trembling, his face turning red. Whatever demons he was wrestling with looked they were winning the battle, and she couldn't let that happen. They didn't need a blow-up now.

"Everybody, we need to pull back and figure out what to do," she said.

"We go find our families," Fel said, his voice taut. "You said that's what we were going to do."

He's losing control.

"We will, but we need to do this smart."

"She's right," Gren said, pulling on his arm. "We'll figure this out."

He obviously wasn't convinced but crawled back with the others until the trees hid them from the camp. They didn't stop there but kept going, all the way back to the small pond off of Dwyer Road, a good ten-minute walk away.

Under the cover of the drooping branches of an immense willow, they discussed what to do next. "Discussed" in the broadest sense of the word. Arguing was a form of discussion, after all. Nika and Rika favored waiting until dark and seeing if they could get close enough to catch the attention of one of the prisoners and find out what was happening inside the camp. The others thought that was stupid as the Krackles could "see" in the dark. Nika pointed out that they'd only seen four Krackles so far, five if you counted the one in the shuttle. Most of the guards were zombies, and as far as anyone knew, they couldn't see in the dark any better than humans could.

Fel favored a more direct approach of breaking into the camp, Gren wanted to observe from a distance, hoping to catch sight of one of their family members, while Calder shifted from one impractical scheme to another. Lemul just listened, not saying much.

They had to break off several times to let tempers cool down. Nika knew the fighting was stupid. The Krackles were the enemy, not each other. But she didn't have a magic plan that would unite them, or more importantly, would work. Her only hope was that with more information, something would come up.

She and Rika sat at the edge of the pond while Gren took Fel aside. It was getting late. Soon, the sun would set, and they still weren't any closer to an agreement in a course of action, and that was frustrating. Sensing her mood, the dog wormed his way between the twins and put his head in Nika's lap.

"Push me your pack, will you?" Nika said.

Rika flipped it over, and Nika pulled out one of the unreconstituted burgers they'd stuffed inside when the processor at the Shrimp 'N Chic ran out of power. The thing was a flat, dense brick of food. Nutritionally, it was the same as any of the prepared sandwiches. It just wasn't in a form conducive for eating. It might be OK for the dog, however.

"Give me Dad's knife."

Rika handed it over, and Nika used it to slice the Chic Special's packaging open. She gave the hockey puck a sniff, then held it to the dog, who licked it, his tail wagging. He tried to bite a chunk off of it, but all that did was knock the burger to the ground.

Nika picked it up, brushed off the dirt, then used the knife to worry a small piece of the burger free. The dog happily took the chunk, gnawing on it like a piece of dried rawhide.

"You got a name for him yet?" Rika asked, patting the dog on the head.

"I don't know. You got any ideas?"

"How about 'Panhandler.' He's always begging for food."

Nika just rolled her eyes.

"I wonder who kept him chained up like that?"

"Whoever it was, they're probably in the depot now," Rika said.

"I don't want to say karma, but . . ."

Rika just smiled and looked out over the pond with her. There was a swirl as a fish came to the surface. Everything looked so normal, as if 500 or 600 meters away, most of the humans in the region weren't being held prisoner.

"You know, we really need to figure out what we're going to do," Rika said.

"And I don't know what that is. Even if we do slip near tonight and manage to find someone to talk to, then what? I sure don't know."

"Like I said, with more information, maybe we'll think of something."

"Hey, you guys," Gren said, coming up from behind them. "I've talked to Fel. He's willing to go along with you for tonight, but then we need to go over all of this again in the morning."

"OK, good," Rika said before pointing over to where Fel, Calder, and Lemul were standing together. "What about Calder?"

"He's . . . he's Calder," she said, as if that answered the question.

Gren motioned Fel over.

"So, we talk again in the morning?" he asked.

"OK," Rika said. "In the morning."

"And it's you and me doing this tonight?"

That took Nika by surprise, and Rika said, "Just like before, this should be Nika and me."

"Nika's got that dog."

Which was a salient point, Nika knew. But there was no way she wasn't going to do this with her sister. She'd tie the dog down here, if she had to.

As if he could sense her distress, the dog started to growl, a low, evil-sounding challenge.

"Stop it. It's just Fel."

She reached down to pet the dog, but he wasn't looking at Fel. He was focused beyond the three of them, looking into the trees, the hackles on his shoulder raised.

What the?

Nika was hit with a wave of . . . itches? As if poked with the straws of a broom. A crackling like that of a campfire reached out to her. She didn't have time to think. She just reacted.

"RUN!" she shouted. "RUN!"

Chapter 10
Rika

Rika felt the needle-like wave wash across her body, realizing what it had to be a split-second after Nika shouted, "Run!" She took off after her twin, mindlessly fleeing.

Krackles emitted a variety of waves to understand their environment. Most could not be detected by humans, but a few, the "cell-cracker" being the most famous, could be felt . . . and heard. The waves penetrated the human body, supposedly revealing everything from bones all the way down to their very DNA. The crackling sound that accompanied the wave was where they got their name: Krackles.

Stupid! Was all she could think as she bolted alongside the edge of the pond. Of course, the Krackles had surveillance out there, and coming this close to the depot probably increased the priority on them being picked up.

"Faster!" she yelled at Nika.

But her sister had to step around the dog, which was running right at her feet, barking up a storm.

Rika risked a glance behind. Gren and Fel were running in the other direction, and she couldn't see Lemul and Calder. But what caught her full attention was three huge shapes emerging from the trees, moving too quickly and nimbly for something so big. One of them turned unerringly toward the two sisters as they ran.

Blatant fear gave Rika a blast of adrenaline. All she could think of was to get away from the horror chasing them.

Nika dodged to the right, Rika on her tail. The Krackle shifted to cut them off. The attempt to shake the thing had ended up costing them a chunk of their lead.

"Keep straight!" Rika shouted.

They were smaller than the Krackle, able to dodge through the undergrowth where it had to plow through. Not that it sounded like it was having much of a problem with that. But it was the only thing that Rika could think of.

Nika was gasping for air, giving out small cries of terror with each breath. Rika knew she could run faster, but the thought of abandoning her twin never crossed her mind. This was Nika!

Rumor was that the Krackles were not as effective in enclosed spaces, and Nika was trying to get them around the pond and to some of the buildings on Dwyer Road. Maybe they could lose the thing in a crawl space or something.

This was a Krackle soldier, armed and dangerous. Rika knew they'd be dead by now if that was its intention. It wanted them as slaves. But if it looked like they were getting away, would it cut them down?

She wasn't even going to consider that. They *had* to get away. From far behind, two shots, then a piercing scream reached them. Rika couldn't tell if the scream was from Gren or one of the boys, but there was nothing she could do about it now. She had to think of the two of them as the Krackle closed in behind.

Rika risked another look and shrieked. It was almost on them

She wasn't going to give up, though. Dodging under a fallen tree gained them a precious second or two as they curved around the pond, getting closer to the buildings. But they had to clear the brook which fed the pond and then some heavier reeds on the other side of it. The small creek was just shy of two meters across. Slow flowing and stagnant, the water was maybe five or six inches deep this late in the dry season, with mud banks on either side.

Nika, in the lead, jumped over, landing on the other side, but slipping in the mud. Rika had already launched herself when Nika went down, and she couldn't avoid the collision. Rika hit her twin, knocking both of them flat, half in and half out of the water. Both struggled to free themselves, but that only got them mired deeper in the muck.

Fully on top of her twin, Rika turned to see the Krackle come to a stop at the edge of the creek. Clad in combat armor, with no eyes in the protuberance that took the place of a human head, it was a nightmare. The emitters—hair-like organs that sent out the more powerful waves—rose from under cutouts in the grey armor. A moment later, as Nika struggled under her, they were hit with the waves again as the thing crackled.

"Stay still!" Rika hissed at her twin as the Krackle stepped into the creek, her skin crawling with itches.

A long lower arm reached out, but despite terror willing her legs to work, she held still. She wasn't quite sure what was forming in her mind, but she knew a plan was brewing trying to break free of her consciousness.

It better break free now! she mentally screamed as the pinchers closed on her upper arm and yanked her free of the muck.

"Freeze!" she yelled at Nika as her thoughts coalesced on an idea.

It was a stupid hunch, but it was all she had. If the Krackle could really see down to the DNA level, it was possible that as it just blasted them, it thought there was only one human there in the creek—twins shared their DNA, after all, so there was only one set there.

That ignored the fact that it had to have known that there were two of them fleeing, but Rika was grasping at any life ring at the moment.

Wet and covered in the fetid mud, Rika writhed and slipped out of the thing's pinchers. She darted to her left, not expecting to get away, but wanting to get the Krackle to shift its position. The upper arm, with the more flexible "fingers," more like miniature octopus arms, snapped out and latched onto her with a strength she knew she couldn't break.

Over the thing's shoulder, Nika had turned and was sitting up.

"Get down, Baba! You need to be free if you're going to be able to rescue us!"

Nika's eyes widened, but she nodded and slid back down into the muck.

Without seemingly much of an effort, the Krackle lifted Rika and held her in front of its torso. Rika could imagine the waves washing over her as it examined her.

Human xenobiologists were pretty confident that while the lower frequency waves were painted a pretty good picture of what was going on around a Krackle, and it was almost in a 360 view, it was nevertheless a low-resolution image. For a detailed reckoning, it had to use the gamma waves, the ones emitted and read by the ferrous oxide system in the body, and this system used more energy.

When the emitters rose again, Rika braced herself for the gamma blast. This time, she could almost feel them dissect her, tissue by tissue, cell by cell. It made her nerves scream, worse than any fingernails on an inkboard could ever achieve.

Whatever it read seemed to satisfy it, and Rika, looking past it to Nika, lying as still as a statue, prayed it would leave with her.

No such luck. It slowly turned around, whether because it remembered there were two of them or if Nika, even in the water and mud, was setting off one of the other systems, Rika didn't know. She screamed and kicked, but to no avail. She was helpless.

The thing turned around and stood still for a moment, as if listening—which it probably was. Its systems could hear noise in almost the same way that Earthlife did.

There was a flicker as the emitters on its body started to rise again, and Rika knew the game was up. Water or not, muck or not,

Nika could not hide from the gamma waves. If the Krackle could see their bones, if it could really see their DNA, then a little muck wasn't going to hide her.

Rika cringed, waiting for the blast when a yellow missile launched itself at the Krackle, latching onto the fingers on its upper left arm. With a horrendous screech, the Krackle darted for the dry ground, whipping its arm back and forth.

The dog was growling, but its jaws were latched tight, and once, twice, the Krackle tried to fling it off, whipping the dog's body back and forth. Finally, it grabbed the dog with a pincher hand and ripped the dog free—at least two tentacle-fingers still in the brave dog's jaws.

The Krackle slammed the dog onto the ground, and with palpable anger, strode over to where it was struggling to get its feet under it. The Krackle leaned over it, emitters extended, then blasted the poor dog with what had to be a hammer blow.

Rika, not even in the direct path of the wave, almost passed out, pain shooting through her. The dog didn't even whimper and just went still.

Rika fought to retain consciousness as the Krackle stood over the dog, toeing the limp body. She couldn't see her twin, but she was praying the Krackle had been distracted. That, or it was depleted from whatever energy fueled the gamma waves. From the way it was heaving like a human runner, she knew that last blast had taken a lot out of it.

After a long moment that seemed to drag on and on, the Krackle straightened up and emitted a staccato series of whistles. Without a backward glance at the creek, and with Rika firmly in its grasp, it started back the way it had come.

Knowing that Nika was safe for the moment, Rika finally let go and sunk into darkness.

Chapter 11
Nika

Nika lay motionless in the mud and water, afraid to move. Tears, long since dried, had formed little rivulets down her face, and her heart was heavy in her chest.

Oh, Rika, what did you do?

During their attempt to escape, Nika had been petrified with fear. Without her twin pushing her, she didn't think she would have made it that far. But when that monster pulled Rika off her, that fear had disappeared, to be replaced with anger, and she had started to get up, to bodily attack the Krackle that dared take her twin.

Until Rika had stopped her.

"Get down, Baba! You need to be free if you're going to be able to rescue us!"

Seventeen words, words she'd repeated a thousand times in her head as she lay in the creek. Seventeen words that had stopped her in her tracks.

Nika was supposed to be the cool-headed one of them, Rika the brash twin, acting on impulse. Yet it was Rika who'd stayed rational. If Nika had been taken, too, then there would have been no hope of rescue. Not that there was much now. What could she do, all alone?

But any chance was better than no chance. Rika had been right. Still, if she'd been captured, then they'd still be together.

Nika had never felt so alone in all her life.

As the afternoon wore on, Nika was numb. She didn't know why the Krackle had left her, and something told her that was important, but her mind was mush, and she just couldn't think. She had to come up with a plan, but there was nothing. Just cold despair.

It was whimpering that finally roused her. At first, she dismissed the sound, not knowing what it was. Each time she noticed it, it disappeared. But despite the situation, her brain was still working.

"The dog!" she said, suddenly sitting up.

She'd seen the dog attack the Krackle, seen it whipped back and forth as it refused to release the monster, and then, she'd seen him slammed to the ground. Nika hadn't been a target of the Krackle's blast, but she could sense it, and she knew the dog was dead.

But dead dogs don't whimper.

She struggled to pull free of the muck, almost losing a shoe in the process, but she finally made it across the creek and to the bank. The dog was still, the slight rise and fall of his chest the only sign of life. Nika knelt beside the dog, taking his head in her lap.

The dog gave a soft yelp and weakly struggled for a moment before it opened its eyes. His tongue emerged to lick her hand.

The floodgates opened as everything hit her at once. The invasion. Their mother. Running from the Krackle. Losing Rika.

She hugged the dog tight around the neck and bawled. She knew she should be quiet, but she couldn't help herself. She'd kept too much pent inside of herself.

After a long five minutes, the sobs slowed down and eventually stopped. Rika wiped a muddy arm across her face, not doing much good at all.

The dog's eyes were open and alert, but it wasn't moving. Nika didn't know if his back had been broken by being slammed to the ground or if the gamma blast had damaged its nerves. It was bad, though, she knew.

"Don't worry, boy. I'm going to take care of you." She gave a short, self-mocking laugh. "And here I am, still calling you 'Boy.' Rika said I have to name you, and I guess you deserve it now. You were a hero attacking the Krackle like that."

His tongue snaked out to lick her hand again.

"What, you like that? That you're a hero? Well, I guess it fits. Hero. That's your name now."

She slowly got to her feet, lifting the dog—no, "Hero." He gave a soft whine as she struggled to find a comfortable way to hold him. He wasn't a huge dog, but he wasn't small, either, and Nika wasn't very big herself. Finally, she held Hero close to her chest, his head over her shoulder.

For lack of anywhere else, she headed back to where they'd been when the Krackles attacked. The light was fading, and she saw danger in every shadow. A bird taking off from a low hanging branch almost gave her a heart attack. But there was nothing to do but push on, and quicker than she expected, she arrived at the spot, and to her surprise, both Rika and her packs were there on the ground, undisturbed. Three more packs were scattered around the small area.

Nika carefully laid Hero on the ground beside her pack, then rummaged inside for one of the Shrimp 'N Chic sandwiches. She didn't know if Hero could eat, but she had to try and get something down him.

The unreconstituted sandwich was dense and tough, and she worried the edge of it with her teeth, hoping to tear off a chunk, when a glint caught her eye, and with a cry of triumph, Rika swooped down to snatch up her father's Kri-Blade, holding it tightly to her chest. It wasn't much, but she felt better having something in her hand.

Plus, she could now cut the Shrimp 'N Chic. The sharp blade sliced through the sandwich, and she held the small piece in front of Hero. The dog licked it, but didn't take it into his mouth, and that worried Nika. Hero had to eat if he was going to heal.

You need to eat, too, she reminded herself when her stomach rumbled.

With a shrug, she put the Hero-licked piece in her mouth. It tasted like packaging and was brick-hard, but if she could get it down, it would provide her with much-needed calories.

It took her at least fifteen minutes, but she managed to swallow about half of the sandwich before she quit. Her jaws ached, and her mouth was dry. Rika pulled out a water packet from Rika's pack, took a long swallow, then offered the rest to Hero. Between the two of them, they managed to get some of the water down his throat with the rest spilling on the ground.

She started to wipe his jaws and noticed that her hands were still covered with dried mud. That made Nika examine the rest of her, and as that reminded her that she was still caked with the rancid muck, it started an itch-fest. She had to clean up.

And there was a pond, not four strides away. A big, giant bathtub.

She slipped out of her shoes and then pulled at her what-used-to-be-khaki top, but the dried mud made it stiff. With a shrug, she walked into the pond until it was waist deep, then sat, the water up to her neck. She'd shed most of the mud in the pond first, then take off her pants and top to wash them by hand.

She shivered in the night air, suddenly feeling vulnerable again. Having second thoughts about being out in the water, she started to creep back to the shore when a sharp crack filled the air. Rika ducked lower in the water, only her eyes and ears above the surface, and froze.

There was silence. No trill of insects, no owls hooting. Heavy, oppressive silence.

Maybe I imagined it, she tried to convince herself.

There was another snap, then the sound of something moving through the bushes.

Nika sprang out of the water and rushed to where she'd left Hero, snatching up her father's Kris-Blade and wheeling just as a dark shape came out of the trees. Nika crouched, presenting a smaller target, and held the blade out, ready to jab.

"Rika, is that you?" a voice hissed.

Nika shook her head in confusion. "Who are you?"

"It's me, Fel!"

Relief swept over her.

"I'm Nika," she said. "What happened to you? Where's Gren?"

He stepped closer, out of the shadows.

"I don't know," Fel said, his voice breaking. "I think the Krackles got her. We were . . ."

Nika dropped the knife and rushed Fel, taking him into an embrace as he broke into sobs.

"It's OK. It's OK," she said, holding him. "They got Rika, too."

"Rika, too? And I heard Cadler screaming. I think they got him and Lemul. That means it's only us."

As big as Fel was, as physically strong as he was, he'd somehow seemed to have shrunk, and Nika was the one supporting him.

"What are we going to do now?" he asked in a plaintive voice.

She pushed him away from her chest, her hands grasped around his upper arms, and gave him a hard shake. She felt a small shimmer of confidence returning, and she tried to fan that ember into a flame.

"What are we going to do? We're going to save our families! That's what we're going to do."

Chapter 12
Rika

"Wake up."

The voice was a million miles away, and Rika ignored it. It was just easier to do nothing. Thinking just seemed like it would take too much effort.

"Wake up." This time a foot nudged her hard in the side.

With a groan, she cracked open an eye . . . and sat up, scootching backward to get away from it. Him.

The zombie looked at her with bored eyes. Despite the shaved head, despite the almost furry-looking one-piece that no human had ever worn, it—he—looked human. His eyes were a pale blue, which just didn't seem right to Rika. They should be jet black, evil eyes.

The zombie raised a small object that looked like a simple pen and pressed it against her arm. Rika jerked back.

"Stay still," the zombie said in weirdly accented and stilted, but understandable Standard.

"How do you speak Standard?" Rika asked, eyeing the pen-thing warily.

The zombie ignored her, taking her left arm in his right, holding it fast and pressing the pen against it. Rika squirmed, but the zombie was too strong. There was a quick stabbing pain before the zombie withdrew, looking down at the pen. Whatever it indicated seemed to satisfy him.

"Are you in pain?" the zombie asked.

Which was not what Rika was expecting. This thing cared?

Then again, farmers on low-tech retro worlds cared about the health of their oxen, too.

She wondered what he wanted to hear and if she could game her answer to her benefit.

"Are you in pain?" the zombie asked, reaching for her again.

"No!" she squeaked, scooting back on the old military issue cot until her back was against the wall."

"Very well. You will now leave to your station."

He turned abruptly away and stalked out of the room. It was only then that Rika realized she was alone. The other five cots were empty.

Hope blossomed, and she slid off the cot, padding softly to the door.

Where another zombie, this one in a rougher-looking one-piece overall, a shiny band around each upper arm, met her.

"You need to come with me," this one said, but within the range of normal human accents.

Rika's mind was reeling. The other one, the one that had jabbed her, looked human but had non-human mannerisms and speech patterns. This woman, from the way she stood with one hand on her hip, the other holding a cylinder of some kind, simply screamed human. Real human.

"Are you a zombie?"

"Just get moving. I don't have all night here."

"But—"

"No damned buts, girl," she said, waving the cylinder. "Or you're gonna get your first taste of a prod. Trust me, you won't like it."

The way she held the "prod" showed an easy familiarity with it, and Rika was going to take her at her word. She put her head down and followed the guard, Rika guessed she was, across a small paved courtyard, a lone dim light the only illumination.

Rika tried to look cowed—which wasn't hard, given that was how she felt—but her eyes darted around, taking everything in. She didn't see any way out of her situation, but she tried to memorize everything as they approached the low, long building on the other side of the courtyard.

The place looked abandoned, with trash blowing around the grounds, but she could hear signs of life.

Her guard stopped by a door, then turned to her and said in a rote voice as if she'd said the same words a thousand times, "Get inside. This is your home for the next, hell, for a while. Don't get used to it. When you're allowed out in the morning, stay clear of the fences. Don't wander outside the immediate area. Don't fight. The bosses don't want their property damaged," she added, the first thing she'd said with any emotion. "Oh, and if you see a Master, you stop whatever your doing and freeze. Got that?"

"Yes, ma'am."

"You've been tagged, so don't you be thinking about any grand escape plan."

"Tagged?" Rika asked.

Did that other zombie inject me with some sort of tag?

"You're DNA. It's in the system now. You try and leave here, and the Masters will know. And if you think this is bad," she said, waving her prod, "you just try and get on *their* bad side."

Rika rubbed her arm where she'd been jabbed. If that was some sort of testing kit, then it worked far faster than any human DNA analysis. Unless the rumor was right, and the Krackles could read their DNA. It didn't seem possible, but then who knew what they could do?"

"That's it?" Rika asked, waiting for more bad news.

"Yep. That's it, unless you want more?"

"No!" Rika blurted out.

"Don't worry, honey. You'll get your training soon enough and be assigned your lifetask. You might as well enjoy your downtime while you can."

With that, she waved the prod in a sweep, indicating that she should enter the building. With a wary eye on the prod, she skirted around the guard and entered the building. The door closed behind her.

It was pitch black inside, and she could hear snoring and the soft rustle of bodies. Afraid to make a move and step on someone, she stood still, waiting for her eyes to adjust.

"It's OK. Just find a spot to lie down," a voice said from beneath her.

"I can't . . . I can't see anything."

"Just sit. You're OK right there," another voice said.

Suddenly weary, Rika slid to a sitting position. Her foot nudged someone, and she pulled her legs in tighter.

"Sorry," she whispered.

"Don't worry about it. Just try and get some sleep. If this is like yesterday, they'll get us all out of the barracks when the sun comes up."

"What's your name, sweetie?" another voice from the dark asked.

Rika hesitated. In the holovids, prisoners never told their names. But these were prisoners, too.

"Rika. Rika Ingersoll."

"Lisbeth Ingersoll's girl?" someone asked.

"Yes!" Rika blurted out. "Have you seen her? Do you know where she is?"

"No, I know her, but I haven't seen her. That don't mean nothing, though. The whole town's in here."

The flash of hope Rika had felt faded away.

"But we'll find her" the voice said. "Don't you worry none."

"We'll help you look tomorrow," the first voice said. "But now, you try and get some rest. It'll be morning soon enough. Come lay down next to me."

Rika leaned back against the woman. She didn't even know her name, but she took some comfort in the woman's presence.

But she didn't fall asleep, worried about Nika, worried about their mother. She lay there, listening to the muffled sobs, snores, and whispers of her fellow captives until dawn.

Chapter 13
Nika

Nika sat beside Hero, absentmindedly stroking his back. The dog seemed more alert, lifting his head and twitching his front paws. His hind legs remained limp and motionless, however.

Fel was on his back, still asleep. Nika wasn't sure how he did that. She slept in fits and starts throughout the night, cold and miserable, her imagination running wild. Most of all, it was the first time in her life she'd been without Rika, and she could feel a physical, empty void in her heart.

Rika had wanted her free so she could rescue her and Mom. But how? They didn't even have the rifle Gren had been carrying. And the last time they'd gotten close, they'd triggered some sort of alarm that had led to the attack on them.

But she had to do something, and do it before the Krackles left with their prisoners. For all she knew, they'd already started.

Where is the Navy?

Arcadia wasn't some frontier planet well off the shipping lines. The Navy and Marines should be able to react. This was the third day since the invasion, and the sector command had to know what had happened. When would they come to the rescue?

The Krackles probably had that answer, and they'd have already put to space before that. The thought drove Nika into a deeper depression and feeling of helplessness.

"Fel, wake up," she said as the boy snored.

If she was going to be sitting here depressed, then he was going to share it with her.

She kicked his feet. "Wake up!"

Fel opened his eyes, looked at her from the confused depths of sleep, then sat up as his brain slipped into gear.

"How is he?" he asked, nodding at Hero.

"His hind legs still don't work. He seems better, though."

The dog licked her hand as if he understood they were talking about him.

Fel frowned, then looked out from under the trees to the sky. A few towering clouds were orange and red in the dawn sun's light.

"Looks like it could rain later on today."

"How can you tell?" Nika asked. They were out in the open, with only the trees for shelter, and she didn't relish getting soaked in a downpour.

"The clouds. I've seen enough of them growing up here."

Which was probably true. He'd been born on Arcadia and had never been off-planet. Although technically birthright citizens, she and Rika had only arrived a year-and-a-half ago.

Arcadia's mid-belt had two rainy seasons: the spring rains where the days were overcast and misty, and the late summer and fall when the whompers hit.

Nika peered through the trees. The handful of scattered clouds might be bigger than normal, but not excessively so. She tried to remember back to last summer what the clouds were like, but she drew a blank.

Her attention switched back to the pond in alarm. She and Rika had been given the standard safety brief last year: stay out of creek beds and gullies. Even if the sky was clear overhead, a whomper ten klicks away could send a flash flood down any creekbed.

"Do we need to move Hero?" she asked. "If the pond floods, I mean."

"Don't worry about it. A pond like this will take some time to flood over its banks. We can move him if it comes to that."

She started to argue, then stopped herself cold. She was avoiding the real issue, and that was what to do to rescue the prisoners. But she didn't have an answer to that. Normally, she could talk it through with Rika, but now, all she had was Fel.

It can't hurt, she thought with a mental shrug.

"So, we know where everyone is being held. What we have to do is get them out before the Krackles leave, then keep them free until the Navy arrives."

"You've got an idea?" Fel asked hopefully.

No, I don't.

"I'm just working it through. I need to get a better idea of where our people are in the camp," she said, immediately knowing that was true. She had to go back and try and find out.

"OK, then, let's go. We don't have time to waste," he said, standing up.

"No! Just me." Nika wasn't quite sure why she said that, but it felt right.

"No way you're going alone. In fact, no way you're going. I'll go. You stay here with Hero."

"You're too big," she blurted. "You can't go."

"What do you mean?"

She didn't know what she meant, only that she was certain she was right.

"You're too easy to see," she said, fishing for a reason that made sense.

"What? That's BS. I can stay out of sight, like yesterday. Back in the trees."

And yet they spotted us. They didn't need to see us.

And it clicked. She knew why her subconscious had objected to Fel going.

"Look, they don't need to see us. They'd got the place under surveillance. They've got drones or sensors or whatever, and they're keyed for bigger bodies."

"Bigger bodies? I don't get it. What are you talking about?" he asked, his brows furrowed in confusion.

Nika realized he was not following her train of thought. Rika always maintained this was one of her problems, that she assumed everyone immediately saw things as clearly as she did

She took a deep breath and said, "We've got animals running around here. The Krackles don't want their surveillance sensors giving false alarms every time some dog or rabbit wanders by. They'll have got their systems set to a minimum mass. And you'll set them off, as big as you are."

Fel shook his head as he took that all in. "But you're still bigger than a rabbit."

Which was true, and that was only one possible fault with her logic. She was sure they had some sort of parameters on whatever sensors they were using, but it didn't have to be mass. But even if she was right, she was still seventy-seven pounds, and that was not insignificant.

"But not big enough to set them off," she said, trying to sound confident.

Fel scrunched his face as he tried to point out flaws in her logic. There were plenty of flaws, but he couldn't seem to pick any of them out.

"Look, let me give it a shot. I'll try to spot your mom and Mace, but you stay here, out of sight. Watch Hero in case it rains. I'll be back before *we* do anything," she said, with emphasis on the "we."

"But . . ."

Nika could tell he really wanted to disagree, but he didn't have a rational argument to make.

"I won't take long."

"How long is that?"

"Two hours. Three tops."

He stared at the ground for a long twenty seconds, and Nika could almost see the gears turning.

Finally, he said, "I still don't see why we both can't go." He looked at her to see if she'd give in, and when she just stared back, he sighed and said, "Two hours, then. No more. But don't do anything stupid on your own, OK?"

"I don't like to do stupid things."

Which isn't agreeing that I won't do them.

If the opportunity arose, she knew she'd do whatever it took.

"OK," Fel said, clearly unhappy with it.

"I need you to protect Hero. And don't let any Krackles come up from behind me."

"Yeah, I can do that," he said with more than a hint of relief as he twisted to look behind him. "I can do that."

Nika gently shifted Hero's head off her lap and stood. She started to pick up her pack, but then dropped it. If she was right about mass, she had to minimize it. Her pack wasn't part of her, so-to-speak, but she didn't know what the Krackles considered as part of a reading.

If I'm even right in this theory in the first place.

Nika took only her father's Kri-Blade. No food, no water. Nothing else.

"Well, I guess that's it," she said.

"Be careful, Nika," Fel said with a catch in his voice.

This has got to be hard on him, she realized. *He thinks he should be the one to rescue his family.*

Without thinking it through, Nika reached up, grabbed Fel's collar, and pulled him down.

"I'll be back, and we'll figure this out together, both of us," she whispered before giving him a firmly planted kiss on the cheek.

She released the stunned boy, wheeled, and disappeared into the woods.

Chapter 14
Rika

"Keep tee moving," the zombie said, giving the pregnant woman a light shove in the shoulder.

"Listen to her. She sounds like a freaking Quavarian," Rika whispered. "Keep *tee* moving."

"Probably is," Anna Reiker said.

"What do you mean? Quavarians aren't zombies.

"A quisling."

"A quisling? What the heck is a quisling?" Rika asked.

"You know, the old meaning. Someone who ends up working for the enemy," Anna said, disgust dripping from her voice.

"Like a human?" Rika asked, shocked.

"Yeah. One of us."

"But . . . but . . ."

Rika turned to look around. There were about twenty zombies supervising their meal. That didn't seem like very many. There were at least 300 women filing through the line at the moment. If they wanted to, the humans could overwhelm them, but to what end? The fences around the camp were high and sturdy, and there was the knowledge that Krackle combat troops were in the camp, ready to react to an escape. The zombies had told them that as long as they stayed in the camp, they would live. If they tried an escape, thousands would be cut down, and not only those who tried to break out.

She took a moment to look at the zombies, really look at them. There were some differences. Some of them wore the lighter, smoother overalls. They didn't talk much. In fact, the one who'd examined her the night before was the only one of them who she'd heard speak. The others were in heavier textured overalls with shiny bands on their upper arms. Like the one last night with the cattle prod. The one who spoke like a human.

"I can't believe it," she said.

"I heard they already got some of us to turn."

"No way! Some Arcadians?"

A Quavarian, maybe. Some other human? Maybe. But not one of them. It was impossible.

"Why would anyone do that? Work for the Krackles? The very thought makes me want to puke."

"Who knows," Anna said. "Better treatment? Better food? You haven't had any of the Krackle shit yet, so don't judge until you've tried it. You might be turning, too, just to get something decent to eat."

Rika started to protest, but she realized Anna wasn't being serious. Just bitter.

Rika didn't know Anna well. She'd been two years ahead of Nika and her at school, but at least she was a familiar face. There were others in the barracks she knew, but Anna was the only one close to her age, so she latched onto the more experienced prisoner. Two days in the camp made her an expert.

They reached the front of the line where a dispenser spit out what looked like nothing more than a green sausage. Rika stopped and brought it up to her nose to sniff.

"I said, keep tee moving," the zombie—the quisling—said, tapping her wand suggestively in the palm of her free hand.

Rika didn't need a translation. She jumped to follow Anna to the side.

"What do I do with it?" Rika asked, turning it over in her hands.

"Bite the end and suck out the middle. Then you finish up with the skin. Or, you can try the chopping method," Anna said, pointing to the woman a few meters away.

She was taking big bites through the skin, trying to take in chunks. A significant amount of the middle gushed out, running down her cheeks to drip to the ground.

"Unless things are different today, this is all we're going to get, so I'd go with the sucking method. You don't want to waste anything."

"And we can eat this?" Rika said suspiciously. "We don't have the same biology as Krackles."

"But we do with the zombies. And if it's poison, it's sure slow-acting. We ate it yesterday morning, and no one's keeled over yet."

Duh! Don't be such a dummy, Rika Ingersoll.

She brought the sausage to her lips, then gave the outside a tentative lick. Nothing. No taste. Building up her nerve, she bit off a tiny portion of the end.

Here goes nothing.

She squeezed on the skin and sucked at the same time. Something gushed into her mouth, and she gagged, spitting it out. It wasn't that it tasted horrible. It was like rice gruel in a way, but more . . . *green*. Slimy.

"You don't want to waste it," Anna said, sucking her skin dry, which she then folded up and bit off a chunk. "Guaranteed nutritious, at least according to our guard there."

"You're right. I can't waste it."

She'd do anything for one of their Shrimp 'N Chics now, even the unreconstituted ones. She gathered herself, put the end of the sausage in her mouth, and slowly squeezed this time. And it wasn't horrible. It wasn't good, but she'd had medicine worse than this.

She managed to suck down the insides, singing to herself to help her blank out that she was eating Krackle food, or at least what they provided to their zombies. With all the green gook gone, she dutifully folded up the skin and ate it. It was like eating paper. Once again, not horrible, but nothing she really wanted to do.

"Is there any water out here?" she asked Anna, wanting to wash the taste out of her mouth.

Anna pointed to a spigot coming out of the barracks where at least twenty women were lined up.

"That's for drinking and bathing," she said. "But, from the looks of it, we might get a whomper by this afternoon. Good for showering."

"Really?" Rika asked, looking around. There were heavy clouds in the air, but they didn't look substantial enough for any real rain. "I thought we were a couple weeks away. Last year, the first whomper hit after school started."

"Tell that to the terraformers. They still can't control the weather, even after all these years."

"Will they send us inside if it rains?" Rika asked.

Anna and the rest told her that after breakfast, they'd be left to wander about the quad commons with the rest of the prisoners, and Rika was anxious to look for her mother. She wouldn't be able to do that if they were confined to their barracks.

"Don't know. It didn't rain yesterday."

Again, Rika, don't ask stupid questions.

Nika laughed at her questions sometimes, which got Rika's goat, but she'd give anything to have her twin with her now to poke fun of her.

No, I wouldn't! She's got to be free to help us.

Which wasn't 100% true. Rika was pragmatic enough to know that unless the Navy and Marines got there soon, there would be no rescue. Nika needed to stay free until the military came so she wouldn't live out the rest of her life as a slave.

Tears came to her eyes as she tried, unsuccessfully, to block off the thought that she would almost assuredly never see Nika again.

If she let herself acknowledge that, she knew she'd lose it right then and there.

"Looks like it's party time," Anna said sarcastically. "Just like yesterday."

Rika pulled herself out of her self-pitying. This was her chance to find her mother. With tens of thousands of prisoners, it might take some time, but she didn't care. She'd keep trying until she found her.

It turned out she didn't need to make much of an effort. Within thirty seconds of entering the mass of people milling about, she heard a familiar voice.

"Rika!"

Rika wheeled about and ran to the familiar figure rushing at her. She collapsed into her mother's arms crying, but feeling safe for the first time since the Krackle captured her.

Chapter 15
Nika

Nika lay on her stomach at the edge of the brush that had grown up around the camp. Initially, the entire buffer had been cleared of trees and bushes, the grass continually cut short. After the depot was closed down, the buffer wasn't maintained, and bushes had reestablished a foothold. At the moment, a myrtle gave her concealment.

She hoped.

For all she knew, the Krackles could have detected her and had her marked for capture. The thought sent her heart racing, and she considered scooting farther back.

Come on, Nika Ingersoll! If they've already spotted you, then retreating isn't going to do a hill of beans. Just stick with it.

Despite the fact that the gathering clouds had cut off the direct sunlight, she shaded her eyes in an attempt to make out more of what was going on in the camp. It didn't do much good. She wished she'd been able to find her twin's binos, but if her fairy godmother was around to grant wishes, she'd wish the Krackles off Arcadia—and maybe a million credits while she was at it.

The camp fence was about fifteen meters in front of her. On the other side was another hundred meters or so of grass where the Krackle shuttle had landed yesterday, then the backs of a row of lookalike, Spartan buildings. Between the buildings, she caught glimpses of movement, but she couldn't make out much more than that.

"I've got to move," she muttered. "But which way?"

The main gate to the camp was somewhere to her right, so she chose left. It looked like the buildings were closer to the fence. Maybe she could see more there, even get the attention of someone inside.

Keeping low, she pushed herself back, then started crawling, paralleling the fence line. After a minute or two, she was breathing hard. After ten minutes, her hands and knees were aching and raw. She stopped to take a break and get her bearings . . . and almost cried out in frustration. She'd barely made any progress. The grassy field still stretched out a good bit in front of her.

I promised Fel I'd be right back. I can't just crawl.

Nika knew she was making excuses, but she didn't care. She wasn't going to crawl all the way around the depot.

I'm small. I just need to keep low.

Nika slowly stood, then took a few steps farther away from the fence. The recovering brush gave her some cover, and by crouching, she thought she couldn't be seen by anyone inside the camp. She just hoped she wouldn't trigger any sensors.

Crouching like that made her thighs ache, but it was a heck of a lot better than crawling. And she was making progress. She edged closer to the fence a few times to orient herself, and she'd made it almost around the field. Now, she was only thirty or forty yards from the backs of the buildings. This close, the bars on the few windows were pretty good indications that these were not barracks, where she thought the prisoners would be being held. They were probably warehouses of some sort.

The third time she oriented herself, she spotted another gate. No road leading out. Just a gate.

I wonder if that's a way in? Her heart raced.

Nika was still at an oblique to the gate, and she couldn't see what was on the other side of it. She had to get closer.

In her excitement, Nika didn't bother to go deeper into the buffer area. It was as if she lost sight of the gate, it might disappear altogether. She retreated a few steps but kept her eyes locked on it the best she could as she made her way through the tiny bit of cover offered by the vegetation.

She wasn't sure what she'd do if the gate was clear of Krackles and zombies, but at least it offered potential, and that was something she'd been otherwise sadly lacking.

The area around the gate was overgrown with grass and a few bushes. Nothing had been going in and out of it even before the Krackles invaded. That wasn't necessarily a bad thing, however. It meant she could probably get down on her belly and crawl up to it. After that, she'd play it by ear.

Nika reached the area opposite the gate and studied it for a long moment. It wasn't very wide like she remembered the main gate was. There was maybe enough space for a single hover to get through, but that was about it, and without a road leading out, she didn't think it was there for vehicles. There was an old-fashioned lock securing a chain that held it shut. Nika wasn't a locksmith or thief, able to pick the lock, so she ignored it. But there was more than one way to get past a gate, and that was over it.

The entire camp was covered by surveillance cameras. Every year, some kids or drunks got picked up for trying to get inside. Nika never knew why they wanted in and thought they were idiots, but the fact was that they made it in. Nika wasn't drunk, and she was pretty sure she could shinny up the vertical slats, just as she and Rika had climbed the coconut palms on New Saipan.

With the power grid down, she doubted the cameras were even on. If they were, they certainly weren't being monitored by the camp staff. The Krackles could be using them, she guessed, but she thought they'd be relying on their own tech.

Only one way to find out.

Nika got on her belly and started to edge out from cover when motion caught her eye, and she froze. A zombie was approaching the gate at a jog. He pulled a small yellow instrument out of his overalls and held it against the frame of the gate. There was a flash of blue light, and then the zombie pulled out a larger tool or instrument and held it against the chain. A moment later, the chain fell to the ground.

The zombie looked behind him and then struggled to get the gate open.

Is he trying to escape?

She'd never heard of zombies escaping. It was generally accepted that they were thoroughly brainwashed by the Krackles. But maybe some did, and that knowledge was classified.

She started getting to her knees, ready to flag him down when she saw what the zombie was looking for. Two Krackle soldiers in full combat gear were rushing the gate. The zombie, in full panic mode now, struggled to get it open.

She started to shout for the zombie to hurry before the Krackles reached the gate, but it was too late, and she dropped back to her belly.

They shouldered the zombie aside, knocking him flat on his back, then easily pushed the gate open.

And Nika realized that the zombie wasn't trying to escape. It was opening the gate for the Krackles, who were . . .

I blew it, she thought bitterly. *Too careless. What did I expect, that I was going to march in like some superhero?*

Tears ran down her cheeks as she hugged the dirt, expecting the Krackles' hands to haul her up any second. She froze, trying to be a rabbit, hiding in the bushes. She'd been lucky once with Rika, but it was probably too much to hope for luck to strike again.

The ground shook under their heavy tread, her belly picking up the vibrations. She kept her eyes tightly closed. She didn't want to see them.

And the vibrations dissipated. She knew the Krackles were just standing over her.

Just do it already.

At least she'd see Rika and her mother again—if they didn't just kill her and be done with it.

The time stretched on and on until she heard a shot and shouts.

Tentatively, she opened her eyes, expecting to see a Krackle looming over her. But there was nothing. She dared to raise her head off the ground. She could just barely see the zombie on the other side of the gate, his attention focused somewhere to Nika's left.

What the heck is going on?

She had to move. Slowly, just using her hands to push, she edged back farther away from the fence. She'd barely made it five meters when she caught motion to her left. She froze again, afraid even to breathe.

The two Krackles were striding back, pulling a limp figure between them. For a moment, Nika thought that Fel had left the pond and come forward, but no, the clothes were different.

Nika didn't recognize the man, and for a moment, she thought the Krackles had killed him, but he weakly struggled in their grip as they dragged him back to the gate. A moment later they were through the gate and disappeared into the camp.

The zombie watched them for a moment, then ignoring the chain, held up the yellow tool to the frame of the gate. The blue light flashed again, and the zombie turned and walked away.

Nika let out the breath she hadn't realized she was holding as she processed what she'd seen.

First, there were others out here doing the same thing she was doing—or attempting to do, at least. There were probably still more as well. Maybe they could band together?

Second, she was probably right about the Krackle sensors. The man, almost three times her size, had triggered something, but she, right in front of the access gate, had not. She didn't know if the difference was in body mass or something else, so she couldn't get too complacent, but she was pretty sure she had some sort of advantage.

Third . . . she wasn't quite sure what the third thing was. The zombie had done something to the frame of the gate before the Krackles barreled through. After they returned, he'd done something again. The only thing that made sense was that he'd deactivate something that could stop a Krackle, much less a seventeen-year-old human. And then he'd activated it again.

Whatever thoughts she'd had about scaling the gate, or anywhere along the fence, for that matter, had just gone up in smoke. She'd have to figure out something else.

A crack of lightning made her jump, her nerves were wound so taut. It was only then that she noticed the sky. The clouds had gotten denser, and the day was dark. Fel had been right. A whomper was on its way.

Nika shivered, and not just from the breeze that suddenly picked up. She looked back at the gate. Maybe a whomper would give her the cover to get closer to it and see if she could see a way through. But she'd promised Fel to get back, and she was already late. For all she knew, the big lug was coming after her, and he wasn't that much smaller than the man she'd just seen captured.

She had to get back to him and find some shelter, then come up with a plan. Any plan.

Nika gave one last look at the dark sky and turned back into the forest.

Chapter 16
Rika

The lightning made Rika jump, and she wasn't the only one. The gathering clouds had everyone on edge. Whompers could be dangerous, knocking down tree limbs, upending hovers, and causing flash floods. The normal course of action during a whomper was to take cover, something no one knew if they'd be allowed to do.

At least 20,000 people, probably closer to 30,000, were in the depot, now milling around outside. For two days, they'd been told when to go inside and when to leave their barracks. There weren't any trees in the common areas to fall and hit anyone, but routine precautions were hard habits to break, and there was a slight surge of people returning to their assigned barracks.

"Let's go," Rika's mom said, pushing her gently on the back.

Rika stopped and looked back to the fence surrounding the camp.

"She'll be OK," her mother said. "She knows what to do."

"I know," Rika said, reaching back to give her mother's hand a squeeze.

Lisbeth Ward wasn't a native Arcadian. A St. Regis citizen, she was working just past the main gates of Camp Prokowski-Mellon as a clerk at the Marine Shop, a commercial chain that sold higher-quality uniforms and insignia than the official exchange did, when she'd met the young Captain Ingersoll. The sparks flew, as they say, and three months later, they were married.

Seven months after that, the twins were born.

Neither Nika or Rika ever commented on the math, just grateful that they had both of their parents. A father who had risen in the ranks, gained the respect of all those who knew him, and who would do anything for his little girls. An extremely competent and capable mother who raised them—often alone while their father was out saving the universe. A woman who loved her daughters until the end of time.

The twins had learned, after moving from one base to the other, that not all kids were so lucky. Military life was difficult at best, and some people didn't handle the stress so well. Divorce was a much bigger issue within the service than without.

Not that family problems were only in the military. A month after they'd arrived, the police had come and taken Fel and Gren's father away, and he'd served 90 days in jail before being transferred to a halfway house while undergoing counseling. Gren told the twins that she missed her father, but Fel wanted nothing to do with "that bastard."

Rika couldn't understand that level of animosity toward a father. She knew it existed, but she was glad it was beyond her comprehension. She and Nika had spent more than half of their lives missing their father, wishing he'd come home again from some far-off corner of the galaxy, fearing that he'd get killed on every mission.

Tears started to flow as she realized she would never see her father again. Never see Nika. She turned and embraced her mother in a hug as sobs wracked her body.

"It's OK, honey. It's OK," her mother softly crooned, stroking her daughter's hair.

"Get out of the way," a large woman said as she shouldered the two aside in her rush for shelter.

"Come on, Rika. It's going to hit any moment."

As if on cue, the sky opened up, and the whomper hit like a hammer. Rika and her mom joined the mad rush for the nearest barracks. The zombie guards had segregated them by gender, but that didn't matter now as people just wanted out of the pounding rain.

No one knew if they'd be allowed inside, but the guards joined the rush as well, and the mass of people caused a traffic jam at the doors with most of the pressing people out under the deluge. Rika's mother pulled her daughter aside under the wide eaves.

"We'll go in after that mess gets situated," she said, pointing to the others.

Rika pressed her back up against the wall of the building. Just half a meter from her, the rain fell like a curtain. Under the eaves, she was somewhat dry, with only rain splatters splashing back on her legs.

Already, the drainage system was working. Arcadia had been settled for 82 years, long enough for the citizens to understand how to handle the runoff. Water was pouring off the roofs of the buildings and through a web of small drainage ditches, barely noticeable under dry conditions, but like capillaries and veins, designed to channel the water into progressively larger flows into underground pipe systems and out of the grounds where creeks would transport it to holding ponds. The creek where she'd been captured was part of the system and would be a raging torrent now as water was transported to be stored in the pond where they'd stopped. Rika had been fascinated with the system when they'd arrived, but now it was just part of the landscape.

At the moment, she could barely see the nearest buildings in the downpour. Shadowy figures ran back and forth as people sought shelter. Rika shifted her gaze to the fence, but it was completely lost from view.

I wonder . . .

"Mom, why don't we, you know, make a break for it. I mean, no one could see us in this, right? We could get over the fence, find Nika, and be long gone before the whomper ends."

"And the fence will fry you, lass," an older man with a three-day grizzle of beard on his chin said.

"What do you mean?" Rika asked. "The power's gone. They wouldn't know."

The depot's fence had been set up with sensors, but with the power gone, they wouldn't be activated.

"Don't need no power. Didn't you hear what the zombies said when we got here? Didn't you see what happened?"

"She was just captured," her mother told the man before turning to Rika.

"They rigged the entire fence with some sort of power barrier. They said if we touch it, we'll die."

"And you believe them?" Rika asked.

"They demonstrated," her mother said in a subdued voice.

"But how? I mean . . ." Rika said, trailing off. She realized how they would have demonstrated it, and she didn't want to know anything more detailed than that.

So, the fence could kill. That sucks bit time. But the rain—surely, we can make use of that. The Krackles have to have a problem with sheets of water falling.

"What about . . . say, getting some plywood or something. Build a platform and jump over. Don't touch the fence itself," she said, unable to give up and grasping at any straw.

"They know where you are all the time, lass. They'd know you're gone," the man said.

"What do you mean? They've got a cam on us? I mean, each one of us? Thirty-thousand people? I don't buy that."

"They don't need no cams. They registered us. Got our DNA."

Rika had forgotten what the zombie had told her about that. It just seemed too fantastic.

"And you believe that, Mom?" she asked. "It takes a lab, what, twenty minutes to run a DNA analysis? And that's with our own DNA.

Yet somehow, the Krackles, who don't have our DNA, can read ours just like that?"

"Who knows what they can and can't do, honey?"

Rika stood in silence, watching the rain fall. She didn't buy it. The tech for that was so far out of human capabilities that if the Krackles could do it, then they had to be so far past humans that nothing they did would be enough, and Rika refused to believe it.

"I think it's worth a shot," Rika said. "I think what the zombies said, it has to be a bluff. There has to be a way out of this mess."

"No, lass. I like your spirit, but we are well and truly screwed here," the man said bitterly. "We've got no hope, so best you begin to accept that."

"I won't accept anything!" Rika yelled. "My dad, he's going to rescue us!"

"Well, lass, whoever your father is, he'd better get here quick," the man said before sidling down along the wall, farther away from them.

Rika wanted to yell after him, but her mom whispered for her to let it go. She was angry, but that was probably born more out of frustration, not on the old man. Rika had been trying to come up with a plan of some sort, but her outburst was telling. She realized she was counting on her father and the Marines. Despite coming to the camp, despite her ideas, that had been what was going on in her subconscious.

She hoped Nika had come to the same realization, but knowing her, she'd try to do something stupid.

Like I would if our positions were switched.

But she wouldn't know about the fence, she realized, her heart catching in her throat.

"Nika and I talked about maybe scaling the fence," she told her mother.

Her mother gasped, grabbed her shoulder in surprise, and squeezed hard. "Oh, God, I hope she doesn't try it."

Rika didn't answer, but in her heart, she knew Nika would attempt it if nothing else came up.

Please, Baba, just stay away.

Mother and daughter stood in silence, lost in their thoughts as the rain continued to fall.

Chapter 17
Nika

Nika ran through the woods, half-blinded by the rain. It wasn't the water that she feared, but getting killed by a falling branch. More modern trees had been genmodded to better withstand Arcadian tempests, but the downed branches and trunks she had to hop over were all she needed to know that this was an older-growth forest. She hadn't come this far to be taken out by a falling branch.

She was soaked, her short hair plastered to her face, but she pushed on. By some miracle, she managed to navigate back to where she left Fel, who was huddled on the ground. For a moment, she thought he was hurt, but wiping her eyes, she saw he was bent over Hero, trying to protect him from the rain.

He looked up in surprise as she touched his shoulder, and then gave a huge, relieved smile.

"Oh, my God! I was so afraid for you, Nika! You can't know how many times I almost went after you," he shouted to be heard over the whomper.

"You'd have been caught, Fel," Nika yelled back, giving him a hug. "I saw someone else get caught, an adult."

Hero wiggled his upper body, trying to get close enough to lick her hand. She gave him a pat on the head.

"Did you see my mom? Gren?" he asked eagerly.

"No, Fel. I'm sorry. I didn't see anyone I know. But I didn't have much of a chance. I've got a better idea for when the rain ends."

She didn't have a clue of what to do next, but she couldn't tell him that.

"But people are alive, right?"

"Yeah. They're alive. We knew that."

A sharp crack made her wheel around just in time to see a branch hit the ground not ten yards away.

"We need to get out of here. Maybe get inside one of the buildings," she told Fel, pointing across the pond.

It wasn't just the fear of falling branches. Despite what Fel had said, the pond was filling up. Unless the rain stopped, the little cleared area would be underwater soon.

"Can you carry Hero?" she asked.

"No problem."

He stood, holding the dog who gave a soft yelp of pain.

"Careful!"

"Sorry, boy," Fel said.

Nika slung Rika's pack onto her back and said, "Follow me."

The rain might have slackened ever-so-slightly, the wind a bit weaker, but Nika kept a wary eye on the swaying trees as she traced the path she and Rika had taken while fleeing the Krackle. She belly-slid over the fallen tree, the victim of past storms, then helped Fel manage it with Hero in his arms.

The roar was the first sign that the stagnant trickle of a creek was no longer. The two stepped up to a raging torrent, one that Nika could not hope to cross. It would be too dangerous even for Fel, especially carrying Hero.

"Don't worry. It'll go down soon," Fel said. "After the whomper passes."

Rika was almost mesmerized by the rushing water that bounded down to the pond. It was hard to imagine that this was the same trickle of mud from the day before. Their entire world had changed, however, so why not this?

"I can't believe that this much rain fell here. I know this is a whomper, but this?"

"Not just here in the woods. This is probably runoff from the depot, too, or at least some of it," Fel said as he sat down, Hero in his lap.

"From the depot? Where our families are?"

"Well, yeah. I bet this creek is fed by the drainage system, at least partly."

"The drainage system? From the depot?"

Nika wasn't raised on Arcadia, and she wasn't as versed as to how the population dealt with the whomper season. She knew cities and towns were riddled with drainage systems, with buildings built on higher ground and lowlands kept to store runoff. The open-aired drainage ditch she and Rika had climbed through to see their mother captured was just one example of them, so commonplace that Nika had never noticed that one before.

"The rain has to go somewhere, Nika. That's what these ponds are for."

Which she knew, but it had never sunk in. And something about that was important. She couldn't put her finger on just what that was. She stood, looking upstream.

"So, this leads back to the depot," she said, more of a statement than a question.

"Sure. Probably," Fel said, hunching his shoulders to give Hero some protection from the rain.

"Wait here. If the water goes down, cross over and find some shelter on the other side."

"Why? Where're you going?" Fel asked, struggling back to his feet.

"I just need to check something out," Nika said, wishing the boy would stop talking so her brain could figure out just what was tickling her mind.

"Where?"

"Up the creek," she said, pointing. "I need to see for myself."

"Then what?" Fel asked.

"I don't know," she said, turning back to the boy and putting a hand on his arm. "I need you to stay here. I was right about the sensors, and you're too big. And someone has to watch Hero."

"I don't like this," Fel said. "Maybe you should stay with me. You know, we can wait for your father to get here."

"And if the Krackles take off before then? With our families?" she snapped fire dancing from her eyes.

The answering pain from Fel's eyes dampened her anger. The boy had lost as much as she had, and it had to kill him to be sitting here doing nothing.

"I'm sorry, Fel. I know you didn't mean that we should just give up. Look, let me go see what's going on. I think it's something important, but I'm not sure what. Maybe looking over the depot again will jog something loose in my mind."

Fel didn't look convinced, but he didn't say anything.

Nika pulled him down for another kiss on the cheek, dropped Rika's pack, and turned away before he could ask anything else. She really didn't have a plan, just a hope that something, anything would surface that could be useful.

She walked away in silence, making her way alongside the creek as the rain started to diminish, along with the wind. Which was one less thing to worry about. An errant branch might still fall and crush her, but the biggest danger of that was over.

As if in counterpoint to that thought, a huge branch appeared in the creek flow, bashing its way downstream. Something like that would've crushed Nika like a bug underfoot. She swallowed hard and pushed on.

The rain stopped before she was halfway to the depot. The creek still raged on, fed by rain that had fallen not only in the woods, but in the vast depot itself, if Fel had it right.

Rika came to a fork. Two streams of water met to form the creek. Without dithering over it, Rika chose the right fork and followed it on.

The roar reached her before she saw it. Water was gushing from a culvert of sorts, spraying into the air before falling back to feed flow. Tiny rivulets fed the creek from the woods themselves, but it was obvious that this plume was the main source of water for this branch of the creek.

Rika edged closer, wary of falling into the torrent. The culvert was made from ferrocrete, narrowing down to a pipe sticking out of the ground. If she had any doubts before, she now knew the creek was manmade. It wasn't natural.

She let her eyes rise, following the general direction of where the pipe had to run. Through the trees, she could see the top of the depot fence.

And it all came together. The water had a way out of the depot, so there was a way in as well.

Rika tried to gauge the diameter of the pipe. It was small, but then again, so was she. It would be a tight fit, but she thought she could crawl through it.

Not at the moment, though. She could not make it through the water, but already the plume was lower. Without the rain to feed it anymore, the pipe would empty.

Rika sat at the edge of the culvert to wait.

Chapter 18
Rika

The whomper stopped as suddenly as it began, and the people slowly emerged from whatever building in which they'd taken shelter. Rika and her mother just stepped away from the side of the barracks.

She took a tentative step on the ground, but it held firm. On most other planets, a downpour like that would have rendered bare ground a mass of mud, here on Arcadia, they knew how to prepare areas like this. As a few rays of sun broke through the clouds, and the final drops fell from the structures, it would be easy to forget that the place was under a deluge just a few minutes ago.

"I want to try and find Gren and the others," she told her mother.

"I should go with you."

"It's OK, Mom. I won't go far. Just a quick look around this quad."

The depot was quite large, with the ammo bunkers taking up a huge amount of space, but mainside, where most of the buildings were, had a smaller footprint. There were four quads, each with a line of buildings surrounding a common area, and several stand-alone buildings like the headquarters, the chapel, the gym, and the commissary.

"OK," her mother said, sounding unsure of herself. "I'm going back to H203. If anything happens, you hightail it back there."

"What's going to happen?" Rika asked automatically.

Her mother grabbed her by the arm and jerked her close. "They start loading us out, that's what could happen. And I don't want to lose you again."

That sobered Rika up. Things were not normal, and getting shipped off-planet for a life of slavery was a definite possibility. No, not possibility: *probability*. The only question was not if, but when.

"Of course, Mom. I didn't mean to make light of this."

She oriented herself, spotting H203, their barracks. If anything happened at all, she'd make sure she got back to it.

Her mother let go of her arm, and Rika started making the rounds, all the time keeping the direction back to H203 clear in her mind.

"Do any of you know Gren Grafton?" she asked a group of about a dozen people standing together chatting.

They shook their heads, and she asked, "Lemul Adoud? Hiyori Singh?" to the same response.

Storyville and the surrounding area wasn't that big, so it shouldn't be hard to find someone who knew her friends. But it took almost twenty minutes before a young man said he knew Hiyori, but hadn't seen her. In the next group she asked, however, she found Mark Fortnight, a classmate. He'd seen Gren right before the rain.

At least now I know she's in this quad, she thought, scanning the area around her. *It shouldn't be that hard to find someone. Maybe they should start some sort of finder wall or something.*

If someone hadn't already tried to create one and the zombies closed it down, which was something more probable. They didn't mind people milling about, but they didn't seem to like anyone organizing something.

As she scanned the crowd, she locked eyes with a young zombie, who immediately looked away. He was a "shaggy," the nickname some of the people had given the quislings, due to the longer nap of their overalls. He'd been captured himself on some world, and now he worked for his captures.

Rika kept her face emotionless. There had been more than a few instances of the shaggies using their wands on people for perceived—and intended—slights. As a group, they seemed more prone to anger than the "smoothies," the original zombies.

She started to walk across the commons, wanting to put some distance between her and the zombie. He gave her the creeps. She refused to look back, but she could feel his stare burning into her back.

It took asking more people, but finally, an older lady said that Gren was in H222. With a spring in her step, she rushed to the barracks, but with the rain over, the people had been sent back outside. She wandered around for another ten minutes, wishing for once that she was taller so she could see through the milling people.

In the end, it wasn't her who spotted her friend.

"Nika!"

Rika turned to see Gren pushing through to her.

"No, I'm Rika," she said, rushing to hug her.

"Well, I knew I had a 50% chance there," Gren said, hugging and lifting Rika off the ground. "Oh, my God, it's good to see you."

"Me, too. I've been worried sick about you and the rest."

"Have you seen anyone else? Fel? My mom and Mace?"

"No. Just you. Oh, and my mom."

"You found your mother? What about Nika?"

"She wasn't captured. At least, I don't think so."

"I hope not. But it's great you found your mother. I saw Hiyori—"

"What was up with her?" Rika interrupted her friend.

"Like we thought. She left us that night in the park, then got picked up in the city."

"And left us without a look-out."

"Yeah, she says she's sorry about that, but you know Hiyori."

Rika was not sure she'd be so dismissive about what Hiyori'd done. It was unconscionable to put the rest of them at risk like that.

"Nothing about your mother or Fel?" she asked to change the subject.

"Lots of people who know her, but no one's seen her or Mace. Fel, either. They have to be in one of the other quads. I'm going to try and get to one of them tomorrow after breakfast."

One of the few rules given to the prisoner was to stay in their quads. Rika didn't know what would happen if that was disobeyed, but it couldn't be good.

"Are you sure you want to do that?"

Gren nodded.

"Boy, you'd better be careful."

"Don't I know it. But I have to find them."

Rika nodded. She'd do the same thing in her position.

She didn't know what to say, however, so she looked away . . . and saw the same shaggy zombie, and this time, he wasn't hiding his stare. He'd followed her across the quad, and when he saw her looking at him, gave her a little smile.

Shocked, Rika grabbed Gren by the arm and pulled her away.

"What's going on?"

"Just come with me."

She led Gren to the barracks and around the corner.

"Will you tell me what this is all about?"

"There's this guy following me," Rika said, her heart beating wildly.

"Maybe he knows you."

"A zombie guy. A shaggy. Not a regular guy."

"Oh . . ."

"I don't know what to do."

"Are you sure?"

"Yes. I'm sure. Look around the corner. See if he's still there. Young guy. Maybe 20. Five-ten, maybe 200 pounds. Round face."

Gren nodded, the slowly poked her head around the corner.

"If that's him, then yeah, he's still there, looking right at me."

Rika pulled Gren back. "What do I do?"

There was a thud, the sound of a baton hitting the fleshy part of a hand. Rika's heart stopped beating, and she slowly turned around to see a zombie, an older woman, looking at her with a wry smile as she rhythmically slapped her baton into her hand.

"What are tee gonna do? Nothing, I be wagering."

"Yes, ma'am," Rika said, trying to wish the situation away.

"Hah! I weren't no ma'am, and tee all call us something different, right. No use playing polite and civil-like. So, which one of us shaggies is looking at tee?"

The shaggy laughed when Rika's eyes got big. "We know what tee call us. No matter. Where's this shaggy."

"Right around the corner. Standing there," Gren said, keeping her voice even and without inflection.

The zombie sauntered up to the corner and took a look. She raised her baton in a salute, then turned back to the two girls.

"That be Ben Westerman. About time he grew some balls," she said with a laugh.

"Ma'am? What do you mean?" Rika asked, afraid of the answer.

"I mean he be finally getting some gonads, girl. About time. This be our fourth roundup since Galant, where we both were taken, and he be finally marking his claim."

The rational part of her brain made note of that. Galant had been hit three years before, on the other side of the realm of humanity. There had been a large Quavarian population on the planet.

Rika's lizard brain, however, silently screamed.

"Marking his claim?" she squeaked out.

"Tee're a young-un, but to each his own," she said, taking Rika's chin in her hand. "Mighty small, too."

"Why?" Gren asked with a little steel in her voice.

"Tee know why, honey. That's why we're, tee know, doing what we're doing. We can serve the masters as slaves, or we can serve them like this. And let me tell tee, this has a lot more benefits. Like choosing breeders," she said, looking up and down Rika's body.

"Tee might want to consider it, hun," she told Gren. "Tee'll have the chance when we get on the ships."

Rika was weak at the knees, unable to say anything.

Breeders?

"I could never do what you're doing," Gren snarled. "You're a traitor to your own kind."

The zombie stopped with the tapping of her wand and glared at Gren, and for a moment, Rika thought she'd use it on her friend. She grabbed her Gren's arm and tried to pull her away.

The zombie suddenly smiled and started tapping again. "Suit yourself. But I tell tee, serving the masters this way be much, much better than the other. Think on it."

She walked past the two as if they didn't exist.

Rika held up for a few more moments, but then started breathing heavily and bent over at the waist. She thought she was going to throw up.

This isn't me. Be strong, Rika Ingersoll. Be strong.

But that was easier said than done.

"That Quavarian bitch," Gren snarled, watching the zombie walk away. "I can't believe it. I mean, who would choose the Krackles over fellow humans?"

Rika didn't have an answer for that. But with the zombie gone, the reason they were hiding around the corner of the building came back and hit her like a freight train.

"Is he still there?" Rika asked.

Gren, still seething, looked around the corner. "I don't see him."

Rika took her friend's arm and asked, "Can you take me back to H203? I need to see my mom."

"Yeah, yeah. Sorry, I let that traitor get to me. Let's go."

Gren put her arm around Rika's shoulders, and together they pushed through the people to cross the commons.

With every step, Rika felt vulnerable as she'd never felt before.

Chapter 19
Nika

Nika straddled the little rivulet that trickled out of the pipe, peering inside. Twenty minutes ago, the water still gushed out, arching into the air before falling to the ground. Now, it was almost nothing.

The pipe was smaller than she'd initially thought. Small enough for her to crawl inside, but not much more than that. She'd have to crawl on her belly, in the dark, for a long, long way.

The thought gave her the shivers. It had been hard enough to crawl on the ground by the fence. But what scared her the most was the thought of another whomper while she was still inside. With no room to turn around, she'd drown.

Nika looked up at the sky. The clouds were parting, rays of sunshine reaching down, but she knew they could quickly form again, and the thought of being caught inside when the rain returned made her knees weak.

Her heart was pounding in her chest, so hard that she thought it would burst free. She could turn around, leave the depot, and try to hide until the Krackles left. That could save her, but not her mom. Not Rika.

The thought of that was too much to bear. Rika had sacrificed herself to save her, and she couldn't do any less.

"He who will not risk, cannot win," she muttered, a quote from an ancient sailor on Earth, and one of her father's favorite sayings.

Before her doubts could overwhelm her, she stuck her head in the pipe and pushed with her legs, wriggling inside. Her body blocked most of the light, and she could see nothing ahead of her.

"No way to get lost, at least," she said, her voice swallowed up in the dark.

The trickle of water was cold under her as she started to crawl, and grit dug into her hands and knees. She would have thought that the pipe would have been scoured clean, but there were patches of grit interspaced between thin patches of slick mud. Normally curious, this would have her mind pondering a reason for why some places were grit and some were mud, but not now. All she could think of was how far she had to go.

Arms out, left leg slightly bent. Pull with the arms, push with the leg. Repeat. Repeat. Repeat.

Nika had no idea how long she'd been in the pipe. She'd tried counting how many times she edged up, but she kept losing track. She couldn't even concentrate on the math. If every pull forward was about eight inches, and the distance she had to cover was about a hundred yards, then that was . . .

Nika loved math. She could do math in her head. But not on her belly in a dark pipe with no way to turn around. She didn't even know if she could crawl backward if it came to that. Committed, there was only one way, and that was forward.

The itsy, bitsy spider crawled up the water spout. Down came the rain, and washed the spider out . . .

She softly sang the ancient song as she crawled. Not the best song to be singing in her situation, but it was cemented in her mind, a brainworm. She tried to come up with something else, something about sun, but the itsy, bitsy spider refused to let her out of its web.

Pull with the arms, push with the leg. Pull with the arms, push with the leg. She switched to her right leg, but that didn't seem to be as effective in propelling her down the pipe. Back to the left.

Nika began to appreciate the cold mud. It didn't tear at her hands, and her belly slid over it easier.

Pull with the arms, push with the leg. Pull with the arms, push with the leg.

Her neck began to ache, craning as she was to see any hint of light ahead. Nika gave up and straightened her head. Either she'd reach the end and emerge inside the depot, or the rain would come and then . . .

It was neither. Her mind numb, she was surprised when her reaching hands hit something hard. She looked forward, but couldn't see anything. Her hands told the story as she ran it over the obstacle. She was at a metal grate.

"Oh, my God!" she shouted, the folly of what she'd been doing sinking in.

Panic, which had been swirling around in her subconscious, waiting for the opportunity, pounced. She was stuck, and she didn't see a way out.

She shook the grate, rattling it, but nothing more. Tears started rolling down her cheeks.

The spaces between the grate were just large enough for an arm—a small arm— and she pushed her right hand through, hoping to find a latch, but reaching a mass of cold, clammy . . . she didn't know what. With a scream of frustration, she punched forward, and the mass moved. With her left hand grasping the grate, she pulled herself up and punched again with her right, and to her amazement, she saw light. Not much, but real light, and she cried out in relief.

She renewed her efforts, and as she cleared more, she realized that it was just garbage: paper, an old shirt, plastic, leaves. The detritus of the camp, washed away into the drain.

As she cleared some on the bottom a rush of water hit her, making her jump back, but the water quickly petered out.

Stupid engineering, she thought as she cleared away more of the mess, letting more light into the pipe. *Too much garbage, and it would block the flow.*

Why would they design it like this?

And it hit her. The grate was not there to catch garbage. The depot had been a military installation. The grate was there to keep people out.

Not that many people could fit inside the pipe. Nika barely fit. But drones could fit. Little robots carrying explosives. Nika didn't know the details of what armies actually had to do something like that, but she'd seen enough tridee shows to get the idea.

Which means I'm still stuck.

Whatever boost seeing the light gave her dissipated like the trickle beneath her. She was at the end of the pipe. On the other side of the grate was a slightly larger chamber, and beyond that, a square box-like catch basin. There was a lid on the basin, but she could see light coming in along the edge. On the other side of the lid, maybe ten feet from her, was the way out and into the depot. It might as well have been a hundred miles

Unless this thing opens.

Nika felt along the inside of the grate, hoping to find a latch. Nothing.

Of course, stupid. Why would they put a latch on this side?

She stuck her hand through and felt along the bottom. Nothing. On the left side, she felt two large hinges. That gave her a tiny bit of hope. If there were hinges, the grate was designed to be opened.

She shifted to one of the openings on the right side, immediately finding the latch . . . which was secured with a lock. She gave it a tug, but of course, it didn't conveniently open.

Pressing her cheek up against the grate, she could just make out the lock in the dim light. No one had opened it in years, maybe decades, by the look of it. The shackle itself shone bright in the light, but the body of the lock was dark and corroded.

She ran her fingers over it. Tiny pieces of metal flaked off. All the more proof that the lock had been there a long time. Every lock Nika had ever seen had been made of ceralloy or plastic, neither of which corroded.

If it was in this bad shape, then maybe it could be broken. If she only had something—

I do!

She wormed her hand down to her hip and pulled out her father's Kri-Blade. It gleamed in the dim light.

Kri-Blades were among the best known to humankind. Expensive, too. Very few individuals could afford them, and the Marine Corps brass chose to spend their credits on more practical weapons. But her father's Marines had chipped in to buy him this one as a farewell present, and it was among his prized possessions.

This one was for show, but it still was a working knife, and Kri-Blades had a reputation of being able to cut almost anything.

Let's see if that's true.

She pushed the knife through the grate, then her arm to the elbow, bending it up. The tip of the blade just touched the lock. She tried to cut in a sawing motion, but that just pushed the lock away. She couldn't get any purchase.

As she withdrew the knife, she considered trying to saw away the grate. She could get a better angle on it, but she'd have to cut through at least a hundred sections for it to fall free.

Nika wanted to see if it was even practical. She applied pressure to a section of the grate, sawing with the edge of the Kri-Blade, until her shoulder screamed in protest. When she examined the grate, there was a cut. Not a big cut, but a cut, and the knife looked OK.

She ran her finger over the tiny gash. Fifty more times, and she might be through. And then repeat a hundred more times.

There was no way that was going to work. She'd still be sawing away a year from now, and that was only if the whompers didn't return and wash her away.

It's got to be the lock.

But how? She tried using different openings to get a better angle. She tried to pull herself up, her head pressing the top of the pipe. Nothing worked.

After her last failure, this time on her back, she jabbed at the lock in anger. The tip caught for a moment, knocking the lock aside, and another small piece of metal fell off.

What if . . .

Nika repeatedly jabbed at the lock in desperation, knocking it about, but no more pieces fell off.

"You need to be more focused instead of going bat-shit crazy, girl."

She shifted onto her side. Instead of sticking the entire knife through the grate, she only put the front part of the blade through, leaving the handle on her side. With her left hand, she placed the tip of the blade against the body of the lock.

"Here goes nothing."

With her right hand, she hit the butt of the handle with all her might. The jolt as the knife hit the lock shot pain up her hand, but she knew she'd finally gotten a good blow.

Nika checked the lock. It was still whole, but maybe she'd done some damage. The lock's most corroded spot was where the shackle went into the body.

If I can just go for that spot.

She carefully positioned the tip of the knife, then hit the handle again. She felt it dig in. Hopefully, that meant she was making progress. Once, twice, three times.

It was awkward lying on her side, but she didn't have much choice. She missed sometimes, the tip skittering past the lock. But when she hit true, she could feel the Kri-Blade chip away.

Hit it harder, Nika Ingersoll. Show it what you're made of.

She used her legs to push her back against the far side of the pipe, and that gave her a little more room to swing. She hit the handle with all her might.

The tip skittered free, and the force of the blow knocked the knife out of her hand and through the grate where it disappeared into the trash on the other side.

"No!" she shouted, reaching through the grate, hand groping for the knife.

Nothing. Garbage, but no knife.

She jammed her arm all the way to her shoulder, compacting flesh to gain and extra half-inch, her hand questing for the blade.

A biting pain made her jerk back in surprise. Her finger was bleeding, and she stuck it in her mouth, tasting copper.

What cuts like that? The Kri-Blade! she thought, triumph overcoming her immediate fear of infection.

She edged her hand back out until she felt the hard tip of the blade amongst the other detritus. She tried to squeeze her fingertips together like tweezers, but her blood was slippery, and she couldn't get a grip.

Almost crying out in frustration, she shifted to her back and used her right arm this time, snaking it out until she just reached the knife. Any mistake now, and the knife would be forever out of reach. Using her index and forefinger, she carefully squeezed them, pinching the blade. Slowly, she tried to draw it back, but after a moment, it slipped free from her tenuous grip.

"Did I move it?"

She thought she did, but it took reaching out again to confirm that. It wasn't much closer, but now she could get a little better grip. It took two more tries, but finally, it was close enough for her thumb to reach. With her thumb and forefinger, she locked on, and a moment later, she was cradling the blade with relief.

"That was too close," she said, closing her eyes and trying to calm her breathing.

It took almost a minute before Nika was ready to try again. She placed the tip of the knife against the lock, and gripping the handle tighter this time, hit the butt again. This time she could swear she heard a click of some sort over the sound of the knife hitting it.

When she placed the tip against it again, it seemed to lodge tight. Once, twice more. Another piece of lock body broke free.

Taking a deep breath, Nika gave it one more hit, and this time, the body seemed to disintegrate.

With a cry of triumph, Nika reached through and grabbed the broken body, yanking down. It didn't open. Now snarling in frustrated anger, she pulled down again. She could feel what was left of the body shifting, but the shackle wouldn't pop free. She shifted her grip and felt the shackle twist.

Instead of yanking down, Nika put her fingers around the shackle and pulled out, away from the lock body. The shackle lifted free. Almost numb, Nika lifted and twisted the shackle through the latch, dropping it to the ground.

Nika pushed on the grate. It barely budged. After decades, it wasn't going to swing open easily. She'd had more than enough of the grate by now, though, and she attacked it, using all of her power to push, hit, and jar it open.

A mere grate could not stand up to the anger of a 17-year-old military brat. Each attack pushed it open a little more until it suddenly gave way, slamming against the side of the containment box.

With an incoherent shout, Rika shot from the pipe as if from a circus cannon, scrambling around until she was sitting, her back screaming in protest. She didn't care. She shuddered as the reaction set in.

Leaning back against the wall, she half-sobbed, half-laughed in relief.

"Is someone down there?" a male voice called out.

Nika froze. She'd forgotten for a moment that she was in enemy territory.

"Are you OK?"

What if that was a zombie? The voice sounded normal to her, but zombies were essentially human. She'd never heard one talk.

"I'm going to open up the cover," the voice said.

"Wait!" Nika shouted, her mind whirling.

She eyed the pipe, wondering if she should get back in it. But no, she came all this way. Of those were zombies there ready to nab her, so be it.

"I'm Nika Ingersoll."

"My God, Nika. What are you doing down there? It's me, Derek Sythington. From the Friendly Mart."

Another flood of relief washed over her. Derek ran the night shift at the Friendly Mart down on Highway 32 and Rippart Lane.

"I crawled down the drainage pipe from the outside. Have you seen Rika or my mom? Do you know where they are?"

"Nika, you stay down there. Don't move."

"But what are you going to do?"

There was no answer.

"Derek?"

Part of Nika wanted to just give up. Open the cover to the containment box and step out, surrendering. Just get it all over with.

But that wouldn't do anyone any good. That wouldn't rescue anyone.

Nika still didn't have a plan, but she was a lot further now toward making one than she had been this morning.

She sat back to wait and see what would happen next.

Chapter 20
Rika

"Think your boyfriend's still looking for you?" Gren asked.

"Don't even think that!" Rika said with a snarl.

Gren's eyes widened in surprise at Rika's reaction, but then she nodded. "Sorry. You're right. My mind is just trying to cope with all of this. I know you don't like that zombie. I was just . . . forget it. Stupid joke."

Rika started to snap back again, but she bit it off. They were all under a lot of stress, especially knowing that they could be taken off Arcadia at any moment, never to return.

And Gren was just being Gren.

"No, I know you were joking. I'm just wound tight right now."

Gren leaned over and put her arm around the smaller girl. "You gonna tell your mom what happened?"

Rika had planned on telling her mother about the shaggy, but with Gren asking, she had second thoughts. First, so what if some zombie boy had looked at her? She was probably making a big deal out of nothing. Second, that other zombie, the woman, she'd probably been just digging on her about the breeding stuff, trying to get a rise.

Rika had calmed down, but she was somewhat embarrassed that she had reacted as she'd done. She had to regain control, or she was just going to lose it.

Others had lost it, screaming or falling catatonic. Those were hauled off by zombies, and Rika didn't want to contemplate what their fates would be. The rumors about them were not good.

"No. It was no big deal, and even if it was, there's nothing my mother can do about it. No use worrying her.

"But speaking of my mother, let's go track her down. She said she'd be waiting back at our barracks."

"Yeah, I'd like to see her," Gren said wistfully.

Rika gave her a quick glance. Her friend had to be fighting to hold it together herself, not being able to find her mother, Mace, or Fel.

She snaked out a hand to take Gren's in hers, then started to cut through the mass of prisoners.

"Rika! Rika Ingersoll!"

Rika turned to see Derek from the Friendly Mart, followed by a young woman she didn't recognize, pushing through the people to get to them.

"What does he want?" Gren asked.

"I'm surprised he knows I'm me and not Nika. He always says he can't tell us apart."

"No one can tell you apart," Gren said as they waited.

"My mom can."

"Rika," Derek said as he reached her. "You need to come with me."

"What for?" Rika asked warily.

She trusted Derek as far as it goes, but knowing that some people had become zombies had torn down a little of the natural trust she'd always had for others.

Derek looked around like an antelope trying to spot the lion. "I'd rather not say out here in public. You just have to trust me."

"You just have to trust me" is what every villain said on the tridees before turning on the hero.

"You're going to want to come," the woman said, a slender, dark-skinned woman of about twenty-five years.

"I don't know you," Rika said, her eyes narrowing.

The woman gave a half-laugh, but she didn't bother to introduce herself. "Suit yourself. But Derek here's trying to help."

"This is Leona, my cousin. I went and got her before I came for you. She's right, though. I am trying to help. Just come with us, OK? Try to act normal, though."

What is this? Try to act "normal?"

She wished he'd just come out and tell her what was going on, but his cheap tridee theatrics intrigued her. She gave Gren a questioning look, and her friend shrugged.

"OK. I'll act normal. Can I ask where we're going?"

"Over by the cafeteria. Just follow me."

Not that the "cafeteria" was in use, but it was where they were given the morning sausage thing. Rika and Gren followed Derek and the woman, all the time Rika wondering what "normal" looked like. She felt out-of-place, her walk stilted and stiff. The more she tried to look normal, the more awkward she felt. Everyone had to see that something was up.

Derek didn't walk right to the chowhall but between it and the next building. Ahead of them was the fence, and for a brief, glorious moment, Rika thought he was leading them to a hole in the fence or something, a way out. But he stopped at one of the catchment drains where runoff was collected and carried out of the depot.

She frowned as he stopped, put his hands in his pocket in the worst acting performance of nonchalance she'd ever seen, and said, "I'm back."

"Back from where?" Rika asked.

A quiet, muffled voice seemed to come from the catchment. She couldn't make out the words, but the tone . . .

Before her brain could make sense of her instincts, Rika bent over the drain cover and lifted it up.

"No!" Derek's cousin yelled as she lunged forward, slamming her foot on the cover.

But Rika had seen enough. A pair of brown eyes, a mirror image of her own, staring back up at her.

Chapter 21
Nika

Nika started to stand the moment she saw her twin, but someone yelled, and the cover slammed shut, just grazing her head.

"Look. You down there, you can't just pop out like a jack-in-the-box. The EA's PC will pick up the anomaly."

What?

"EA" stood for "Enemy Alien," government-speak for the Krackles. But "PC?" "Politically Correct?"

"What're you talking about," her sister asked. "That's Nika there. I don't know how she got there, but we've got to get her out."

"I'm OK, Baba!" Nika shouted.

"Will you can it?" the other voice said. "We don't know yet what other bands they use."

"What are you talking about?" Rika asked.

"Look. I'll make it short, but you've got to trust me. The EA's have cataloged all of us in the PC, their Prisoner Control system. If we leave the compound, they'll know it. If someone new enters the compound, they'll know it. "

"And just how do you know that?" another voice, Gren's, she realized, reached her.

Nika gave a happy gasp. Not that Gren was a prisoner, but that she'd met up with Rika. She tried to shift her body to see through the gaps in the drain cover, but all she could see was Derek's chest.

"If anyone knows, it's Leona," Derek said. "She's a Krackle scientist. That's why I went and got her."

"Not exactly. I am a systems engineer with the AIU," the woman, Leona said.

"You? What are you, all of twenty?" Rika asked. "I want to see my sister, and I don't care what line of bull you fed Derek here."

"No bull, Rika. She's already got three Ph.D's. And she's thirty."

"Twenty-eight, but close enough. What matters is that I understand how they set up their transit camps. I've been to Galant, Pangoria, and Armister. I just never thought I'd be in an active camp as a prisoner myself. But here I am."

Nika frowned. She knew there was a small AIU detachment at the NMCRC, but she'd never thought about what they actually did there.

"But believe me, we don't want to have you . . . uh, what's your name again?"

"She's Nika, my sister," Rika said.

"Look, Nika, we don't think their camp scanners penetrate the ground, so, you're probably safe where you're at. Otherwise, you'd have an EA snatch team here already. But if you pop your head out, they'll pick it up and come investigate."

"So, you're saying that they have some sort of reading on us, and that's how they keep tabs. And if Nika gets out of there, then she'll set off some sort of alarm?"

"Yeah, you can put it that way, if that makes it easier to understand."

Nika almost snarled at the woman's condescending attitude.

"And how do they do this? DNA?"

"Uh, it's not so easy to tell. Maybe DNA, maybe bone structure, body chemistry. But most of us think DNA."

"Most of you?" Gren asked.

"Not me. That would take a quantum leap in technology. But we can't tell for sure based on what we've been able to reverse engineer from the traces they've left. Personally, I think they've tagged us all with a unique isotope."

"They never picked up on me around the depot. Body mass has to be a factor," Nika called up from her hole-in-the-ground.

"Out there, maybe, but in here, once they've cataloged us, I don't think it could be just body mass. We've got babies in here," Leona said.

"But it could be DNA?" Rika asked.

"Well, yes. We just can't be sure of that."

"Well, luckily, Nika and I have the same DNA."

A moment later, the cover flung open, and Rika jumped in to the shouts of alarm from the other woman.

"Stay down, Baba," Rika said as she stood, chest and head out of the hole.

Nika crawled forward and hugged her twin's legs, sobbing. She felt whole again, even inside an enemy camp, even with the universe closing in on her. She was with her twin.

"Stupid move, girl," Leona said. "I told you we don't know if they read DNA, and for all I know, you opening that freaking hole there is giving their scanners access to the other one now.

"Derek, I'm out of here," she added. "You'd better come, too."

"It's good to see you, Nika," Gren said, stepping up to look inside the hole.

"Good to see you, too," she said before tackling the question she was afraid to ask. "Did you find mom?"

"I did, Baba. And she's fine. She's worried sick about you, but you know her. I'll tell her you're safe."

"I want to see her," Nika said.

"You can't. You heard Miss All-Knowing. You can't get out of this hole."

"Maybe you can, you know, go get her and bring her here?"

"I can get her," Gren said. "She'll be overjoyed."

Rika hesitated for a moment, and Nika knew what she was thinking.

"Never mind. Stupid idea. But tell her I love her."

"I will. And you need to get back out of here. Miss All-Knowing could be right."

"Why don't you go? Take my place. I'll stay here," Nika said.

"Ah, Baba, you know I can't. Maybe they read DNA somehow, but maybe not. Miss All-Knowing said bone scans. You broke your arm, and I didn't. A simple X-ray can spot that. We can't take the chance."

Nika felt horrible. She never thought she'd see Rika again, and now, hugging her legs, that made all the more difficult. It was the universe dangling something she knew in her heart she'd lose.

Nika brought her legs under her to give Rika a closer hug, and pain shot through her right calf.

"Yow!" she gasped, turning around to her butt and trying to straighten the leg. The pain was intense as the cramp locked its hold on her.

"Keep breathing, Baba," Rika said, stroking her sister's hair.

The twins were in surprisingly good health overall, but they did suffer from cramps on occasion, and Nika had just crawled the length of the dark pipe to get there, and she hadn't been keeping herself hydrated.

Nika grabbed her toe and tried to stretch out the calf, but the cramp refused to relinquish its hold.

"I've got to stand, Rik," she said.

Rika knew that when her sister used "Rik," she was serious, but Nika knew she was thinking about what Derek's cousin said and didn't want her to expose herself.

"Look, you hug me and slide down while I slide up. I've got to put weight on it."

She could feel Rika's hesitancy, and she understood it. But she couldn't crawl anywhere like this, and the thought of going back into the pipe and having another cramp hit terrorized her.

"I mean it, Nik."

"OK, OK. Turn back around."

Nika managed to turn belly down, her right leg stretched out behind her.

Rika shifted her position to keep her body between Nika and the main part of the depot and said, "OK, try and hug me, then slide up. I think I need to keep most of me up over the edge of the hole."

"Be careful," Gren said, sounding frightened.

Nika pulled her left leg up and used it to lift herself, all the while keeping her front plastered onto Rika's. As her face passed Rika's belly, Rika started to lower herself into the hole.

"I hope this works, Baba," Rika whispered as their faces passed each other.

"Me, too," Nika said, kissing her sister's forehead.

And then Nika was standing, while Rika crouched at the bottom of the hole. Nika started to put weight on her toe to try and stretch out the cramp.

"Nice seeing you, Gren. I'll tell Fel you're looking good."

"Fel? You've seen Fel?" Gren asked, her face coming alive.

"Oh, yeah. I guess I should have told you. He's back with Hero at the pond."

"Who's Hero? And is Fel OK?"

"Yes, he's fine. He wanted to come, but we think the Krackle sensors are based on mass. The Krackles went right by me this afternoon to nab a big guy."

"Ah, you finally named the dog. Appropriate, given what he did," Rika said. "I thought he'd been killed, so it's good to know he made it."

"He's waiting for me to get back. I'll tell him I saw you. What about your mom and Mace?"

"I haven't found them. Still looking. Tell him . . . tell him I'm fine. Don't let him come closer."

"From the looks of this, there's no way your moose of a brother would fit in this," Rika said, peering into the pipe. "And that looks like a grate there. Luckily it was open, Baba."

"It wasn't. But Dad's Kri-Blade did the trick."

"Impressive, Baba, impressive."

Nika put a little more weight on her foot, leaning into it. The cramp was finally fading.

"I think it's getting better. Maybe—"

Whatever Nika was going to say was lost as she caught sight of two Krackles running toward them, a couple of zombies rushing to follow.

Her heart caught in her throat as panic started to take over.

"What?" Rika said, turning away from the grate.

"Get inside the pipe, then freeze," Nika said, her voice brooking no argument.

"Oh, crap," Gren said, turning to face the Krackles.

"What's going on?" Rika asked.

"Stay down, Rik. I mean it," she said, reaching over and releasing the Kri-Blade's scabbard. "We've got company, and I don't think we can make the switch again."

Nika didn't have to say that they'd already messed up.

"But—"

"No buts, Rik. Now. Get in the pipe. We don't have any more time."

"Baba!" Rika said, her voice laden with pain, but a moment later, Nika heard her twin scramble into the pipe opening.

She couldn't look. She had to stare down the Krackles. She just had time to scramble out of the hole when they were on Gren and her. But they ignored Gren, their focus entirely on Nika.

The huge Krackle on the right's tendrils raised, and an instant later, Nika bore the full brunt of its gamma waves as a buzz of clicks assaulted her ears. She staggered under the onslaught, and her nerves itched, her mind fuzzy. It wasn't painful, per se, but it was horrible, nonetheless. It felt as if every cell in her body was being torn apart.

The smell of apples hit her, which seemed like an odd thing to notice in her position.

The blast quit, and Nika drew herself up defiantly. She was all too aware of the catchment hole behind her, and just inside the pipe, her twin. She couldn't give the Krackles a reason to check the pipe.

With more courage than she thought she possessed, she started to walk between the two aliens back to the buildings. She felt like she was going to pass out, but she held her head high—at least until one of the Krackles grabbed her with its pincher hand.

Nika couldn't help it. She squeaked in terror and tried to pull away, but the thing was too strong. The tendrils rose again, and Nika feared the blast would be lethal this time.

"Go, Rika," she said before a zombie grabbed her free arm and gave it a yank.

"I claim her," the zombie, a young, slightly overweight man said as a small tab on his collar emitted a series of clicks.

The Krackle holding her froze for a moment, as still as a statue.

"I claim her," the young man said, his voice cracking in fear.

His tab responded with the clicks again, and in a flash of clearness, Nika realized the tap was a translator of sorts. She didn't know who the zombie was, and she didn't know what being "claimed" was, but it had to be better than whatever the Krackle had been about to do. About what it still could do.

But the Krackle released her. She felt one more wave, much subtler, then the two Krackles abruptly turned and strode away.

Nika would have collapsed had the man not been holding her.

"Tee wasted teer claim on her, Ben?" another zombie, an older woman asked. "Stupid, if you ask me. And when she was trying to escape? That went beyond stupid."

"I wasn't trying to escape," Nika said automatically.

"Sure, tee jus' happened to be looking into one of the drainage pipes. Tee might even be small enough to fit through, fat lot o' good it would do tee. The masters, they've got you cataloged, and when they tracked tee down, well, there be only one penalty for running."

She turned back to the young man and said, "Tee made teer choice. Tee have to live with it. If she don't pass screening, teer outa luck."

"I got it, Vickie," the young man, Ben, said.

The zombie woman gave a harrumph, then told Nika and Gren, "Get tee back to the others. Don' try this again or tee won't have your young knight there to protect tee."

She nodded at the last zombie, and the two walked back to the buildings.

"Thank you," Nika said.

"You can't claim her," Gren spat out.

Nika was surprised to see the anger on Gren's face. She was even more surprised to see the embarrassment turn the man's face red.

"It's not . . . I mean . . ." he stammered, dropping Nika's arm as if it was radioactive.

"I know what you want. That zombie, the one you called Vickie, she told us. Ni . . . Rika's not a breeder, and she never will be."

Breeder?

That didn't sound good at all.

"No, it's not like that!" the man protested.

"It's not like that? Give me a freaking break. We saw you stalking her like some pervert."

"No!"

"No? You lying piece of—"

"Is that true, Ben?" Nika asked, rounding on him.

"No. I mean yes. But not like that."

Gren glared at him.

"OK, maybe I was stalking you," he told Nika. "But not because of anything perverted. I just wanted to know more about you."

"To make her your breeder," Gren snarled.

"No! I would never—"

"I heard you say you claimed me. What does that mean?"

"That I want you as my breeder," Ben said miserably. "But that's not what I wanted. Not like that."

"So, you claimed her. How convenient if that's not what you wanted," Gen said.

"I'm sorry. I didn't know what else to do."

"What do you mean?" Nika asked.

"The alarm went off—"

"The alarm?"

"When you tried to escape, there was an anomaly in the prisoner scan. The masters reacted, and when they do, we have to, too."

"I wasn't trying to escape," Nika said sullenly.

It was technically true, too.

"OK, then when you tried to get into that drainage pipe, the system showed a blip in your reading. Like I said, an anomaly.

"I joined the others, and when I got here and saw it was you, I just freaked. And when the master grabbed you . . . well, the masters don't like anomalies. Their system isn't perfect, and I don't think they like that, either. So, when something like this happens, they just, you know . . ." he said, suddenly unable to meet Nika's eyes.

"Kill me?"

His silence was answer enough.

Nika had come very close to dying right then.

At least Rika's free.

"You know I'm not going to be your breeder, or whatever you call it," she said.

"I don't want it like that. I mean, yeah, I know that. I just had to do something."

"You know she's just seventeen," Gren said, sounding somewhat, but not completely, mollified.

"No, I didn't. . . I'm nineteen," Ben said.

Which surprised Nika. She would have guessed at least mid-twenties.

Not that that makes any difference.

"Thank you for stepping in. But Gren's right. I'm not going to be your breeder. Anyone's breeder. I've got my rights."

Do I, though? Do Krackle slaves have any rights?

But she'd cross that bridge when she came to it.

She stepped over and took Gren's hand. "Can you take me to my mother now?"

"Sure thing."

Gren led Nika back to the others. Neither looked back, but Nika could sense the boy standing there in silence, watching them walk away.

Chapter 22
Rika

Rika was afraid when she saw Nika's feet climb out of the box. She didn't know if "company" meant Zombies or Krackles, but she didn't want Nika to face either one. She should be out there, not her twin. At least she had some experience dealing with them.

If she was afraid before, she was petrified when the clicks of a Krackle "seeing" filled the air. Thoughts of being picked up by the Krackle down at the creek flashed through her mind, and she instinctively scooted farther back into the pipe. Guilt flooded her, guilt for leaving her sister to face the Krackles.

She almost crawled forward again to rush to Nika's defense, but a simple "Go, Rika," halted her in her tracks. She'd told Nika to freeze when the Krackle had her, and it had saved her. Now, she had to stay free until she could figure out what to do.

"Sorry, Baba. Stay strong, and I'll get you out of there," she muttered, tears rolling down her eyes as she pushed back. No matter how logical it was, she couldn't help but feel that she was abandoning her sister and mother.

As she retreated, Rika could just hear some voices, human voices, but she couldn't make out what they were saying. She considered crawling forward again, but to what end? Unless Nika came back?

That was enough for her. She sure couldn't crawl backward the length of the drainage pipe, so she reversed her direction, back to the catchment box. She heard a few more snatches of conversation, maybe Gren talking, then nothing. Rika froze, barely breathing, as she listened for something, anything to tell her what had happened. After twenty minutes, she has to accept that whatever happened was done. It was time for her to go down the pipe and find Fel. And Hero.

Rika smiled at the thought. It was so like her sister to name the dog Hero. Not that it didn't fit, but still, Nika wasn't going to name the dog something meaningless.

To get down the pipe and out of the depot, however, meant she had to turn around. That would be impossible while inside the pipe. She had to go past the grate and into the box. She stuck out a hand to start, then paused. The cover to the box was open, and Rika didn't know how or what had set the Krackles off. Derek's cousin, for all of being some sort of Krackle engineer, hadn't any answers, but the cover being off the box making a difference made sense.

So, what are you going to do, Rika Ingersoll?

It was hard to tell from her vantage, but the light looked like it was beginning to fail. Rika wondered if it made sense to wait for darkness before entering the box and turning around. It wouldn't matter to the Krackles, she knew, but what about the zombies? They had human eyes, even the smoothies. If whatever happened had put them on alert, then they might have the box under surveillance.

Decision made, Rika settled in to wait. It was only then that she noticed her father's Kri-Blade, still in the sheath, on the floor of the box. Nika had left it there for her.

Even when she was captured, she was taking care of her twin. More tears fell down her cheek, and she almost angrily wiped them away. She couldn't get emotional. She had to keep her cool if she was going to figure anything out.

The bottom of the pipe was still damp, and Rika started shivering. She hadn't had anything to eat since the green sausage that morning, and the cold was sapping her energy. She knew she should move, so before it was fully dark, she emerged from the pipe and grabbed her father's knife, clipping the sheath to her waist. She couldn't help taking a quick glance at the sky before she entered the pipe. It was a brilliantly glorious orange and blue, the sun lighting up the clouds overhead.

This time, her shiver wasn't from the cold. Clouds like that formed to release whompers. Not yet, but probably sometime during the night.

Nika regarded the pipe once more. It was small, and her fit would be tight. But Nika had made it through, so she could, too. She just had to make sure to be out of the other side before the rain fell.

"Better get going, girl," she muttered, ducking into the pipe and starting to crawl.

Chapter 23
Nika

Following Gren, Nika started to feel faint as it all sunk in. She'd come close to dying, only to be rescued by a zombie. It didn't make sense. She held up her left hand. It was shaking like a leaf. She stuck both hands in her pockets so no one could see them.

She was worried sick about Rika. Her sister was the more aggressive of the two of them, the most fearless, but not in all ways. She hated the dark and didn't do well in confined spaces. Their mother said it was because she had a more active imagination, and now she had to make it all the way to the end of the pipe?

Nika needed to get her mind off Rika and her close brush with death.

"So, who the heck was that zombie?" she asked Gren as they entered the quad.

"An asshole, stalking Rika like that."

Nika frowned, then said, "But he saved my life back there."

"Not by choice. Like I said, he's stalking Rika. Wants her as his own private breeder."

But he didn't seem to want to be serious.

She wasn't going to be anyone's breeder, especially if they were rescued. But the zombie hadn't wanted to press whatever "claiming" was.

"I didn't even know zombies could talk like that. Heck, the woman sounded like a Quavarian."

"She was."

"What do you mean?"

Gren stopped and looked around for a moment. "See that zombie over there? With the smooth overalls? That's a real zombie. You know, the ones who broke off from humans thousands of years ago or whatever."

"OK, and how is that different?"

"The ones with the fluffier overalls? We call them shaggies. They're traitors. Captured by Krackles, then working as guards to keep us prisoner. That woman? She was on Galant, so she's been a guard for, uh . . ."

"Three years," Nika said, astounded. "How can anyone work for the Krackles?"

"'Cause they're messed up. Traitors, like I told you. Just like that shaggy who tried to claim you. Traitor."

Despite the whole "claiming" thing, Nika had been willing to give Ben the benefit of the doubt. He'd saved her life, after all. But now?

She shuddered at the thought.

"That's your mom's barracks. She'll be waiting for you. Well, for Rika. But before we get there, is Fel, you know, OK?"

"Frustrated and anxious, but OK. He wasn't hurt."

"He's not going to do something stupid, is he?"

"I told him not to, but you know Fel."

"Unfortunately, I do. And he's prone to letting his balls take control of him," she said wistfully. "I almost hope the Krackles take us off-planet soon so he won't get swept up in this crap."

"Don't say that. The Navy's coming. If they come before we're taken, we'll be rescued."

"Come on, Nika. You're a military brat. There's no way the Krackles don't know where the Navy is, and they had this all planned out."

"The Navy and Marines rescued all the prisoners on Sunshine. New Promise, too."

"And the Krackles learned from that," Gren said, almost in surrender.

Nika hated to hear the sense of defeat in her friend's voice.

"They don't know that my dad's on the way back, though. That wasn't planned."

Gren shrugged and said, "Maybe. But I'm not counting on it."

Nika didn't know what to say, but she was saved when she heard a welcomed voice call out Rika's name. She immediately broke into a run to where her mother stood with two other women.

"Rika, I've been worried, you've been gone so . . ." Her mother's eyes widened in shock before Nika almost bowled her over in a hug. "What are you doing here? When were you captured?"

"I wasn't. I snuck in."

"Oh, Nika baby, why would you do that? You were free. And where's, you know," she whispered.

"She's out there. We switched places."

Her mother froze, then her voice barely audible, whispered, "There's a way in and out?"

"Yes. No. I mean, I just barely fit. I—"

Her mother put a finger over Nika's lips and quietly said, "Not here."

She turned to the other two women who were looking at them curiously. "This is my daughter, N . . . Rika, I was telling you about. And this is their friend Gren Grafton."

"Rika, this is Gladiola Torrent and Llana Sanchez. Gladiola is a vice president with Arcadia Co-op, and Llana teaches at Deer Run Primary School."

"Pleased to meet you both," Nika and Gren said, almost in unison.

Nika was amazed that even in this situation, prisoners of the Krackles and about to be taken off-planet to live out their lives as slaves, the niceties of society still had to be met.

"Grafton? You Peggy Grafton's daughter?" Ms Sanchez asked.

"You know my mom? Have you seen her here?" Gren asked excitedly.

"I know her, dear. We went to school together. But sorry, I haven't seen her here."

"We were captured together, but after processing, I haven't seen her or little Mace."

"I heard most of the little ones are over at the last quad," Ms Torrent said.

"Really?" Gren asked, spinning around to look down the line of quads. This was the second quad in the line, so the last one was two more down. "I need to go there."

"Hold on, Gren," Nika's mother said. "It's getting late, and they're going to round us up soon."

"And take us off-planet, and I'll never see her again," Gren said.

"Just wait until morning, OK? Nothing's going to change before then."

"But—"

Nika's mother placed her hand on Gren's shoulder and said, "Just wait. Look, they're already starting to round us up."

Nika looked around. Zombies were moving into the quad, and people were entering the buildings.

"Uh, where am I?" she asked her mother. "Can I stay with you?"

"No, honey. You're in H210, over there. I'll see you in the morning, OK? First thing."

"Gren, can you show Rika the way?"

Gren took one last look in the direction of the other quads, but her shoulders suddenly slumped, and she agreed.

Nika gave her mother one last hug, then reluctantly parted. The distant sound of thunder reached her as she crossed to her barracks, and she looked up. Clouds were forming, and clouds like these meant rain. Rain meant the drainage pipes would fill up.

She stopped and turned to where she'd left her twin, even if she couldn't see anything from here.

"Crawl fast, Baba. Crawl fast."

Chapter 24
Rika

Rika stopped, collapsing to the bottom of the pipe. Her hands hurt, her knees hurt, and now her left hip hurt. More than that, the darkness, the walls of the pipe closing in on her, made her mind race with possibilities, none of them good.

She wasn't surprised that Nika seemed unfazed. Not much fazed her twin. She was the even-keeled one of them. Rika was more adventurous, more outgoing. Perform a double somersault into the pond? No problem. Climb the highest tree? No problem. But she also had a few embarrassing phobias, and fear of the dark was one of them, even if she told herself it wasn't. She'd trained herself to deal with it, but here, where claustrophobia set in, the fear was back tenfold.

"Come on, Rika! The sooner you get on with it, the sooner you'll be out!" she shouted.

Her voice seemed to be swallowed up by the pipe, which only added to her unease.

She started moving again, eyes straining to pick up any sign of the end. She'd been crawling forever, and the stupid thing couldn't be that long.

She reached another thin section of mud. She had to spread her hands more to gain purchase on the sides of the pipe, which was a little awkward, but it was better than the grit and small pebbles, which tore up her hands like sandpaper. Her legs and belly had no recourse, though, and the mud was a welcome relief. She almost sighed at the cool wash . . .

It was suddenly cooler than usual, more intense. Rika dropped her hands back to the bottom, and water flowed over them. Not much, barely more than a trickle, but there had been none before.

She froze, holding her breath as she listened. She wasn't sure if she could hear anything. Was that a low drumming she heard, or was that her imagination, fueled by her fear?

Rika wasn't sure how deep underground she was. Maybe a meter or so?

Could I even hear a whomper underground?

Her belly and chest were wet from the mud, but now the wetness seemed to be creeping higher on her jeans. She felt in the dark again. The tiny trickle seemed larger already.

"It's raining!"

This wasn't her imagination running wild. If there was water flowing in the pipe, then that was being fed by something. She tried to turn her head to look back, but there was no room in the narrow pipe, and she wouldn't be able to see anything in the dark anyway.

But she knew what was happening—and what she had to do if she was going to get out of the pipe alive.

Rika started scrambling, rising onto her knees to get better movement, her head bumping on the top of the pipe. Fear drove her, an all-encompassing fear.

Last rainy season, a four-year-old had been sucked into a drainage pipe. The rescuers couldn't recover the body for ten hours, and the newsvid images of the tiny, limp body being handed up to his father had stuck with Rika for months.

"Push it, Rika!"

More water began to flow, working past her as she crawled, and that fueled her panic. She could hear the flow now, the gurgles mocking her puny efforts.

The first substantial wave hit her hard, knocking her flat. With her body blocking most of the pipe, the water pushed her forward. Rika couldn't regain her footing, as the water took control. She'd have tumbled head-over heels if the pipe was larger.

Rika struggled to keep her face clear of the water that made it past her as she shot down the pipe, a powerless piece of flotsam in the maelstrom. Water still splashed up, sending her into a coughing fit.

Rika was beyond panic. The only thing on her mind was to survive. She managed to get in a full breath before the water closed in on her. At that point, she went limp, letting the water take her.

Nika and her often held breath-holding contests, either at home or at their swimming hole on Morales Creek. They'd completely relax, expending as little energy as possible as they floated next to each other, waiting for the other to quit. Rika usually won.

But that was floating in the creek, knowing that she could lift her head at any time and breath. She wasn't being pummeled by water in a constrained drainage pipe. Rika had hit three minutes with Nika before, but that wasn't going to happen now, she knew.

Every blow against the walls of the pipe took a little bit more from her, and her lungs started to scream for air. She didn't have much time left now.

I'm so sorry, Baba. I failed you.

Her last thought was the hope that someone would find her body when she was shot forward, her arms and legs flailing. She couldn't see anything, and for a moment thought the pipe had expanded, but she fell with a stomach-churning belly flop into open water. Rika struggled to the surface as she was swept downstream and took deep, heaving breaths.

Her legs were hitting solid objects, and she managed to get them under her and scramble for the dry land. Or not so dry, but at least not underwater.

The whomper was pounding her from above as she pulled herself free of the fast-flowing water. She lay belly-down on the ground, shaking at her escape. Looking back, she could just make out the plume of water as the pipe emptied into the creek.

Her mind was blank as she stared at the plume. It took her several moments to realize that she'd somehow survived. It was impossible to believe, but there she was, beaten up and out of breath, but alive.

As it sunk in, she leaned her head back and laughed like a madwoman, cackling her defiance to the whomper. It had tried to kill her, but it had failed.

And then she remembered Nika. Her mom. The rest.

She quit laughing. She wasn't sure what she had to do next, but sitting here in the rain wasn't the answer.

Rika didn't know exactly where she was in the dark, but the creek, now grown to a torrent, had to lead to the pond where Fel and the dog would be waiting. With a sigh, she got her battered body to her feet and started following the creek.

Chapter 25
Nika

"Get ready for another lovely day in Paradise," the zombie yelled.

"What time is it?" the older woman in the next bunk asked as she sat up, rubbing her eyes.

Nika hadn't slept more than a few catnaps during the night, and she was exhausted. First, there had been the four hours of downpour, and trying to do the math in her head, she wasn't sure Rika would have been able to be out of the drainage pipe before the whomper hit, and she was worried sick about her twin. After that, there had been too many tears, too many furtive conversations, and too much restlessness, much less the surroundings and situation, for her to sleep well. The same women who had seemed in decent-enough spirits, all things considering, had deteriorated in the darkness.

As far as Nika was concerned, she welcomed the morning light. After breakfast—which sounded dreadful from how it was described to her by others—she'd be able to find her mother, who always seemed to be able to make things better.

She stood up and stretched when the zombie yelled out, "Before you go get breakfast, listen up. I hope you've enjoyed your little vacation here, but that's about to end."

"What's happening?" someone asked.

"What's happening? The rest of your miserable lives is happening, that's what."

There was a murmur of questions, and the zombie shouted, "Just listen up, and you'll see.

"You'll be allowed out in the quad today, but that can change in an instant, so keep your heads up and be ready. If you get the word, come back inside and wait. Or, more probably, be ready to move out as ordered."

"Move out to where?" the same voice asked. Rika couldn't see who it was.

"To the ships, stupid. Where else?"

There were gasps from the women and cries of surprise.

"What, you thought you were going to stay here forever?"

Nika felt her heart fall. It was real now. She knew what happened when the Krackles captured humans, but somehow, as long as she was with the others, she could put that out of her mind. Now, she couldn't. The rest of her life, as the zombie said, was staring her in the face.

"I can't tell you when you're all leaving. Maybe today. No later than tomorrow morning. Just pay attention and be ready to react."

The zombie paused, then seemed to lose some of her harsh tone. "Look, I was where you were once, so I know how you feel. I'm not going to lie. Some of you are going to have it rough, real rough, depending on where the Masters send you. But not all of you. If you obey the Masters and the First Servants—you call them smoothies—then you should be able to live out a normal lifespan. Just don't fight them. Your life as you've known it is over, so let it go."

No one said a word, and she let her gaze sweep the barracks. Her voice once again became hard as she said, "And just in case any of you get some funny ideas of trying to escape while we're boarding, the masters have been lenient so far, leaving all of us alone. They will not stand for anything that interrupts an orderly evacuation. There will be no excuses, no trial, no nothing. You'll be killed where you stand."

"Better to die than be a slave," someone muttered.

The zombie swung her head to lock onto the young woman who'd spoken. "Nothing's worth dying for. But if you want, then be my guest. I promise you it won't be an easy death, and some of your friends might get caught in the backblast."

There was a sudden, if slight, shift, and the women standing next to the one who'd spoken gave her a little space.

The zombie laughed. "See, your friends understand, and all I can use on you is my wand. It's the First Servants or the Masters that will kill you. You and maybe some of your friends who have the bad luck to be standing next to you. The Masters aren't too discerning when they're upset."

Dead silence greeted her, and she said, "Well, now that we've got that out of the way, go get fed. You may not get fed again for a while."

It was a subdued group that filed out the door and into the quad. Nika blinked in the bright sunlight. It was a beautiful day. Last night's whomper had cleaned the air, and it smelled bright and crisp.

Nika looked up at the sunrise and wondered if it was the last Arcadian sunrise she'd ever see.

Chapter 26
Rika

Rika hugged the ground, trying to disappear as the big Krackle transport slowly flew down Highway 32, just a hundred feet above the ground. She was afraid to breathe until it had passed them.

"Do you think it's looking for us?" Fel asked from where he lay beside her.

"I don't know. Maybe."

It had taken Rika almost an hour of stumbling around in the dark until she found the pond—now much larger than it had been—and made her way to Fel and the dog. Tired, wet, and cold, she'd snuggled up against Fel while she tried to sleep. It hadn't done much good, and she'd bolted wide-awake as the big transport had made its appearance.

The threat seemingly gone, Rika sat up, her body a symphony of aches and pains. She'd been beaten up pretty bad in the pipe, but at least she was basically sound, which was a far better outcome than she could have hoped for.

Down the highway, she could still hear the whine of the transport, even if it was hidden from her sight by the trees around her. But then the whine changed in pitch. Something was happening. For a moment, she thought it was turning back, and she brought her legs up under her to be ready to run, but the whine never got closer, and a moment later, it cut off completely.

"I think it landed," Fel said as he carefully moved the dog's head off his lap and stood, peering around a tree. "Maybe it spotted us."

"Maybe," Rika admitted.

But something told her the transport was not there for them.

"We need to go take a look," she said.

"What? Are you crazy?"

"You know I'm crazy. You've called Nika and me crazy often enough."

"Yeah, but that's for climbing the comms towers or jumping from one tree to the other, stuff like that. Not giving yourself up to the Krackles."

"So, have *you* come up with any way to save your mother and Mace? To save Gren?"

"No," he said miserably.

"This might give us something, and we're for sure not getting anything sitting here hiding out."

Fel was a nice-enough guy, but not the brightest fuel cell in the pack, and he never seemed to give Nika and her credit for anything, which drove Rika bonkers. But she knew what buttons to push on him. The guy was going crazy out free when his family was being held captive, feeling guilty on one hand and anger at the Krackles on the other.

"And we're not going to give ourselves up. All we're doing it taking a look."

"That got Gren and Nika . . . I mean you, captured last time we 'just took a look.'"

"And Lemul," Rika added.

"Yeah, of course. Lemul, too."

Rika stood up and tried to straighten out her clothes, which had started to dry and were getting stiff. She knew she should get into the pond and clean up, but she didn't fancy being out in the open like that.

"I'm going. You can come with me or keep hiding here. Up to you."

She saw the resolve in his eyes as he said, "I'm not hiding. And I'm coming with you."

Rika nodded, keeping her face stoic while inwardly, she felt relief. Nika had made some comment about size being a factor in Krackle sensors, but she really didn't want to go alone. Besides, the transport had landed on the highway, not next to the depot.

"What about Hero?" Fel asked.

Rika looked down at the dog, who had raised his head at the mention of his name? Even after only a day, he seemed to know they were talking about him.

The dog had whimpered and barked when Rika had stumbled in during the night, but when she moved to pet him, he seemingly lost interest. He knew she wasn't Nika. It was childish of her, but she felt hurt.

"We're not going to be gone long. I think he'll be OK."

"If we come back," Fel said under his breath.

But he didn't argue. He gave Hero a few pieces of cut-up, un-reconstituted shrimpburger and cupped some water in his hand for the dog to slurp up before he nodded to tell Rika he was ready.

Rika gave the dog a pat on the head and was embarrassingly pleased when Hero licked her hand. She had a smile plastered on her face as she started walking around the pond, Fel following.

The smile faded the closer she got to the highway. Was she being stupid? Maybe she *was* walking into the lion's den. But her curiosity was stronger than her concern—or was she just trying to erase the fear she'd had the night before in the pipe?

Rika was self-aware enough to know that was a possibility, that she was being foolish to prove to herself that she wasn't a coward. Acknowledging that possibility didn't sway her, however. She was going to find out why a Krackle transport had landed on the highway.

The two reached the fork where Dwyer hit the highway, butting behind the businesses there. Rika got back on her belly, setting off the abused nerves and flesh, and crept forward to the edge of one of the buildings. Barely sticking her head out, she looked down the highway, but saw nothing. The transport must have landed around the bend.

She signaled Fel, and they retreated back into the trees before turning and paralleling the highway. It took about fifteen minutes, but finally, a loud bang caught their attention, and ahead, through the trees, they caught sight of the transport. They couldn't see what was happening, though.

"I'm getting closer," she said.

"And I'm coming with you."

Rika suddenly felt guilty for shaming Fel into coming. He wasn't adding any value to the effort, and even without sensors, he'd be far more easily spotted than she would be.

"No, you need to stay back here."

"I'm not afraid," he said defiantly.

"No, but I am, if you come with me." She could see him trying to come up with a counter-argument, and before he could speak, she put her hand on his arm and said, "I know you're not afraid. But let me do this alone, OK? If they spot me, I need to know that you're still free, and you can get word to the Marines when they land."

Rika had finally admitted to herself that her dad and the Marines wouldn't make it back to Arcadia in time, but it sounded good, at least. And to her surprise, Fel seemed to buy it.

Like I just said, he's not the brightest fuel cell, she thought, but with a degree of fondness, which surprised her. She knew that Nika kind of liked Fel, but Rika barely gave him a thought other than as just one other of the gang.

She was too sore to get back on her belly, so she slipped from tree trunk to tree trunk until she had a better field of view. The transport was on the highway, looming large. Where a human ship would have nav lights flashing, the Krackle ship looked dead.

But if it was dead, there wouldn't be a handful of Krackles surrounding it and four armored vehicles lined up on the other side. These were combat troops, and Rika ducked back behind the tree.

Krackles could sense the area around them in a full 360, but with their lower frequency waves. Their higher definition gamma waves projected from the dish-like protuberance that sprouted from their shoulders like a human head. It was those gammas that had knocked her out when she was captured, and those Krackles, who were maneuvering the armored vehicles, would be using them. If one happened to "glance" her way, she'd be spotted, probably even behind the tree.

All she could hope for was that they were focusing on their gamma waves, and not paying attention to any of their other sensory waves that might pick her up.

She looked back in the direction of where she'd left Fel, wondering if she should just leave.

No, I've got to see what they're doing. That armor may be going to the depot.

She carefully lowered herself to the ground, pushing herself up with raw elbows. Within a minute, it became clear what they were doing. They were loading the armor onto the transport. First one, then the next two were carefully loaded. Most of the Krackle troops embarked on the transport as well, and the back ramp closed. Two Krackles returned to the last armored vehicle and got inside as the transport lifted off the road, spun around on its axis, and took off. Not a hundred feet up like it was before, but at a steep angle, as in going into orbit or making a long-distance flight.

If the transport had engaged its space drive engines, Rika would have been cooked. But so probably would have been that last armored vehicle. Within a few seconds, the transport was gone. The remaining armored vehicle started to move toward town, and it was quickly out of sight as well.

Rika wondered what that all meant. Why would three vehicles be loaded and one left behind? She didn't know. But she did know that nothing she'd seen gave her any idea of what she could do to free her sister and mother.

Reluctantly, she turned and walked back to Fel.

"What did you see?" he asked.

She described the loading of the armor, then the transport leaving.

"Then we don't have much time, do we? They're pulling out," Fel said.

And Rika realized he was right. He wasn't as slow as he seemed. She felt embarrassed that she hadn't put two and two together, and he had. If he was right, and she thought he was, then their families would soon be taken off-planet and out of reach of any rescue. The thought made her want to sink to the ground and cry.

Oh, no, you don't Rika Ingersoll. As long as there's hope, you don't give up!

"Maybe we can find a hover, and as soon as the Krackles start loading our people, crash the fence," she said. "That might let some people get out, at least."

"But how can we tell if our folks are the ones to escape?"

"We don't. But at least some could escape."

Now it was Fel's turn to look embarrassed. "Of course. Sorry about that. If we can save anyone, then we need to do that."

"I'm not a good driver," Rika said, trying to think things through.

"Not a good driver" was an understatement. She'd had a few lessons, but she didn't have her license yet. And this would take manual driving. The autopilot wouldn't let her drive into a fence.

"This time, it's on me. I've let you and Nika tell me what to do, but I *am* a good driver. I can do this."

"You'd have to bail before the hover hits, you know. My mom said the fence was electrified or something. Said the Krackles gave them a demonstration on what would happen if someone touched it."

"No problem," Fel said.

And Rika knew he was right. She'd been so concerned about getting things done, she'd inappropriately assumed that she had to do everything. But in this case, Fel was the right person for the job.

"OK, you've got it. Now, all we have to do is find a working hover."

Which might be easier said than done. Most personal hovers grabbed power from the grid. But there were some, mostly outside the cities, that were hybrids with fuel cells for when they couldn't draw from where transmission loss made the grid impractical.

"Let's check for a delivery truck back near the pond," she said.

They should have remained stealthy, but Rika didn't have it in her anymore. They walked back as if on a weekend hike. No Krackles jumped up at them, however.

They started searching the buildings. They found an old Hyperbolic, but this one looked like it hadn't been driven in decades. The fuel cell was dead, and there was no power to check if it could even be recharged.

There was a locked garage behind a floral shop, and they both decided that offered their best shot. It probably had a delivery vehicle, which were usually hybrids. The problem was that they couldn't break in. Finally, Fel found a sturdy-looking bar and started attacking the lock, hoping to break it.

Rika watched eagerly, happy that they finally had a course of action.

"Freeze!" a mechanical voice sounded behind them.

Rika gave a soft shriek of surprise as she spun around, and Fel stepped in front of her, bar raised threateningly.

But these weren't Krackles, she realized with joy. Rika knew who they were: Regency Marines in Mk4 Combat Suits.

So, why were they drawing down on the two of us. It makes no sense.

"We don't allow looting," the first Marine said through their throat speaker.

"We're not looting,' Rika said as Fel lowered his arm and shifted the bar around behind him, as if they hadn't seen it yet.

"Right," the other Marine said. "You just happen to be breaking into that garage for fun."

"Look, we don't have time for you now. You need to go find someplace to lay low. And don't loot property," the first one said.

"Are you with the 109th?" Rika asked. The Marines' unit would be stamped on their combat suit's back shoulder, which she couldn't see.

"Why?" the first Marine asked.

"Oh, shit, that's the colonel's daughter," the second Marine said. "One of the twins. I didn't recognize her looking like that."

Rika knew she was a mess, and she couldn't help but tug on her blouse and wipe a hand through her short hair.

"I'm Rika Ingersoll. Colonel Ingersoll is my father. Is he here?"

The two Marines rotated to look at each other. Rika knew they were on their comms, either to each other or back to their command.

She didn't have time for military protocol. If her father was here . . .

She stepped up to the first Marine, dwarfed by his combat suit.

"I need you to take me to the colonel now. I've got vital information for him."

Chapter 27
Nika

"When do you think it will happen?" Nika asked her mother.

"I don't know, hun. It sounds like you got more information than we had."

It was a very subdued crowd in the quad, with small groups of people forming, breaking apart, and forming again in new groupings. Nika had followed the rest of her barracks to get breakfast, but after one bite, she'd given hers away. She was too worried to eat.

She wasn't the only one. Many never even got their food.

It was probably a stupid move. Their zombie had insinuated that they would be going for a long period without any food. Nika knew that, but she still couldn't force down the green sausage.

Instead, she left to find her mother. When the call came down, she'd already decided that she'd stick with her, rules be damned. They'd have to force the two of them apart.

The zombie's warning stuck with her, and she could be courting serious punishment. But it wouldn't make any sense. If the Krackles had a need for human slaves, then why would they waste one for something like that? It wasn't as if she was trying to escape.

"You know, you could go out the way you came in when we're evacuating," her mother said.

Nika didn't even wonder that her mother made that statement right when she was thinking of escape. People said that twins had some sort of telepathic bond, and maybe that was true, but it had always seemed to Rika and her that their mother always knew what they were thinking even before they did.

"They'll know I'm gone."

"But how hard will they try to get you back? Are they going to dig you out of the ground?"

"From what our zombie told us, yeah, maybe."

"Ours didn't say anything like that."

Which both of them knew didn't mean anything.

"It's just . . . baby, I'm not trying to tell you what to do. But if you have the opportunity, then maybe you should take it. Find Rika and wait until your father gets here."

"I don't want to be without you, Mother," Nika said, turning in to hug her tightly.

"Neither do I, but it looks like that's going to be out of my hands."

Nika felt like she was five again, coming to her mother to make things right.

"I hope Rika made it out OK," Nika whispered.

"She's a capable girl. I'm sure she did."

Nika had always thought she'd somehow know if something happened to her twin. She'd tried to mentally reach out to her during the night, but there was nothing. Nothing good, nothing bad.

"Hi Gren," her mother said. "You holding out?"

Nika wiped her eyes and turned around, trying to smile.

"I'm going to the fourth quad," her friend said without preamble.

"But they told us to stay here," Rika said.

"If we're leaving, I need to be with them. Our zombie said that we're all going to different places, wherever the Krackles need us most. I can't take that chance. I know Mom and Mace are over there. I'm sure of it."

"But if you get caught leaving . . ." Rika said, leaving the rest of the sentence unspoken.

"Then I get caught," Gen said with a shrug of her shoulders. She gave Nika a long stare, then asked, "If you knew your mom was in the next quad, what would you do?"

She still had one arm around her mother's waist, and she pulled her in tighter. She already knew what she'd do. Sticking with her mother and going into her barracks wasn't that much different than trying to reach another quad.

"You know I'd try," Nika said.

"Damned right you would. And so will I."

"Then . . . we may never see each other again," Nika said as realization hit.

Gren nodded sadly. "That's why I had to find you first. To say goodbye."

Gren held out her arms, and Nika joined the embrace. She held her friend as tightly as possible, as if she would never let go. Tears flowed onto Gren's blouse.

"I'm never going to forget you," Nika said, trying to hold back the sobs.

"I'm not going to forget you, either, Nika. You and Rika."

They stood there for a full minute before Gren slowly disengaged from Nika. They stood apart, holding hands.

"Ms Ingesoll, you take care of Nika, OK?"

"I will, hon. And find your mother. And Mace."

Gren nodded, dropped Nika's left hand to wipe her eyes. "Well, that's it, then. Take care."

She abruptly turned and strode off.

"Fair winds and following seas," Nika said, the words her mother always used when their father left on a deployment. She wasn't a hundred percent sure what that meant, only that it was traditional.

Mother and daughter watched in silence as Gren disappeared into the crowd.

Chapter 28
Rika

Rika broke into a run the moment she saw her father huddled with several other Marines over a command pad. One of her escorts futilely grabbed for her shoulder, but she was too quick. Her father just started to turn when Rika hit him like a rugger. Her shoulder screamed in protest after smashing his body armor, but she didn't care.

"Rika girl, Rika girl, it's OK. You're safe now," her father said, gently wrapping armored arms around her. He looked up at the others and asked, "Can you give me a moment?"

He hugged the crying girl for a long moment before he gently pulled her away from him, kneeling so they were face-to-face.

"I couldn't believe it when Corporal Annison said you were here. I was so afraid for you. Are Nika and your mom with you?"

"They were captured," she said with a sob as her father's face fell. "I mean, I was captured, but then Nika took my place. She's in the depot."

Her father looked confused. "Nika took your place?"

"She came in through the drainage ditch, and the Krackles can't tell us from DNA, but she stood up and I went down the—"

"Slow down, Rika," he said. "I can't understand what you're saying. Start at the beginning. You too, Fel. Come here, son."

Fel had been hanging back, holding Hero—he'd refused to follow the Marines unless he could get the dog and bring him.

"Major Nguyen, Sergeant Major, come back to hear this. The rest of you, get going.

"Now, you two, tell me what happened."

With fits and starts, Rika and Fel gave him a running account of what had happened since the invasion. Her father's face had hardened when the two described the families being taken, and Rika could see him struggle to contain his anger when she told him how she was captured.

"Nika," was all he said when she explained how she and her twin had exchanged places. Rika hesitated then. She still felt guilty about the switch, and for a moment, she wondered if her father blamed her for it, too.

"Go on, Rika," he said quietly.

For whatever reason, she didn't tell him of being caught in the pipe when the whomper hit. He was carrying enough on his shoulders as it was.

She told him of finding Fel, then watching the Krackle ship load up.

"That's what we thought it was doing," Major Nguyen told her father. "They're preparing to diddiho out of here."

"Any sign of their transport ships?"

"Not yet, sir. But we've got limited resources still functioning. Some of the ASP's and the inerts. The second they go active, however, without a Navy umbrella, they'll be taken out. The Krackle ships could already be in system, and we wouldn't know it yet."

Rika didn't know what an "APS" or an "inert" was, but they had to be some sort of space surveillance, and the "ships" the major was talking about had to be the transports to take the prisoners off-planet.

"And no changes in their combat fleet?"

"No, sir. The Navy thinks they'll have the strength to win if the Krackles put up a fight."

"The Navy's coming?" Rika asked, her hope rising.

"Just a second, Rika," her father said, holding up his hand.

Rika was embarrassed. She knew better than to interrupt.

"And if they're loading out their armor, how much time does that give us?"

"I don't know. On Phylox, they loaded out immediately and were gone before the Navy arrived. On SL-80, the process took four days. I don't think the armor load-out is a concrete sign they're about to depart immediately. Probably more like trying to get ahead of the game. If I had to guess, I'd say as early as tonight, as late as the next night. They have to know how long it will take Third Fleet until then to reach us."

"Thank God they didn't realize the regiment was already en route back here," the sergeant major said.

"With no new data, then we proceed as planned," her father said, pursing his lip, a telltale sign that he wasn't happy.

"If I may, Colonel? I'd like to ask Rika something."

"I want to get her and Fel to safety," her father said. "But, be quick."

The major turned to Rika. She was a reservist, the regimental assistant operations officer. Rika had met her at a few functions, and she knew her father had a high opinion of her.

"If I showed you a map of the depot, could you point out where all the civilians are being held? And the Krackles?"

"I don't know. I never saw the entire place. But I can try."

"That's all I can ask of you."

She flipped out her CC screen and opened a line drawing with "Yaakov A. D. A." written at the top. Rika gave a little shudder. She wasn't very good with maps. What was the use of that? Anytime she needed to get somewhere, she could ask her wristcomp.

Except during times like now, when the wristcomps were all knocked offline.

She leaned over the display. It made no sense to her, just boxes arrayed in patterns. Try as she might, her mind refused to make the leap from lines to the actual depot. Until she saw "Main Gate" written at the bottom of the map.

If that's the main gate, then . . .

She closed her eyes and imagined she was walking through the gate. If that was so, then the quads had to be to the left. She opened her eyes and looked back at the map, putting her finger on the gate, then running it to the left.

Suddenly, as if by magic, the map gelled into something she understood. The first group had to be the first quad, then the second was her quad.

"Right here," she said, touching the map. "That's where we were."

"How many people?" the major asked.

"I don't know. Let's see, we had about a hundred in my barracks, and there are . . ." she paused, counting the buildings. "Maybe two thousand?"

The major looked at her father and said, "That means eight thousand here. Either there are more places where they're being kept, or they didn't bother with capturing everyone."

Rika looked at the major in surprise. She was inferring that maybe the Krackles had simply killed large numbers of the city's population. Despite all that had gone on since the invasion, she'd never even considered that. The Krackles wanted slaves, after all. At least that was what everyone was being told.

"What about the Krackles? Where are they?"

"I don't know. I never saw many. Mostly just zombies."

The major looked at the map for a moment.

"You know, not all the zombies are the Krackle humans. Some are what they call quislings."

"We know, honey," her father said.

They know? If the Marines know, then why isn't this common knowledge?

Rika didn't like being left in the dark. She wanted answers.

"What's going on? Are you going to rescue our people?"

"Rika, we can't . . ." he started, then paused to consider it. "Hell, why not.

"We were already on the way back when the Krackles invaded. We don't think they knew that. The Third Fleet is on its way. Our mission, ours and the 91st's, is to stop the embarkation of the prisoners if that starts before the Third Fleet gets here, and if the fleet catches them before that, to protect the prisoners during the fight."

The 91st was the active-duty regiment on the planet, stationed over on Nuevo Monterrey near the capital.

"How did you make planetfall, though?"

"Dropped, during the whomper. For cover."

Rika's mouth fell open. Each battalion had a drop-qualified company, able to surreptitiously insert on a planet. It was dangerous, and in a whomper, it had to be almost impossible.

"Did anyone get hurt?" she blurted.

The quick, pained glance between her father and the sergeant major was all she had to see. Not every Marine made it. They'd undertaken an extremely dangerous method to insert in an effort to save the prisoners.

"We've got two companies at Riesetown, and one here. The 91st Marines are on the continent. The rest of the Marines are cloaked and in behind the Cat." The major said, referring to the smaller of Arcadia's two moons. "They'll land if fighting breaks out."

Which will be more dangerous, landing on a transport in a hot zone.

"Did you get what you need?" her father asked the major. "I want to get these two to safety."

"This helped, but we still don't know if there are others, and we don't have a clue where the Krackles and zombies are."

"Don't you have your little microdrones?" Fel asked.

"Yes, but we can't deploy them without letting the Krackles know we're here," she told him.

"Oh, sorry," Fel said, his face reddening.

Rika thought it was a good question. No reason to be embarrassed.

"That's still going to cause us some problems and raises the probability of civilian casualties." She looked down at her CC, inputted some numbers, and then said, "If we only go with eight thousand in the depot, the fifty-percent PCM is just shy of fifteen hundred. If there's more, then that will change."

Rika gulped. A Projected Casualty Median of one thousand, five hundred people dead. And a 50% chance that even more would die. Maybe Nika would be one of them. Maybe her mom.

"If you knew where the Krackles are? Would that change the numbers?" she asked the major.

"Yes. I can't tell you by how much. It would depend on numbers and where they were. But yes, certainly."

"I can find out," Rika said before she had a chance to reconsider.

"What? No!" her father said. "You and Fel are getting out of here to safety."

"The major said if you know where the Krackles are, that can save lives."

"No. You're not a Marine. I'm not going to risk you."

"I made it out. I can go back the same way. Change places with Nika and find out."

"No. We'll send someone else if you know a way in. What about Lance Corporal A'Tae? She's small," he asked the sergeant major.

"No, Dad," Rika said, taking a gauntleted hand in hers. "I can barely fit as it is. And even if this Marine could fit, as soon as she shows her head inside, the Krackles are going to pick her up. It has to be me."

Her father pulled her into him. "I can't lose you, Rika."

"I don't plan on getting caught. Besides, if something happens, then you'll have Nika."

She was surprised at how calmly she said that. Maybe the guilt of being out here while her twin was in there.

"But I want both of you. Your mother, too."

"This is the best chance."

He was still hesitating.

"Remember what you told us when you deployed to Sacramana? That sometimes, you had to do what you didn't want to because of duty? You have to make this decision as a commanding officer, not my father."

Her father's eyes filled with tears, and he looked over at the sergeant major.

"You know I love your girls like my own, sir. But she's right. This could save a lot of lives."

Her father closed his eyes and tilted his head back. The sides of his buzzcut were graying, she noticed. She'd heard about the weight of command, and for the first time, she thought she realized what that meant. When she saw him sigh, then the command attitude take over, she knew she'd won.

"Major Nguyen, tell Captain Neller that I want two Marines to escort my daughter to the opening of the drainage pipe, and they're to stay there until she gets back.

"And you," he said, turning to Rika. "Find out what you can, but don't take any chances. Everything you find out can be important, but we'll get none of that if you get caught. Agreed?"

"Yes, sir. Agreed. No taking big chances."

The colonel disappeared for a moment, and the father reappeared. He lifted Rika up to give her a kiss. "Just make it back, baby girl."

"I will," she said, kissing the stubble on his cheek.

"And if you see your mother, tell her I love her."

She ran the back of her hand along his jawline as he lowered her back to the ground.

"Sergeant Major, if you can take my daughter? And Major Nguyen, I'm not happy with the rally point. Let's see if we can't find somewhere with more cover."

Rika knew he was trying to use his "command voice," but she could hear the break in it. She hated forcing him to do this, but it was the best decision she could make.

She looked back at him for a second, taking in the image of her father, wondering if this would be the last time she saw him.

"I should go with you," Fel said.

"You know you can't. I'll have two Marines with me. You take care of Hero. Nika will have your ass if you let anything happen to him."

"That she would," he said with a forced laugh.

He wasn't happy. That was obvious. Rika knew that both he and her dad were against her going back. But it had to be done.

"I'm ready," she told the sergeant major, who was standing by.

"You said that both you and your sister can't be in the depot at the same time," the sergeant major said.

"Yes. One or the other of us, but not both."

"Are you going to be able to get her to the catchment basin? From what you said, it wasn't within the quad itself."

"Yes, Sergeant Major. We've got our own way of doing that. I just need your help in getting something together."

"Well, in that case, I suggest we get going."

"OK, here's what I need . . ."

Chapter 29
Nika

Quiet fell over the quad as the lone Krackle strode across, people parting before him like the Red Sea. Nika knew they were all wondering the same as she was: was this the end? Were they about to be taken off-planet?

The Krackle never wavered in its course as it cut between two barracks, heading into the mechanical shop area. Slowly, in fits and starts, the people started to talk again, relieved that they were still there.

"Where do you think we're going, Rika?" Anna asked.

Nika had never told her that she wasn't Rika. Nika didn't want to be paranoid, but she didn't think she should advertise the fact that there was a way in and out. She and her mother had discussed it, but given the size of the drainage pipe and the fact that they'd all been tagged, there was no advantage to spreading the word.

"I don't know. No one does."

"Maybe the zombies do, huh?"

"Maybe. But they don't seem to be free with information," Nika said.

"I know, the assholes. You'd think the quislings, at least, would be sympathetic and help us out a bit. They were prisoners, too. I mean, what would it hurt to tell us what's going to happen to us?"

Nika didn't want to think about that. Some people had tried to question the guards, but as a group, they tended to be tight-lipped. But why? Like Anna asked, what would it hurt?

There was a possible reason, and the thought gave Nika a hollow pit in her stomach. If their future was so bleak, so horrible, that people would riot and try to break free, then keeping quiet might forestall that. Nika had no doubt that the Krackles would react with lethal force, and with the fence powered up somehow, she didn't think anyone would escape. By keeping them in the dark, they could be kept docile, like lambs to the slaughter.

Nika and Anna had been slowly walking, and although the older girl didn't realize it, their route wasn't random. They were passing the cafeteria. Nika was still concerned that Rika might not have made it out of the pipe before last night's whomper hit. Rika would know she was worried, and Nika was sure her twin would try and give her some sort of signal, out beyond the fence, that she'd made it. A small pink cloth or plastisheet, up in a tree, would do it.

Since they were babies, Rika's color had been pink, Nika's, lavender. It was an open secret that their father needed the colors to tell the two of them apart.

The two girls rounded the cafeteria, and Nika scanned the forest. Nothing. She tried to push down the image of her sister, drowned, her body stuck in the pipe. Her eyes drifted to the catchment basin and . . .

A small lavender ribbon fluttered weakly in the breeze.

Lavender? It should be pink. Lavender's for me.

And why would Rika come all the way back through the pipe just to tell her she was OK? Something was wrong.

Anna was nattering on about what food she would miss, of all things, and Nika didn't want to check out the ribbon with her following.

"Hey, Anna, I hope you don't mind if I cut this short. I think I need to spend more time with my mom, you know, in case . . ."

"Oh. Yeah. I understand," Anna said, sounding disappointed. "But try and find me later, OK? I don't know many people here."

Nika felt guilty as she cut away from the girl, heading toward her mother's barracks, but this was important. As soon as she felt she'd gone far enough, she stopped and spun around. Anna wasn't in sight, so she turned and started back to the cafeteria.

Just before she reached it, however, she caught sight of Ben, who was watching her. He immediately looked away and walked off. Nika should think it was creepy, but she felt he was harmless.

You'll feel different if you get to some Krackle planet and he claims you as his breeder.

She shook off the feeling, and trying to seem casual, she walked between the cafeteria and the next barracks. Rika could feel thousands of eyes on her, and she kept expecting to hear someone call out her name, or a pair of Krackles to come running. Each step was agony.

To her great surprise, she reached the catchment box without anyone calling her out. The lavender ribbon had been tied to the lid.

"Baba?" she whispered.

"About time you came, Nik. I've been here almost an hour."

"What the hell are you doing here?" she asked, shocked to the bone.

"Nice to see you, too, Baba," Rika said.

"I was so afraid for you, after the whomper last night."

"Yeah, almost got me, too."

"So why on God's green planet are you back?"

"I saw Dad."

Nika froze, unable to say anything. Finally, she got out, "He's here?"

"No, I took a liner out to Telluride to see him. Of course, he's here, and with a company of Marines."

That didn't make any sense. Their father was a *regimental* commander, not a company.

"Why a company? And are they going to rescue us?" she asked, hope blooming for the first time since the invasion."

"They dropped. During the whomper."

"Oh, my god!"

"Yeah, oh, my god is right. Some didn't make it. One company here, two down at Riestown. The regulars are at the capital."

Nika's heart threatened to pound out of her chest to know the Marines were back. A company might not be enough, though, to rescue everyone.

"So, they're going to break us out?"

"If they have to. Best case is that the Navy and more Marines arrive. But if the Krackles try to take us off-planet, they'll act."

Nika tried to digest that. It wasn't great, but any shred of hope was much more than what she'd had five minutes ago.

"So, why did you come back? Just to tell me?"

"No, Baba. I came back because Dad needs intel. Where the Krackles are. Where more of us are. If he and Major Nguyen don't get it, a lot of people are probably going to be killed. Maybe fifteen hundred."

"Fifteen hundred? That many?"

"Maybe more," Rika said.

Nika took a moment to absorb that.

"And how are you supposed to get that kind of intel?" she finally asked.

"You and I are going to switch again. Then I'm going to find it."

"No! It's too dangerous. Last time we switched, the Krackles came to investigate. If it weren't for Ben, Gren and I might not be here."

"Wait? You were almost killed? And who's Ben?"

"The zombie boy, the one that likes you."

"That shaggy who wants me as a breeder? What the—"

"He's not like that. Well, he likes you. Me. But he's not making a claim. And he saved me with the Krackles."

"We're going to have to talk more on that later. But now, let's switch so I can get this done."

"What kind of information?"

"Like I said. Where the rest of us are, not just in the four quads. Where the Krackles are. Zombies, too."

"You wait there," Nika said. "I'll find out."

"Nik!" Rika yelled as Nika turned and walked off. She wasn't going to let her sister come back into the depot, especially not with the fact that at any minute, they might be loading transports to leave the system.

But how was she going to get the information? She'd seen Krackles going into where the mechanical shops were. The shaggy zombies had their own barracks at the end of the quad. The smoothie zombies? She had no idea.

One person could help if anyone. Her mother.

Rika returned to her mother's barracks and corralled her, pulling her away from the rest of the people.

"Nika's back," she said, then when her mother grew agitated and opened her mouth, she said, "Not in the depot. In the drainage ditch."

With a force of will, her mother regained her composure and quietly asked, "And why the hell did she come back?"

"Dad's here, with some of the Marines."

Her mother went white and almost stumbled. "Here?" she said in a squeak.

Rika nodded.

"Are they going to be able to rescue us?"

"That's the plan."

"Oh, thank God."

"But there's a problem. They need to know where all of us are, where the zombies are, and where the Krackles are. Otherwise, a lot of us are going to die. I need that information, and quick."

Her mother shook her head and took two deep breaths before saying, "Then we'd better get that for them. Wait here."

Nika was relieved to see her capable, in-control mother back, the one who could do anything. She really hadn't known how to proceed, and she was happy to pass the baton to her.

She settled in to wait.

Thirty minutes later, her mother hadn't returned. Forty-five minutes. An hour. Nika couldn't help but wonder if her mother had gotten caught trying to get the answers. She started pacing, wringing her hands.

Finally, seventy minutes after her mother let, she came back. Nika jumped to her feet. "Did you find out."

The look on her mother's face was all the answer she needed.

"I tried. I asked everyone. We knew the shaggies are in H225. Someone said her son told her there're more in I250.

"And some of the Krackles have gone into machine shops, but no one knows if they're bunking there or not."

"Which isn't telling Dad much."

"I know. But let's keep digging. Maybe I can go to the next quad."

"I don't think we have time. Let me get this to Rika and see what she thinks."

"I'm coming with you."

"No, Mom. Too dangerous. I don't want to call attention to us."

"But—"

"No. I'll be right back." She stood on her tiptoes and kissed her mother on the cheek. "Love you."

And before her mother could argue, she wheeled and left her, half expecting her mother to follow. But she stayed put.

Nika didn't know what she was going to do or how Rika was going to react. If she knew her twin—and she did—Rika was going to insist on getting the information herself. Nika wasn't going to allow that. She'd walk off if it came to that.

As she made her way back to her sister, she felt eyes burning her. She spun, and sure enough, Ben was standing in front of a barracks, staring at her. He looked away, and inspiration hit her.

She turned and strode right at him. He looked back, and panic set in as he tried to find an escape route, but Nika cut him off.

"Come with me," she said, going around the barracks.

Please follow me.

She reached the back end, stopped, and turned around. Ben was tentatively following, looking unsure of himself.

"Look, I'm sorry if I've been watching—"

Nika held up a hand to stop him short.

"I don't care about that. I want some answers."

"What?" he asked, taking a step back in confusion."

"Answers. I ask a question, you give me the answer. That's what humans do, or have you already forgotten?"

This was pretty aggressive talk for Nika. More like something her twin would say.

Rika would be proud of me.

"No, no. I know what an answer is. But what are you going to ask? We're not supposed to tell you anything of, well, you know."

"I don't give a crap about that. I need to know where the Krackles are? Where they sleep—if they even sleep."

Ben's face went white, and he stammered out, "The Masters? Why do you want to know that?"

"Look, Ben. You like me, right?"

Ben nodded nervously.

"If you ever want to get to know me better, you need to answer me, now!" She tried to use her command voice, copying her father.

"But they don't want us to tell you anything about them."

"But they don't want us to tell you anything about them," she repeated in a sarcastic and overly dramatic falsetto. "Are you even human?"

"Yes, I'm human," he said with a bit of backbone.

OK, ease up a little, Nika.

"Of course, you are. So, why do you care what they want?"

Other than the fact that they'll kill you in a second if they want.

She didn't voice that thought, though.

"And what harm will it do? It's not like I'm going to attack them."

"Well . . ."

She could feel him wavering. It would be stupid of him, given his situation, but boys often did stupid things for girls.

"Come on. For me?"

"You're not going to try and do anything to them? The Masters are invincible."

"Yeah, look at me. I weigh all of seventy-seven pounds dripping wet. What can I do?"

"Well," he said, looking around to see if anyone was around to hear. "I do know, and I guess it doesn't hurt to tell you. The ones here in this camp are in the depot pool."

"The pool?" she asked, surprised. Not the headquarters, not in one of the ammo bunkers, but the pool?

"They like the humidity," he said with a shrug. "Sometimes, some of the combat Masters come in to hang out there, too."

"And they don't think Arcadia's humid enough. What are they? Amphibians? No, don't answer that," she said when he opened his mouth to talk.

"What about the other zombies, the smoothies?"

"Them?" Ben asked, and for a moment, his distaste showing through. "The First Servants. Some of the rector class are in the pool

with the Masters. Others are scattered around, like at the library.
Different places. Why do you want to know about those worthless
dogs?"

"You don't like them?"

"They're not even human!"

Almost the same as us. Enough to interbreed.

"And they treat us like garbage, oh so superior to us."

Nika knew she'd touched a nerve, and she didn't want Ben to
get riled up—and remember that he was the guard, and she was the
prisoner. There was still one more vital piece of information she
needed.

"It's OK, don't worry about it," she said, putting her hand on
the boy's arm.

Her mother had once told the twins that the simple act of a
hand on an arm could have an almost superhuman effect. Nika had
yet to figure out why it worked, but it did. She could see Ben calm
down.

"I look around here. There's a lot of us, but not enough."

"What do you mean?"

"Storyville has over twenty-thousand people, and there's
another ten thousand in the surrounding area. There are not that
many in the four quads. Were the rest, you know, killed?"

"What? No! Of course, not. The Masters aren't like that."

"Then, where are the rest of us?"

"In the bunkers," he said matter-of-factly.

The depot was a vast collection of ammo bunkers. Whereas
the pool was open to organized youth groups, and the dept was
invaded by most of the town's population for the Landing Day BBQ
and fireworks display, the bunkers were off-limits.

"You've seen them?" Nika asked.

"Me? No, I'm assigned here. But everyone knows it's true.
Like you said, the quads don't hold that many." He paused, then
asked, "Why are you asking me all of this."

"I deserve to know, right?"

"I guess so," he said, but he didn't look convinced.

"And now I do. Thank you. I know now that we'll all be going
together to serve the Masters," she said, biting her tongue as she said
the word.

"It's not so bad. You'll see."

"You don't wish you were back home on . . . where are you
from?" she asked.

"Galant."

"You don't wish you were back on Galant?"

"No. I know you don't believe me, but Galant was a pretty rough place. Anything's better than that."

"Even serving the Masters?"

"Maybe. I don't have much choice now, though, do I? I can't think of what could have been, only what is."

His voice became hard, and Nika couldn't afford to let him revert to guard status. She had information, and she had to get it to Rika.

"Thanks, Ben," she said. "You've really reduced my stress level. I think I was about to lose it."

A huge smile broke over his face, and the nice Ben reappeared. "I'm glad I helped you."

"I've got to go now. Maybe I'll see you around."

"What, oh, yeah. Sure. Maybe."

Nika started to walk off when Ben said, "Hey, stop!"

Don't do anything. Just let me go.

She plastered a smile on her face and turned around. "Yes?"

Ben looked at the ground, coughed, then asked, "What's your name?"

The question surprised Nika. "You don't know it?"

"No," he said. "Why would I?"

"Well, you came to help me with the K . . . the two Masters."

"I have your number, that's all. Well, not really a number, but that's how our wands translate it to us."

It seemed improbable that her name—well, Rika's name—wasn't somewhere, but maybe he was telling the truth.

"I'm Rika. Rika Ingersoll."

"Thanks, Rika."

Nika slowly turned around and walked off, expecting him to call out for her again. But she made it to the end of the barracks and slipped into the crowd. She kept her focus straight ahead, still waiting for Ben to come after her. She risked a quick glance behind as she approached the cafeteria, but he was nowhere in sight. She gave a huge sigh, then headed to where Rika was waiting.

She passed the catchment, then stopped as if she was simply looking past the fence. "I'm back."

"About freaking time, Nik! I was about to lose it," Rika said from under the cover.

"Sorry. It took longer than I expected."

"Did you get the info?" Rika asked.

"Yeah. At least part of it. The Krackles are—"

"Keep it to yourself, Baba."

Nika frowned, then said, "What do you mean? I've got to tell you what I found out, and I've got nothing to write with."

"You'll tell Dad."

"No! That's stupid. You're down there. You're going to tell him," she said, almost turning around to look at the catchment.

"Remember the Telephone Game? You have to do it," Rika said.

The Telephone Game was a simple party game. One person started with a long and convoluted sentence and whispered it into the ear of the next person, who then repeated it to the next and so on until the last person said aloud what they were told. The end sentence was never what the first sentence was, usually humorously different. The point of the game was that the more times something was recounted, the further from the truth it became.

"That's not fair. This is just you and me, not twenty people."

"Still, it's better coming from you. Anyway, Major Nguyen will be asking you questions to pull more out of you. I don't even know what questions to ask," Rika said.

"You know as much as I do. You were in here first."

"And you were here later than me. Your memory is fresher."

Nika didn't know what to say. Rika was right, even if only by a little, but she was leveraging it.

"Besides, I never got to say goodbye to Mom. You need to give that to me. And Dad's going to want to see you."

Nika stood there, trying to come up with a good counterargument, but there was nothing.

"This is stupid. We shouldn't risk making the switch again."

"And yet, we're going to."

This was wrong, Nika knew. But there was a tiny bit of logic to what Rika was saying. And there was the strong pull to see her father. She'd already dismissed the possibility, but now, he was out there, waiting for her.

"I don't even know where he is, and you sure can't explain it to me. Neither of us is any good at directions."

It was a weak argument, but that was all she had.

"There's two of Dad's Marines waiting at the end of the pipe. They'll take you."

And even that argument vanishes.

"If we switch, you have to come back here so we can discuss who stays."

Rika hesitated for a moment, and Nika knew her twin had no intention of switching back.

"OK, I'll watch for you."

"Watch and come when I return. Twinny swear."

There was a sigh, then "OK, twinny swear."

Nika took a long look around. As far as she could tell, they were unobserved. That didn't mean much. The entire place could be under scrutiny.

"Open the cover partway," she told Rika.

Nika took off her belt, then started to use it to stretch, twisting her body one way and the other. Rika got the cover a third-way open, and Nika put the belt down on the ground beside the opening, hands locked on each end, then stepped on the loop. She made a show of pulling up, stretching her back.

"Whatever you're doing, get on with it," Rika said, looking up through the gap at her.

Nika made another show of pulling back on the belt, then let one end "slip" from her right hand. With a nudge of her foot while releasing her left hand, the belt disappeared down the hole.

"Take off your belt and leave it," Nika said.

"Smart girl, my twin."

Nika got on her belly and reached into the hole, then stood up. If anyone was watching, she hoped it looked like she wanted to retrieve the belt.

There were too many things that could go wrong. After the first reaction by the Krackles, this little area could be on a higher alert status, for all she knew. If things went bad, she'd just get down the pipe as fast as she could and hope the two Marines could protect her.

"I still think this is a bad idea," she said.

"When have bad ideas stopped us before?"

She opened the cover again, then stepped inside. As soon as her head cleared the edge, Rika stood up, holding Nika's belt.

"Now, get out of here, Baba," Rika said.

Nika grabbed her twin's belt and scooted to the open grate where Rika had left the lavender ribbon. "Leave the cover off, and watch for my signal. Twinny promise."

She listened for a moment, but Rika was gone. A tsunami of loneliness crashed over her as she started down the pipe.

Chapter 30
Rika

Rika walked away from Nika with a smile on her face. She knew getting Nika out of the depot was going to be a tough one, and she was proud of how she'd painted her sister into a corner. It wasn't as if she lied or anything. Major Nguyen would interrogate her, asking for more details or how sure she was about the information. Rika couldn't answer those types of questions.

Only then did she wonder how her twin had gotten the info. Maybe she should have asked, but no matter. She was merely curious; it was their dad who needed it.

She stepped around the cafeteria and into the mass of people. They were more subdued than they had been the day before.

Well, not everyone. A couple was leaning up against the nearest barracks in a fervent embrace, hands almost angrily roaming over each other's bodies. They didn't seem to care that they might as well be on a stage, what with all the people about.

"OK," Rika said, wanting to look away, but unable to.

No one else seemed particularly interested in them, which seemed odd in and of itself. She knew to be prisoners and staring at a life of slavery was wearing, and the stress was clearly showing, but this was worse than yesterday. She wondered if anything new had happened.

Rika knew how to cheer them up, to break the malaise. All she had to do was shout that the Marines had landed. But she couldn't, of course. OPSEC, the Marines called it: operations security. The Krackles couldn't be allowed to find out that the Marines were there.

She broke her gaze from the two lovers only to see her stalker beckoning her over. She stopped dead in her tracks to decide what to do. She could have ignored him, but it was too late for that. He knew she'd seen him. She could turn and run away, which is what every instinct she had told her to do. Or she could go and see what he wanted.

As much as she hated to admit it, she knew she had to go to him. He was a guard, after all, with authority over her. She couldn't afford to make him an enemy, even though he made her nerves crawl. She had to play nice, at least for the moment.

Rika slowly walked up to him, ready to bolt if he made an aggressive move. Like the two lovers, he may not care if there were witnesses all around them.

"What do you want?" she asked as she reached him, stopping out of reach of his baton.

He seemed a little nervous. Antsy.

"About what I told you. You won't tell anyone else, will you? You've got to keep that to yourself."

"I don't know what you're talking about," she automatically blurted out, then almost bit her tongue.

This Ben guy must have told Nika something, and now she'd just denied knowing what that was. She could have just screwed things up big-time.

The zombie's brows furrowed in confusion, and he opened his mouth to speak before understanding seemed to flow over his face, and he smiled a goofy grin.

"Ah, yeah. That's right. What am I talking about? Nothing here. Good."

What the hell did he tell Nika?

He stood there like a big lunk, smiling at her.

"Uh, so, can I go now?" she asked.

"Sure, sure. Since we have nothing to discuss here," he said, reaching out to give her a light tap on the shoulder before deepening his voice and saying in a dramatic, official tone, "You can go now, prisoner."

Rika wasn't going to argue. She turned and faded into the crowd.

That was sure strange. I need to ask Nika what that's all about.

And it hit her like a gutshot. There was a good chance that she might never see her twin again. Yes, the Marines were there, but only a company, fewer than 200 Marines, and the Krackles—and their prisoners—had to be leaving soon.

Maybe that's why everyone's so quiet. Do they know something I don't?

Rika picked up the pace to find her mother. She reached the barracks, but couldn't find her. It took another ten, stress-filled minutes before she spotted her, and it took a force of will not to break out into a run.

Her mother spotted her as she approached, but her momentary smile faded into an intense frown.

"What are you doing back?" she hissed. "And where's your sister?"

"She's gone to give Dad the information he needed."

"And you maneuvered her into switching with you?"

Rika was taken aback by her mother's vehemence.

"She needed to be the one," she protested.

"Right. And saving her had nothing to do with it. I know you too well."

"Are you . . . do you want her with you, not me?"

A look of horror came over her mother's face, and she grabbed Nika, pulling her in tight.

"No, no, no. I'm so sorry. I didn't mean it like that, baby. I'm just . . . this is so hard. I'm sorry."

Nika hugged her mother back, relieved. It was weird to be relieved that she may be taken by the Krackles off-planet to who-knew-where.

"It's OK, Mom. I understand."

"And even if you did that to save Nika, I'm happy for that."

"I hope we're all saved," Rika said.

"We got word this morning that we need to be ready to move at a moment's notice."

Rika pushed away from her mother's chest and looked into her eyes. "They said that? When? When are they taking us?"

"Maybe this afternoon. We don't know." She paused before asking, "Is your father ready to rescue us?"

"I don't know. He's only got the one company with him. He's supposed to wait for the Navy, but if the Krackles move, so will he. Only . . ."

"Only what, Rika?"

"Only a lot of us may die in the attempt."

Her mother nodded and said, "Better that than being slaves."

"Maybe what Nika tells him and Major Nguyen will help. Let them plan better, so fewer of us die."

The finality of what she'd done coming back into the camp hit her hard at that moment. She wouldn't have changed things, getting Nika out, but it had just registered that she might not live out the day.

"I hope so, Rika. I truly hope so."

Chapter 31
Nika

"And you trust this guard?" Major Nguyen asked.

Nika looked over at her father, who nodded for her to answer.

"I think so. He likes me. I mean, he likes Rika. He . . . I don't think he was lying."

Nika's father raised an eyebrow at that, but he didn't say anything.

"But just to make sure I'm clear on this, you've never actually seen the pool complex and the Krackles going in and out," the major continued.

"No, ma'am. I was only in the second quad, that and outside the fence, and you can't see the pool from there."

"It's OK, Nika. What you've told us is good intel," she told her before turning to her father. "And it makes sense. A natatorium would be more comfortable for the Krackles with the warmer temps and higher humidity. Without anything to the contrary coming to light, I'd have to concur that's where they are for the most part."

The major turned to the map floating above the small field projector. She touched the image for the pool building, turning it red.

"Of course, not all of them will be in there. Nika here's seen them out and about, and our recon teams have caught glimpses of them moving around."

"Let's just say . . ." she said as she punched into the control, and several small red circles appeared scattered on the map. Nika assumed they were symbolizing Krackles walking around the depot.

"And for the zombies, we've got these."

She touched four buildings in the quad and the library. Those turned pink.

"That leaves us with human prisoners here and here."

She lit up the rest of the four quads in green, then swept the bunkers green as well.

"I think we can use this as a base to adjust the ops order," she said.

"That makes part of our job easier," a master sergeant Nika didn't know said, pointing to the bunkers. "Those are Class A2. They could take up to a Hellfire barrage without damage. Call for naval gunfire and sweep the area of Krackles. And if not that, we've got our Lancers."

"That's if the prisoners are inside them. From what Nika here's said, the people are outside during the day, at least in the four quads. That matches New Promise, and we all know what happened there."

Nika knew there had been a rescue on New Promise, but from the major's tone, she was referring to something bad. She wanted to ask what happened there, but she stood back trying to fade into the woodwork. She did know what a Hellfire and a Lancer were, however. Not the details, but the Hellfire was a space-to-ground missile, a big one, and the Lancer was the Corps' man-packed rocket system.

"That's why we hit them at night," the master sergeant said as if the answer was obvious.

All eyes turned to Nika's father, but he just said, "Go on, Major."

Nika had seen her father at parades and ceremonies, but this was the first time she'd ever seen him doing his real job. And it was confusing. Instead of just giving orders, he'd spent the entire debrief, as the military referred to it, listening to the others as they argued, rarely interjecting a word.

"If I can interrupt," Captain Keller said.

The captain was one of Nika's secondary school teachers in real life, and it was odd to see him in uniform. He was the Golf Company commander, in charge of the Marines who would be doing the actual fighting.

"Go on, Captain," Nika's father said.

"I've been in the bunkers. Eighty-six of them are the A2s. The ten over here," he said, pointing to the back line of bunkers, "are A4s. They'll stand up to small arms well enough, but not a Hellfire. With the A2s, depending on what else is in them—"

"The ordnance has long been taken out," Major Nguyen interrupted.

"True, ma'am, but, well, a lot of them are being used for storage. Old, furniture, comps, things like that."

"That's true. I've seen it, too. Yeah, against all sorts of regs, but it's a civilian crew that's maintaining the place," the master sergeant said as if that explained it all.

"Your point, Captain?" Nika's father asked.

"Well, sir, I can't be sure, but I think each A2 can hold upwards of several hundred people, so there's enough room to house all the rest of the Lorraine Valley with eight thousand in the four quads.

"The problem isn't the room inside, but getting people in and out. The doors are only twelve feet wide. Hundreds of people trying to get in or out at the same time, well, that would be a clusterfu . . . uh, a mess," he said, glancing at Nika.

I'm a Marine's daughter. You really think I haven't heard that word before?

Then again, as a teacher, he was probably used to watching his language in front of students.

Nika looked at her father. She'd been so happy to see him, so relieved. He was her father, and fathers always fixed things up, right? But as she looked at him now, rubbing his eyes, he looked, well, *tired*. She didn't know what the regiment went through on Telluride, but it had to be a shock to each Marine to leave the combat zone to come home, only to find out that the Krackles were there trying to enslave all of their families.

Nika knew enough about military protocol to know that as a colonel, her father would not normally drop with a Marine company. That would normally be left to the company commander, Captain Neller. Additionally, there was another level of command between the captain and her father: Lieutenant Colonel Ribadeaux, the Second Battalion CO. And this wasn't even the largest force of Marines on the island continent. Two companies dropped at Riesetown.

He was here because his family was here, pure and simple. He'd probably get in trouble for isolating himself with one company instead of retaining overall command, but Nika knew her father, and he'd go to hell and back to save his wife and daughters.

She could also tell that it was wearing on him, and she wanted to go hold him, to tell him that she knew he would figure out how to save the rest. It wouldn't just be lip service. She believed it.

"If the Navy arrives and initiates the assault, it'll be in daylight, and the prisoners should be outside. Even if the mission falls to us, however, and the prisoners are outside, we'll have the same problem of getting them under cover, especially in the bunkers. It only becomes a moot point if we hit the Krackles while the prisoners are still inside," Captain Neller continued.

"Like I said, hit them at night," the master sergeant muttered, sounding a little upset that he'd been ignored before.

"And if we go in at night, but the prisoners are being readied for load-out? We have to assume the worst possible scenario, that the prisoners will be at risk," Captain Neller said.

Nika looked at her father to see his reaction, catching the tiniest of nods.

"Can you speed up your deployment?" her father asked the captain.

Captain Neller looked at his company CC, studied it for a moment, and then said, "The blocking force on Highway 32 is in place now, ready to hold off armor coming to counterattack. For the assault element, keeping in stealth mode? Six hours to have everyone in position. Foregoing stealth, then two hours. Maybe less."

"And letting the Krackles know we're here," the master sergeant said. "We lose the element of surprise."

"We stay with stealth for now. Remember, we're just the emergency option in case the Krackles don't wait long enough for the Navy to get here.

"Tell your XO to get the assault element ready, captain. I don't want to break mass cloaking yet, but I want you ready to move out in five minutes if you get the call."

"Aye-aye, sir. We'll be ready."

"Now, do we have a weather update?" he asked the master sergeant.

The Marine seemed happy to have the floor, standing taller as he said, "We've got a heavy low-pressure cell forming to the south. I don't have access to the planetary sats, but I've got a forty-three percent chance that the area will get hit by a whomper—"

"Colonel, I'm getting a Three-Flash!"

All eyes swiveled to Corporal Nwadike, her father's dog robber. Neither Nika nor Rika knew exactly what a "dog robber" was, but they took it to be something like a personal assistant.

"Let me see it," her father said, holding out his hand. A "three-flash" meant it was for commanding officer's eyes only.

The corporal gave him the comms suite, the small, innocuous hand-held pad that could communicate with the President of the Privy Council back on Laramie, if need be. Her father held it up close to his left eye for a moment, confirming his identity, then brought it back down after reading the message itself.

Fire seemed to dance out of his eyes, and Nika could see energy flow back into him. Where a minute ago, he looked old and tired, he was now champing at the bit.

"The Krackle transports are in-system I just forwarded the data to you, Major, and I want a timeline. Best case, worst case.

"It looks like we're on. We're now the point of main effort, and that means we're implementing the Bravo plan. We knew it was a possibility, even a probability that the Krackles wouldn't let the Navy get here in time to play. It's now on us to keep our people here on Arcadia and in one piece until the Navy *can* get here.

"Captain Neller, go to your Marines. We'll have the updated ops order out to you ASAP, but I want thirty-percent of your Lancers targeting the natatorium, and I want you to start moving into position. Stealth mode unless you hear different.

"The rest of you, you know what to do. Get at it."

Nika wiped the budding smile off her face. This was the father she knew, the take-charge, nothing will stop him guy.

"Major, I'm still waiting," he snapped.

She stared at her CC, then said, "The first transport's between eight and eleven hours, depending on their course and if it's for here or the mainland."

"Pass to Captain Neller that he's got five-and-a-half hours. We're launching in six."

"That takes us 30 minutes before dawn at this time of year. But we can't trust that the prisoners will be inside their barracks, not this close to load-out," the major said.

"Understand. If they are, we need to make sure they stay there. If they're not, we need to make sure that they all go inside when we hit. We're not going to have another New Promise here, Marines. We've already decided we can't use drones as messengers without alerting the Krackles. Any good ideas yet?"

That was the second time someone had mentioned New Promise, and from the context, it wasn't good. Nika still wanted to ask what happened, but she knew she had to stay out of the way.

"We've still got Lance Corporal Studyvant," the major said.

"Last ditch. Defusing the grenade and tying the note to it is going to get its trajectory specs out of whack. Getting it through one of the windows isn't going to be easy, and that's going to notify only one barracks," her father responded.

"No word from Sergeant Timothy?"

"No contact with anyone yet," Corporal Nwadike answered. "I've already sent to him that he's got to get everyone to stay inside the barracks and bunkers."

"He can't respond without compromising his cloaking," the master sergeant said.

No one responded, and Nika wondered if he was the kind of person who always stated the obvious. Not that she knew what was obvious or not. Half of what they were discussing seemed to be in a foreign language to her.

She understood, however, that something bad had happened on New Promise. With Rika and her mother in the depot, her mind was racing, but she didn't even know what to fear. She had to find out.

"Sergeant Major," Nika said as she sidled up to him. "What happened on New Promise?"

"You don't know? No, of course, you don't know. It's been pushed under the rug." She looked around for a moment, then lowered her voice. "Not the Navy's fault. The Krackles took the planet, but a pocket cruiser was in drydock on the planet's moon. They skipped lots of steps to fire the cold motors . . . sorry, that's not what's important.

"When they hit the Krackles, they didn't know the bastards were using human shields. Hundreds of thousands of people were killed in the rescue, if you can call it that."

"Human shields? They hid among the humans?"

"Hid among them, or just a coincidence, I don't know. But people died. Lots of them. And we don't want that to happen again. That's why we need our folks to stay separated from the Krackles."

"That many people can die?" Nika asked. Rika had told her fifteen hundred, but this sounded worse.

"Yes, lass. They can. But your father's doing everything he can to keep that from happening."

"So, what he needs is a way to make sure the people are in the barracks, so you know where they are?"

"That's about the long and short of it. We'll figure it out, so don't you worry."

The thought almost floored Nika. To come this far and be so close to rescue, and have everyone die? It wasn't right.

But she knew a way to get the message into the people. It was so obvious.

"Dad!"

Her father looked over at her as if he'd forgotten she was there. "Nika, you need to leave now. You've done great.

"Corporal Nwadike, I want someone to take my daughter and Fel to the rally point."

"No, Dad!"

For the first time since she'd seen him, he looked confused.

"We've got to keep everyone out of the line of fire, right?"

"Well, yes. We're working—"

"I'll go. I've made it in and out before, and I can do it again."

"No! You've done enough. I want you and Fel out of here. Corporal Nwadike!"

The corporal stepped up and took her by the upper arm. Nika shook free of his grip.

"I need to do it, Dad!"

Her father stepped over and took her by both arms, bending so his face was centimeters from hers. "Nika. I can't afford to lose you. I need to know you're safe."

"And I can't afford to lose Rika and mom!" she shouted, pulling away from him. "Or all the rest. This isn't about family, *Colonel*! This is about duty."

Her father's mouth gaped open, and he was at a loss for words. He shifted his gaze from Nika to the sergeant major as if asking her to step in and convince Nika.

But the sergeant major didn't back him. "She's right, sir. It could mean a lot of lives saved."

Her father looked back at Nika, almost as if seeing her in a different light. She straightened her spine.

"First, Rika gives me an ultimatum, and now you. What does that mean?"

"It means you raised them right, sir," the sergeant major said.

"I was gone too much to raise them," he said bitterly. "Too many birthdays missed."

"I'm going, Dad. It would be better if you told me what to do when I get there."

Sadness crept over his eyes, then it morphed into something else. Pride? Nika hoped that's what it was.

"Come here," he said, pulling her back in for a hug, her face smashed against the armor plating of his chest. She didn't care.

"You're still my little girl, but right now, I'm so proud of you. Just . . . oh, just keep your head down and make it out of there."

"You, too, Dad. Let Captain Neller and his Marines do what they're supposed to do. Don't try to be a hero yourself."

Her father gave her one last hug, then stepped back.

"Sergeant Major, if you can take my daughter to her infiltration point? Brief her along the way. We'll use the initial strike as the signal, then we need all civilians out of the way," he said, father hat off and colonel hat back on.

"Major, we've got a lot to do and not much time to get it done," he said, turning away from her and back to the major.

Not completely, though. Nika looked back over her shoulder as she followed the sergeant major out of the machine shop. He was watching her, a tear rolling down his cheek.

Chapter 32
Rika

The tension was palpable. Groups of people stood together, but not saying much. Each time a smoothie came into the quad, hundreds of eyes locked on, wondering if this was it.

Rika looked up at the late summer sun, now descending to the horizon, wondering if this would be the last time she'd see a sunset. She wasn't really bonded to Arcadia. It was small without much in the way of things to do. She often wished she was back on St. Regis, where she'd lived with her family for two of her father's tours. But now, given a chance, she would happily live the rest of her life on the planet.

Soon enough, they'd be herded back into the barracks—unless it would be to loadout to get taken off-planet. Rika felt helpless, and she kept waiting, hoping for the Marines to come to the rescue. She wasn't sure how a mere infantry company was going to do much. It wasn't just the Krackles and zombies inside the camp. Outside, there were combat Krackles, the ones who'd taken the town, armed with armor and who knows what else.

"I need to check something," she told Anna, giving a nod to her mom.

Her mother pursed her lips and furrowed her brow, but didn't say anything.

"What? Do you want me to come with you?" Anna asked.

"No, I meant I have to go to the toilet. Just trying to be polite, you know."

"OK. Probably a big line, though."

With everyone locked out of the barracks during the day, the only facilities in the quad were at three communal toilets. The lines there tended to be long, but Rika didn't need to use one yet. She just wanted to check the catchment basin one last time without Anna tagging along.

She made her way through the groups of people, no one giving her a second glance. Most were too wrapped up in what they were facing. She wanted to stop and tell everyone that the Marines were there, even if only a few, but her mother thought it was better not to let that out. If enough people knew about it, the Krackles would get word.

She rounded the cafeteria, but there was no ribbon fluttering on the ground. Not that she expected anything, but Nika had told her to check. Rika peered past the fence. She knew there were at least two Marines out there, cloaked against detection. And if the Krackles couldn't find them, then she certainly couldn't spot them. That didn't stop her from trying.

With a sigh, Rika started to turn to go back when a tiny movement at the catchment box caught her eye. She narrowed her focus to see the lavender ribbon make an appearance.

What are you doing, Baba? Why did you come back?

But she was glad. It was stupid, and she knew she was being selfish, but she didn't want to be alone. She felt guilty about that, but she couldn't help it.

Taking a quick look around to see if anyone was watching, she put her hands in her pocket, and trying to look casual, walked up to the box.

"I'm here."

"That was quick," Nika said from under her.

"I try to serve. Now, what the heck are you doing back? We're expecting to get rousted any time now."

"I'm just glad I got back in time, then. I was afraid they'd already started loading you."

"That doesn't answer my question," Rika said.

"We need to switch again. I've got something important to get done."

Rika felt a momentary thrill. She hadn't realized how much being inside was weighing on her, and the thought of being yanked off the planet, well . . . that was just too stressful to imagine.

But switching again would just put Nika in the same position, and she couldn't do that to her.

"Not going to happen, Baba. You need to stay free out there with Dad. I'll stay inside and see this thing through."

"No, and stop trying to be a hero. We need to switch, otherwise, there could be a lot of people killed. A lot."

There was a pause, and then Rika asked, "What do you mean?"

"Like on New Promise, when the Navy hit the Krackles."

"But wasn't that a success? They rescued the people there."

"Yes, but over a hundred thousand people were killed in the crossfire, Sergeant Major Murphy told me."

"A hundred thousand?" Rika asked incredulously. "Why haven't I heard that before?"

"The sergeant major said there was a cover-up. But that doesn't matter right now. What we have to do, what I have to do, is pass the word on what dad wants everyone here to do when they kick this off?"

"They're starting the rescue?"

"The Krackle transports are in system," Nika said.

"Which is why they told us to stand by for loading. We knew they had to be there, but that confirms it. Do you know how long we have?"

"Maybe seven hours. Maybe longer."

The finality of that hit Rika. It was actually happening, unless their father could pull off a miracle.

"And Dad's got a plan to minimize casualties?"

"That's why I'm here. And I need to get going. It'll be dark soon."

"Just tell me, Baba. I'll do it," Rika said.

"Sorry, Baba. I need to."

"Just tell me."

"The Telephone Game," was all Nika said.

"But . . ." Rika didn't have a comeback for that. She'd used the same excuse to make the last switch.

"Dad said I'm supposed to do it. Too many details."

Rika stepped forward and looked down the hole. She wanted to see her twin's face. Her emotions warred within her. One side of her wanted to switch, wanted to be free of the Krackles' clutches. The other side wanted to protect Nika.

"We have to do it now," Nika said. "Too many lives are at stake."

And Rika knew her twin was right. The lives of all the others trumped any feeling of guilt or protectiveness on her side. She'd used the Telephone Game as an excuse before, but that didn't mean it was wrong.

It killed her, but she said, "OK. How do we do this?"

"Not the belt. Just kick in the ribbon, then come and get it."

Rika knew that if a Krackle or zombie was monitoring her, then they'd have to know something was up, but she didn't have it in her at the moment to try and come up with something better. She nudged the ribbon back into the hole, then jumped in to retrieve it.

As soon as she was in, Nika scooped up the ribbon, gave her a quick kiss on the cheek, and jumped out.

"Love you, Baba," Nika said as she hurried off.

"I'm not going back," Rika said. "I'm waiting here. If it all falls apart, come back, and we'll get out together."

Rika didn't know if Nika even heard her.

Chapter 33
Nika

"I'm not going back. I'm waiting here. If it all falls apart, come back, and we'll get out together."

Nika heard her sister, but she didn't answer. She couldn't make that promise with things so uncertain.

She looked up, trying to gauge how much time she had. Summer nights were short on Arcadia, but not short enough. It would soon be dark, and before that, the zombies would be herding them back inside. A very faint rumble caught her attention, and she turned around. To the east, clouds were forming. They were a long way off, and while they might never reach the depot, they would bear watching.

Nika wondered how a whomper might affect a rescue. She didn't know if it would be a help or a hinderance.

Mind on the mission, Nika Ingersoll. Forget about all of that.

She checked the tiny comms bud on her collar, given to her before she left the command post. It was for emergencies only, or at least until after the rescue kicked off. The sergeant had assured her that as long as she didn't power it up, the Krackles wouldn't be able to detect it.

It wasn't much, but it gave her a feeling of security. But it wasn't part of what she had to do now, and for that, she needed help. She made a beeline for her mother's barracks, spotting her and Anna in front.

Her mother looked up, then almost rolled her eyes when she recognized her.

"What?" she asked with a resigned look on her face.

"I need to talk to you. Alone."

Anna looked hurt, but Nika's mother dragged her off to the side of the barracks. There were several people sitting, their backs up against the wall, but her mother ignored them.

"So, are you going to tell me why you're back?"

"The Krackle transports are in-system."

"We figured as much. What's the situation with your father?"

Nika looked at the people sitting. None seemed to be listening in on them.

"They're going to initiate the rescue. Soon, I think."

"Oh, thank God," her mother said, closing her eyes for a moment before she asked, "But why did you come back? There's more to it, am I right?"

Her mother always seemed to know what was going on with Rika and her, as if she could read their minds.

"Do you know what happened on New Promise?"

"The rescue five or six years ago?"

"Well, there was more than that. Lots of people got killed, over a hundred thousand."

"So, your father sent you back here to try and minimize that."

No horror at the number, but an immediate analysis. Nika didn't know if her blank face meant she approved or disapproved of her returning. She wasn't sure which one she would have preferred.

"I told him I'm coming back. He argued, but lost."

Her mother was quiet as she reached out and stroked the side of Nika's head. "Of course, you would. Did he give you any projections of casualties?"

"Major Nguyen did. It's bad. So, we need to get to work before we're all inside the barracks. Or loading the transports."

"What do we have to do?" her mother asked.

"We need to get everyone out of the line of fire. That means in the bunkers first, if we can, but the barracks second. No one running around in a panic, no one rushing the fence. Out of the way and hunkered down. No one moves until the Marines tell us to."

"And when do we do this?"

"I don't have an exact time. Soon, probably. But we'll have a signal. When the pool natatorium is hit."

"The pool? Why is that a target?"

"That's where the Krackles are. At least most of them, we think."

"I guess that makes sense. But the bunkers? Why . . . oh, because they can take a hit. I get it. So, what you want us to do is make sure everyone gets the word, right?"

"Yes, Mom," Nika said, glad that her mother was taking over.

"But we can't just pass the word now. It'll get back to the Krackles that something's up. Your father needs the element of surprise if he's going to pull this off. Let me think . . .

"What we need to do is get what are essentially wardens, people who can organize and kick some butt once we get the signal. There's going to be panic, so it's not going to be easy," her mother said, her forehead wrinkled in concentration.

"That's good. But we need people to look to these wardens beforehand, like leaders already, so they're used to listening to them. What if they say they're supposed to be the ones in charge of the loadout?" Nika asked.

"Good thinking. I don't know if the zombies are going to go along with that, but it's worth a shot. And if the zombies squash it, at least the idea's been planted.

"But we need to do it now. It's moving to sunset, and I don't like those clouds coming in."

Rika looked up. The clouds were much closer than they were just twenty minutes before.

"We need to split up, find someone from each barracks, not just in our quad. I don't know how we're going to get word to the bunkers. But let's start now."

"I'll tell Gren first."

"Already left, Nika. She went to find her mother. Try Kat Sen. I just saw her, and rumor has it she's been over to First Quad with the men to see her husband. Maybe she can do it again."

Nika took off at a run, looking for Kat. But she couldn't wait. Time was fleeting. She saw Tareetha Sambol, the Deputy Mayor, and quickly briefed her. The woman took it surprisingly well, and within a minute, she was finding someone else to pull into the web.

One after the other, she recruited, all the time waiting for the recall back into the barracks. The sun went down, but still, they were outside. Nika didn't want to look a gift horse in the mouth, but she felt uneasy, sure that every zombie was watching her every move, sucking her into some huge trap.

Within 45 minutes, she thought they'd covered the quad, and several people promised to sneak off to the others.

That still left the people in the bunkers, however. They had to get the word to them. Nika thought about doing it herself. They had been ordered to stay within their quad, but people had been going back and forth. Maybe the Krackles didn't care, as long as they remained in the depot.

It's worth a shot, she thought, trying to remember how far the bunkers were from her. They had to be distant enough so that ammo going off in one bunker wouldn't damage all the facilities in mainside.

Before she could start, the zombies moved into the quad and started issuing orders. It wasn't to go back into the barracks, however.

The zombies were ordering the prisoners to form orderly ranks by barracks number. It was time to get ready to be taken from Arcadia.

Chapter 34
Rika

Rika sat huddled at the mouth of the pipe. Darkness had closed in, and she was alone with her thoughts.

That was a dangerous path to take. With nothing to do but wait, her imagination was running wild, going over scenario after scenario, almost all of them bad. She vacillated between going back down the pipe and just leaving the catchment basin and giving herself up. Each option had some pros, but the cons outweighed them. In the end, she stayed put, legs drawn up against her chest.

Every sound made her heart beat. Nika had said that the rescue was on, but Rika didn't know what would happen, and importantly, when. She could be sitting here for hours.

At the thought, her bladder made its presence known. She lowered her legs to relieve some of the pressure.

Come on, just ignore it. If it gets to it, well, this is a storm drain. Let it drain.

A faint rumble reached her, and she perked up. It could be a crowd of people. It could be the wind, for that matter. But it didn't sound like the Marines setting off the assault.

She settled back to wait. And wait . . .

. . .*What?* she asked herself, jerking her head up.

Rika realized she'd fallen asleep, and she smacked her cheeks several times. She couldn't afford that now. But what had woken her up?

She listened for a moment, but there was nothing above the wind which had picked up while she dozed off. Rika had just about convinced herself that it had been nothing when the unmistakable sounds of whispers reached her, and then a sneeze.

Rika brought her feet under her, ready to bolt as she strained to make out who was there. All she could hear were furtive whispers.

A dark shadow appeared over the edge of the box. "OK, here we are. You need to jump inside, Tommy."

"I don't want to, Gren."

"Gren?" Rika asked, scooting out into the box.

There was silence, then a soft, "Nika?"

"It's Rika. What are you doing?"

Gren stepped closer, holding a small shape on her hip. It was too dark to see his features, but Rika knew who it was: Mace. It was only then that Rika saw the other shapes, five or six of them.

"Oh, thank God you're here," Gren said. "You need to take them."

"I can't. I mean, they've been tagged, too."

"They're already getting ready to load us out, Rika. We're being taken off-planet. I can't let that happen to Mace or the rest of these kids."

Shit. It's happening.

Rika shook off the feeling of dread that threatened to overwhelm her and said, "But I still can't take them. It'll set off some sort of alarm, and someone will come and check."

"Well, not yet. But when you see the shuttles land, then just do it. Screw the alarms," Gren said, her torment evident in her voice.

The other shadows were small. Too small to be crawling through the pipes alone. "What were you planning on doing? You're too big to get through."

"I know. But Tommy here, he was going to lead the others."

Tommy shifted, catching a tiny bit of moonlight. He looked to be about nine . . . and he looked very frightened.

"Is this all of them?" Rika asked.

"It's all I could take. It's mass confusion out there. People are panicking."

"I can imagine."

Out in the box, Rika could now make out the murmur and sporadic shouts coming from the quad.

"But we've got a few people taking other children to other drainage pipes. Maybe some of them can get through, too. But you've got to make sure that these young ones make it. OK?"

A gust of wind blew past them as Rika thought about it. She'd stayed inside the depot because Nika was there. But she couldn't turn Gren down. The kids needed to get out. Maybe the Krackles would react, but if the Marines were attacking, they might get away with it. And it the Marines failed—a horrible thought that made Rika feel guilty for even thinking it—then it was worth a shot.

"Of course, Gren. I'll take care of them."

"You're a godsend, Rika. You really are.

"You hear that, kids? Miss Rika here is going to take care of you."

"I want my mommy," a little girl said.

"I know you do, sweetheart, but your mommy wants you to go with Miss Rika, OK? Your mommy will find you later."

"Promise?"

"I promise," Gren said, with a hitch in her voice.

I hope you can keep that promise, Gren.

"OK, Tommy. You listen to Miss Rika and do what she says. You need to be a big boy and help her. So, hop in that hole—"

"No! Not in the hole. You just sit there at the edge, OK, Tommy?" Rika said.

"They'll drop off the surveillance if they're down here," she told Gren. "We need them out in the open. Hopefully, no one will notice that they're not with the rest of you."

"If the Krackles or the zombies come, just go. Run for it."

Rika didn't know if that was a good idea. The Krackles could just wait for them on the other end, beyond the fence. There were two Marines there somewhere, but would they break their cloaking to save them? If that would start the rescue attempt before they were ready?

She didn't know the answer to that.

Maybe we can just stay in the tunnel until it's all over.

The thought of that started the panic bugs nibbling at her brain. It had been bad enough crawling through, where she could focus on moving. If she was just sitting there in the dark, it would be almost unbearable. But she couldn't just abandon them.

"Of course, I will."

"Thanks, Rika. I need to go now. No use making a bigger target here than we have to.

"Tommy, I'm leaving you in charge, OK. You need to help Rika with the others."

"OK, Gren," the boy said, but without conviction.

Gren pulled her little brother around to face her. "And you, Mace. You need to be a big boy, OK?"

"OK. I will."

She pulled him into a hug. "I love you, bedbug."

"I love you, too."

She sat him down on the ground next to the hole. "Rika will take you to Fel, OK?"

"Fel?" Mace asked, clapping his hands in excitement. "Fel!"

Gren choked back a sob, then said, "All of you: Ghist, Taylor, Mei Li. Pay attention to Miss Rika. She's the boss."

She hesitated as if she was going to say something else, but she suddenly turned and started to walk away.

"Take care of them, Rika."

And then they were alone.

"Let's everyone sit down, OK?" Rika said, and the little ones plopped on the ground.

"How is everyone? How are we doing?" Rika asked, trying to sound cheerful.

"I'm scared," Tommy said.

"I am too, Tommy, I am too."

Chapter 35
Nika

"What time do you think it is?" Nika asked her mother as the latest warden rushed off.

The confusion was good for one thing. They'd been able to recruit more wardens to help when the rescue kicked off. The question remained if they'd be able to have any effect on the mass of people.

That wasn't the only question. Some of the people who were in the bunkers had been marched over to the rest. When the rescue started, they'd be too far away to take shelter in them.

Another question was how long they had before the Marines kicked off the attempt. Her father had said six hours, about 30 minutes before sunrise, but it had been light for almost an hour. Clouds had moved in, and the far-off rumble of thunder could be signs that the depot would be hit by a whomper. If that happened, Nika didn't know what they could do to control the mass of people. Thoughts of New Promise were constantly at the forefront of her mind.

"I don't know," her mother answered with a concerned voice. "It's late, though."

Military plans never survived the first shot, Marines often said, but there hadn't even been a shot fired yet. There could be many reasons why the rescue was delayed, but she couldn't think of one that was good news.

She fingered the comms bud again. It would be so easy to power it up and ask, but that would be picked up, and the Krackles would not only come looking for her, but they'd probably figure out that there was someone out there as well. She had to resist the temptation.

Nika looked around her. There had to be 10,000 people crowded around the athletic fields. Getting there had been a nightmare. The panicking prisoners were like schools of sardines Rika had seen on a documentary of old Earth, darting this way and that from sea lions, sharks, and dolphins. Except, in this case, the predators were zombies and a few Krackles. The smoothies were the worst, using their batons with abandon. Not many of them could speak Standard, and they seemed to take out their frustration when the prisoners didn't react quickly enough for them. Prisoners were felled, to be picked up and dragged by others.

Two Krackles stood in the middle of one of the ball fields, ignoring the turmoil around them. Nika kept watching them, waiting for something to happen. She just hoped that when whatever was coming did happen, it would be instigated by her father and his Marines.

Another strong gust of wind hit the crowd, eliciting cries of alarm. Smart people on Arcadia sought shelter when a whomper hit, but the Krackles seemed unfazed.

Things were coming to a head, but Nika couldn't tell how things were going to fall out.

One way or the other, she knew she would soon find out.

Chapter 36
Rika

"Hey, what're you kids doing there?" a voice rang out over the wind. "Come here!"

Tommy spun around at the shout. "It's a zombie," he said in a scared voice.

Rika reacted immediately and without thinking. She reached up and grabbed Mei Li, pulling her into the hole and pushing her to the pipe.

"Go," she told the little girl who had started to cry, then to Tommy, "Help me get everyone in."

"Stop," the voice shouted over the growing wind. "You need to come here!"

Tommy didn't question her, and he immediately jumped in the hole. Together, they yanked the other three in as well.

"Get Mei Li moving," she told Tommy. "Get as far in the pipe as you can."

Tommy ducked his head and pushed forward. She could hear the boy prodding Mei Li forward, and she fed the others in like an artilleryman feeding shells into a howitzer.

"Damn it, if you make me come after you," the voice called out, getting closer.

"Come on, kids, move it. Crawl forward!" she implored.

But the children were hesitating, looking back at her from the broken grate. "Tommy, pull in Mace!"

The young boy was half-way in the pipe, and he backed out into the chamber, grabbed Mace, and shoved the small boy inside.

"After Mace. Go!" she told the Ghist and Taylor.

"What the . . ." the voice asked.

Rika spun around. A zombie stood looming over the catchment, surprise on his face.

"You, girl. Come out here. And bring the rest with you," he told Rika, then speaking to his collar, "This is Noom. I've got a problem here. More runaways. Kids, this time."

Rika frantically pushed on the kids, trying to get them into the pipe.

The zombie, a middle-aged man with a growing paunch, got down to his knees and reached into the hole, swiping for Rika. She yelped and jumped back as far as she could, and his fingers brushed her hair.

"Damn it! If you make me come in after you, you're going to be sorry."

Rika looked behind her. Tommy had Taylor and was trying to force the protesting and frightened boy, who had both hands locked on the grate, refusing to enter the dark pipe.

"I've got him," she told Tommy. Go!"

Tommy gave an uncertain look back, then dove feet first past the grate and into the pipe.

There was a thud as the zombie jumped into the catchment. He pushed the lid all the way off, then bent over to look in.

There was no time for niceties. Rika hit Taylor like a linebacker, forcing the boy past the grate. She lowered her head and scrambled after him, forcing the screaming boy farther inside.

"Oh, no, you don't!" the zombie yelled, twisting his big body to get into the chamber. He barely fit but managed to shove his bulk forward, almost to the grate. Rika could hear him huffing and puffing.

"Stop, or so help me, I'll wand you," the zombie yelled. "Don't think I won't because you're kids."

"Go, go," Rika told the others. "Don't stop."

Rika heard the clink of metal on metal behind her, and she knew right then that the zombie had his wand out and was reaching for her. With a shriek, she pushed Taylor, shoving him up against Tommy.

A hot wave of pain exploded in her foot, and then nothingness.

Chapter 37
Nika

"There it is!" someone shouted, and others picked up the cries of alarm.

Nika twisted around, and her heart fell. A dark shape was coming in to the depot, still miles away, but approaching quickly.

Human ships put out too many dirty ions to land at anywhere other than hardened spaceports, which is one reason why shuttles were normally used to bring people from the surface of a planet to the ship in orbit. Krackle ships didn't seem to have the same problem, and they could land anywhere. Smaller than most human commercial ships, they were still plenty big enough to take a lot of people. Not this many people, however. Stacked up behind the first ship, a second could be seen in the far distance.

"Where's Dad?" Nika asked.

There had been no sign of the Marines, and the comms bud sat heavy on her collar, almost begging to be used. Her hand drifted up to it.

"No," her mother said. "Don't use it. Not yet."

"When's too late?" she asked, but let her hand drop.

"Trust him. He's never lost a battle," her mother said, but from her tone, Nika wondered who of the two of them she was trying to convince.

If the Marines had been discovered, if there'd been a fight, surely they would have heard something inside the depot. Battles were noisy affairs, after all.

People were reacting in different ways to the ships that were coming to take them away. Some were cursing. Some were crying. Some were stoically staring at their doom.

Zombies were crowding the rear of the mass of prisoners, swinging wands to keep people from running. More Krackles were present than before. They seemed to be inclined to let the zombies be their enforcers, however.

If there were more Krackles present here, then if the Marines still hit the pool, there would be fewer there. Nothing was going to plan, and Nika was losing hope. She looked back up at the oncoming ship. It looked evil to her, something out of a nightmare. Not the shape, which could almost be a human ship, but what it represented.

As if welcoming the invaders, the whomper that had been threatening them hit like a ton of bricks. People cried out and huddled together as the rain pelted them.

Rika used her hand to protect her eyes, and she could no longer see the ship. For a moment, she had hope, hope that the whomper had knocked the thing from the sky, but with a whine that broke past the roar of the whomper, the ship appeared coming out of the rain like a demon emerging from hell. It didn't seem bothered in the least by the onslaught.

To her left, the zombies were pushing a large group of prisoners forward into the first ball field. Batons were flashing, driving the people.

Rika had to turn away, the rain was hitting her face so hard.

It was over. Something had happened to the Marines, and now they'd be long gone before the Navy arrived. Leaving a system could be done in minutes rather than hours. All they had to do is to get in orbit and then engage the Krackle version of the human's star drive.

It was hard for Nika to accept it. She'd been so sure that they'd be rescued, and now it was a gutshot, taking away her breath. She gave a sidewise glance at the ship, now coming over the woods on the other side of the fence when a lance of fire, almost too quick for the eye to see, reached up to the ship. For a moment, she thought it was a trick of the rain in her eyes, but then the big ship started to crab sideways.

"Look," someone shouted.

The ship slipped and fell, crashing into the fence on the far side of the playing fields, its spine crumbling. There was no huge gout of flame, no explosion, but Nika didn't have to be an expert to know that the ship was dead.

A cheer went up from the prisoners, a cheer drowned out by an explosion behind them . . . in the direction of the pool!

"Dad!" Nika shouted as she spun around. The zombies behind them looked confused and unsure. Even the Krackles did for a moment, before they turned and rushed off to meet the threat.

Now was their chance—it was go time.

"Wardens! Into the barracks! Don't let anyone stop you!" Nika shouted at the top of her lungs.

With the rain pelting down, she didn't know how many of the wardens heard her, but people near her heard "get into the barracks." Arcadian citizens knew to get inside in a whomper. It was almost in their DNA. With the ship crashing, and now her yelling, they turned and rushed to the nearest buildings, the First Quad barracks. The zombies tried to stop the charge, but they might as well have tried to stop the tide. People fell, but so did zombies as they were overwhelmed.

More explosions reached them through the rain, but Nika couldn't tell where they were coming from. She just kept urging people forward. What had been a couple hundred became a thousand, two thousand. Within a minute, every human who'd been at the playing fields was on the move—all that were alive, that is. Crumbled bodies lay in the rain. Evidently, the batons had a lethal setting.

Rika hesitated over the first body, a young, fit-looking man. His face and shoulder were blackened, his mouth frozen open in death. Much-too-white teeth shone like macabre pearls nestled in the black skin.

Not now, Nika. You don't have time for this.

She gulped and ran past, repeating her calls to take shelter in the barracks. She caught a glimpse of the vice mayor doing the same.

There were logjams at the closest barracks as too many tried to get inside at the same time. Nika started pulling people back, telling them to move to the other barracks.

One man swung and connected with her jaw when she pulled at his shoulder, flooring her. She struggled to get back up, and by the time she was standing again, the man was gone.

There was a bright flash of blue along the fence line on the other side of First Quad. A moment later, a squad of Marines poured through.

"Over here!" Nika shouted, joining the others who spotted them.

But the Marines kept moving, firing their weapons at an unseen foe. It looked like one of them might have gone down, but it was hard to tell with the rain still pouring down in sheets.

Nika tried to wipe her face clear of the rain, but it was just coming down too hard. The collection system was already full, trying to whisk the water . . .

"Rika!" she shouted. She'd left her twin in the drainage pipes, pipes that would be filling with run-off.

She looked around. The prisoners were in full flight mode, and there wasn't anything else she could do. At least that's what she told herself. She understood about the greater good, but this was Rika. They had done everything together since they were born, and she couldn't imagine a life without her Gemini twin.

Nika bolted past the barracks and tried to get her bearings. She had to get back to Second Quad and Rika.

Bright beams lit the rain as she crisscrossed the commons, but Nika ignored them. If one of them had her name, then she couldn't do much about it. She just ran with a single-minded purpose. An explosion opened up the ground in front of her, and she could feel the heat wash over her, but she was unhurt.

Just get me through this, she prayed.

She caught shadows in the rain but didn't know if they were Krackles or Marines. Not that it mattered. She'd be cut down by Marines just as easily as by Krackles. She could be a victim like the ones on New Promise.

Nika knew she was being foolish. She should just take shelter in one of the barracks. She would be safe there, but her heart told her that her twin needed her.

A looming shape appeared in the darkness, lit from behind by flames. Nika skidded to a halt, her feet slipping on the rain-covered grass, and falling on her ass. The Krackle must have sensed her. It spun around, and Nika felt the wave of needles as it acquired her.

She tried to scramble out of the way, knowing it was useless as the Krackle brought up a beamer clutched in its left power arm pinchers.

"No!" she shouted at the thing when its right power arm just disintegrated in a burst. Something wet and glompy hit her in the face.

The Krackle spun like a ballet dancer and fired its beamer in the other direction.

Thankful to still be alive, Rika scooted away on her butt, watching the duel in morbid fascination. The Krackle jumped to the side, quicker than Rika could have imagined something that big could manage. Two more flashes reflected off its armor as it took more hits. Something thudded into the ground next to Rika, sending up a gout of wet mud into the air.

She went flat, trying to stay small, but still staring at the Krackle as it fought for its life. It took another hit, then one more, but still, it refused to give up the fight. It was like watching a tridee—except that it wasn't. This *was* real.

Something small and fast reached out from the rain, and the Krackle was covered with blue light that crackled with energy. The creature stiffened straight, then fell over with a crash. The smell of ozone burnt her nostrils, even through the downpour.

Rika stared at the Krackle, expecting it to get back up, but finally she accepted that it was dead. Still, she gave it a wide berth as she got back to her feet and started running again.

There was a dead Marine at the edge of First Quad, water running off their armor. Rika wondered if this Marine had been in the fight she'd just witnessed. Maybe they were the one who'd taken it under fire, diverting its attention from her. If so, then this Marine had saved her life. Part of her wanted to stop and pay her respects. Maybe she knew them. But she didn't have time. All around her, the drainage web was in full swing as it fought to keep the depot from becoming inundated.

Nika crossed over to Second Quad, passing the library. It was a smoking ruin, fires flickering in defiance to the whomper. This was one of the zombie targets. She figured that most of them had been taking part in embarking the prisoners, but she hoped the strike had caught some of them inside, taking shelter from the whomper.

But just as with the dead Marine, she had to shove that aside in her thoughts. She had to focus on her goal and keep going.

Jumping over a covered drainage ditch, she heard the water rushing through. She didn't think this one led to the pipe that she and Rika had been using, but it was indicative that a lot of rain had fallen—a lot.

She bolted down the line of barracks. Something big passed overhead with a buzzing sound as the ground ten feet to her right and on was torn to bits. Nika dove to the ground, but the plane was already gone.

The Marines didn't have aircraft yet, which were with the rest of the regiment, so it had to be a Krackle craft. The combat Krackles in the area wouldn't let their prized prisoners escape without a fight.

She took a couple of deep breaths. She'd barely escaped with her life twice. If she got killed and Rika needed her . . .

She refused to consider the consequences. Bolting to her feet, she took off at a dead run. The sounds of combat surrounded her, but in the darkness and rain, she could almost ignore them. They were just background noise.

Nika reached the cafeteria and slowed down. The drainage web was in full force, and their pipe had to be full by now.

She made one more quick prayer and ran around the side of the cafeteria, deathly afraid of what she was going to find.

Chapter 38
Rika

The ground shook, jarring her, and Rika tried to claw her way back to consciousness. It was so hard, however, and it would be easier just to go back to sleep.

"Rika?" a voice called out, barely registering. "Rika? Are you OK?"

Rika ignored the question, hoping the voice would go away.

"Miss Rika?"

"Taylor, give her a little kick."

"I'm afraid to," a querulous voice said.

"Do it. You won't get in trouble. I promise."

That sounds like Tommy. Good boy, that one.

There was a nudge against her head, then a harder one.

"Stop!" she muttered.

"Miss Rika, what do we do?"

She wished Tommy would leave her alone. It was nice and warm in the bed. Well, not quite, she realized. Her front was cold, just a bit, but the cold seemed to be spreading. She tried to shift her position, but someone was on her head. When she tried to push whoever it was off of her, her hands first hit something hard, then something wet.

Wet?

Something wasn't right, and her mind tried to make some sense of what it could be.

She jerked her head up, banging it on the top of the pipe as her mind came back online. She was in the drainage pipe, and the zombie had wanded her.

"Tommy, where's the zombie?" she asked, her voice breaking as she tried to draw in her legs. One foot was numb, resisting her efforts.

"I think he left. He said some bad words."

"He said 'shit,'" Ghist said from ahead of her. "I heard him."

Water was running past her, a couple of inches deep. From the sound out in the catchment box, a whomper had hit. That meant the pipe would be full within moments as the web of drainage lines filled up with run-off.

"Don't worry about that," Rika said. "He's gone. We need to get out of here."

She hoped the zombie was gone, but regardless, they needed to get out, or they would drown. Rika had almost drowned before, and now flashbacks threatened to overwhelm her.

Use it, Rika! Channel the fear!

She grabbed Taylor's leg and started backing up.

"Tommy, get Mace out! Fast! Mei Li, and Ghist, follow Tommy!"

Taylor was screaming and kicking in fear, but Rika had a hand latched to his ankle and pulled him after her. She reached the catchment basin—water was coming in from a dozen smaller drainage pipes, rapidly filling it.

With a heave, she almost threw the boy out of the hole, spinning around as Mace and Tommy emerged. An explosion—*an explosion?*—momentarily lit the area, and she could see Mace's wide-eyed fear through the pelting rain. She didn't have time to calm the little boy down.

"Get out of the box," she yelled at Tommy, then bent over to look inside the smaller chamber and the pipe.

"Ghist, where are you?"

"Here," a sputtering voice said as the girl's butt appeared, water up to her thighs.

Rika reached for the girl, grabbing her ankle as well, and yanked her back. The girls screamed as she went flat to her stomach, the shriek cut off as her face went under the rising water.

Rika didn't have time for niceties. She pulled back into the catchment and stood, still holding Ghist's ankle, dangling her. Ghist was heavier than Taylor, too heavy for Rika to throw the girl out, so she lost a few precious seconds getting her to her feet, then boosting her out of the box.

"Mei Li!" she screamed, ducking back to the pipe, which was now half-full of quickly-flowing water.

When she'd been caught before, it had taken seconds for the water to fill the pipe, and once it had, the force had been too much for Rika to resist. The force had kept her from drowning, that and the short distance to the end, but was it already too much for a small girl?

"Mei Li!" she screamed again as she scrambled into the pipe. Already, the water was an implacable force, pushing on her, a wild animal trying to bend her to its will. She braced her knees wide against the walls of the pipe and crawled forward, hands questing in the dark for the girl.

The water rose, and Rika knew she was running out of time—for both Mei Li and herself. But she couldn't give up.

She craned her head up, grazing the top of the pipe so she could breathe, and her fingers brushed something. Instinctively, she closed her fingers and pulled back against the flow of the growing torrent.

Nika realized she had Mei Li's hair, but had the girl already drowned?

People can be brought back, she told herself, fearing the worst, but then two little hands closed tight on her wrist. Mei Li's head was under water, but she was alive.

For the moment.

The water threatened to take them both down the pipe, and part of Rika just wanted to surrender, but she had someone else depending on her now, and she had to fight. Rising on her knees, her back hit the top of the pipe. She pushed as hard as she could, bracing herself against the flow.

She tried to raise Mei Li higher, and she was rewarded with a gasp as the little girl took in a breath, but then she was forced under again.

Rika couldn't just stay in place, though. She had to move, or the water would become too forceful to resist. But if she released her brace, the water was already too strong for her.

She had to compromise. She pushed with all her might, scraping her back along the pipe. Once, twice, three times. Her legs hit the edge of the grate. She was almost there, but the water was now full force. With her knees against the open grate, she gave one last superhuman push, and she and Mei Li fell into the chamber.

Her brace gone, the water again tried to take control, but as it threatened to take them, she managed to get her feet out against the vertical edges of the grate frame. Legs spread, she stood against the flow, her body horizontal, her head above the water, and Mei Li dangling from her straining arm.

One small hand slipped from around her wrist, then the other. Rika knew she could let go of the child, and in the chamber, she could get free before it was filled, too. But Mei Li would be gone, drowned long before she could reach the end of the pipe.

If she's not gone already.

She forced that thought from her mind. She refused to let go even as her hand cramped.

"No!" she shrieked. "Never!"

She felt more than heard a splash behind her over the noise of the rain.

"Tommy, get out! It's too dangerous."

Arms wrapped around her, familiar arms, giving her just the support she needed. Water swirled around her as she was able to pull back, bringing Mei Li with her. All three popped out into the catchment basin. The water still tried to retain its hold over them, but in the larger basin, it wasn't as powerful.

They were able to fight the water's grip and manhandle the gasping little girl to Tommy, who pulled her free.

Exhausted, and trembling, Rika tried to climb out, but she fell back, her legs cramping. She inhaled water, and scrambled sputtering back to her feet. A hand reached down, which she eagerly took, and with a jump and a heave, she fell onto the grass, turned to her side, and coughed out water as the rain continued to pound her.

It took a moment before she was in control of herself, but she turned and looked into the face she knew as well as her own.

"Thanks, Baba. I think you might have just saved my life."

"You are *my* life, Baba," Nika said before hugging her tight.

Chapter 39
Nika

Nika held her twin tight, shaking at how close she'd come to losing her. She'd come around the cafeteria and saw four kids looking in the catchment, and she knew her sister was in there. Without hesitation, she bolted to the catchment and jumped into the waist-deep water to see Rika struggling. She didn't even see the little girl as she wrapped her twin in a death grip and helped pull her back.

She'd been running on adrenaline since the first Krackle ship appeared. Physically and emotionally, the fire was gone, and she was drained. She finally let go of her twin, then looked around at the five children. She recognized Mace, but none of the others.

The little girl they'd pulled out was softly coughing, snot running down her lip.

"What's your name?"

"Mei Li Tanner," the girl said, coughing again with the effort.

"Are you OK?"

"Yes, because Miss Rika saved me," she said with certainty.

"I could because you were strong, Mei Li," Rika said. "You never gave up. And you, Tommy, I couldn't have done it without you."

"You look just like Miss Rika," the other girl said.

"They're twins," Mace said. "They're my friends."

"Yes, we are, Mace," Rika said, reaching over to hug him.

Another explosion made the children jump, and Nika said, "We can't sit out here exposed like this. Let's get the kids out of the way."

"To where?" Rika asked.

The rain started slackening, and Nika looked down the slight slope to the fence line. She wanted to say "Over there," but even with the Krackle ship smashing part of it, she didn't know if the rest of it was still powered up and protected.

"In one of the barracks, if we can get inside. They're no-fire zones for the Marines."

"OK, kids. Did you hear that? Let's get out of the rain."

"Are the Krackles coming to take us away?" Tommy asked. "My mom said I've got to make sure me and Ghist get away from them."

"The Marines are here, and they're making sure the Krackles don't do that," Rika said.

"And our father's a Marine. He's out there," Nika added. "But we have to move now. Let's go."

Mei Li was still coughing, but the rest followed the twins in silence as they moved back to the rear wall of the cafeteria. Nika poked her head around the corner of the building. The rain was slowing, and she could see almost to the end of the quad now. Something flashed across it, a trail of flame, and the rattle of gunfire told her the battle was going full tilt.

"We can't go out there now," she told Rika. "Let's just stay here for the moment."

Right then, an air burst made them all duck, and shrapnel peppered the ground from just this side of the catchment all the way to the fence.

"Whoa," Tommy said. "That was close."

Whoa is right, Nika thought.

If they were still out there, they'd have been riddled.

Nika was overjoyed that the rescue had been kicked off, but she hadn't realized that she'd be in a battle, with all the danger that created. Thirty minutes ago, the thought of dying was sad, but almost acceptable. It was far from that now. With freedom so close, it would be beyond tragic to die now.

Except that it wasn't really close. The Marines were fighting, but that didn't mean they had things in hand. Another gull-winged Krackle fighter swept over the fence, guns chattering as it did its run. Nika didn't want to think of who might be on the receiving end of those guns.

Mace started crying, and that set off the other girl. Nika pulled them in tight, arms around their shoulders, their backs to the cafeteria wall. She felt extremely vulnerable sitting there and looked out at the forest on the other side of the fence.

"Do you think the fence's power is off?" she asked Rika.

"Power? I don't know. Why?"

"The first transport. The Marines shot it down, and it took out a bunch of fence with it. If they powered up the fence in a series, the whole thing might be down. We could climb it."

"With the, you know," Rika said, tilting her head to indicate the kids.

"I don't know what I was thinking," she said.

"I can climb it," Tommy said. "But Ghist can't, and I need to stay with her."

"Of course, you can. But you're right. You need to stay with your sister," Rika said.

They sat in silence, except for Mei Li's constant coughing. Nika knew she'd inhaled water, but there wasn't much she could do about it now. Every few minutes, Nika looked around the corner of the building. The battle seemed to have shifted farther toward the depot headquarters, but there was still fighting close by, too. Once, three Krackles crossed the commons in some sort of choreographed maneuver that looked more like a dance than a battle formation. Nika kept hoping to see them fall, but they made it intact and out of her sight.

The rain slowed to a stop. They were soaking wet and cold, but it was better than being pounded by the rain. At least that was what Nika thought when it let up. But with the increased visibility came more exposure, and she started longing for the rain to hide them again.

All seven of them startled when four Marines in full combat armor came pelting around the corner. One drew down on them, then yelled out on his shoulder mic, "You kids stay there. Don't move!" before they disappeared around the next building.

"We're still in this," Rika said.

Nika didn't know for how long. There had been just shy of 200 Marines left in Golf Company, and now that the Krackles had been reinforced, how long could they hold out?

She tried to remember how far the Navy was still out. Their drone ships would come in first, screaming in G's no human could stand, engaging the Krackle Navy. Then the manned ships would follow, to destroy what was left of the Krackle's space going ships, take control of Arcadian airspace, and land Marines. If they could hold out that long, then their chance of getting rescued would skyrocket. Nika couldn't remember the exact ETA, but she knew it was still hours away.

A huge explosion to their left and beyond the fence rocked the landscape, and a roiling black cloud reached up to the sky.

"I think that's the blocking force," Nika whispered to Rika.

"Is the cloud us or them?"

"I don't know."

They stared at is as it rose higher and higher.

"I'm hearing fewer and fewer M87s," Nika told her twin.

"You noticed, too."

The M87 was a kinetic slug-thrower, two to every four-person fire team. Over the last twenty minutes, they had slowly faded in frequency. That didn't bode well.

Nika reached around Mace and took Nika's hand. "If . . . you know . . . well, I'm glad we're together."

"Me, too," Rika said, squeezing her hand. "We came into the universe together, and we'll go--"

"Don't say it, Baba."

"Go out together," Tommy finished for her.

"Go *outside* together, right Ghist?" Rika asked.

"We are outside, Miss Rika."

"Oh, so we are. You're right."

Tommy frowned, but then it dawned on him that the little ones shouldn't have to worry. "Yes, go *outside* together. That's what I meant."

Nika gave him a nod, and he smiled.

"Here come more Krackles," Rika said in a deflated voice.

Nika turned. To the south, the sky was filled with fighters swooping in, a dozen, maybe more. The entire region must have scrambled to save their precious cargo of human slaves.

"Do we try the pipe?" she asked.

"Still full of water," Rika said.

Nika got to her feet. She wanted to face them. There was no way any surviving Marines could stand up to this next wave. They'd put up a gallant fight, but their chance of success had always been low, no matter how much hope she had put in them. In her father.

As the fighters screeched in, they started to spread out, firing big blasts from a cannon of sorts toward the depot.

"That's a little odd. Why would they . . . oh my God!"

"They're Falcons!" the twins shouted in unison, jumping up and down as the Navy landing craft got closer.

Two of the children started crying, but Tommy stood beside Nika and asked, "Are they Marines?"

"They're full of Marines, Tommy!"

A Krackle fighter rose to meet the incoming shuttles, firing a brace of missiles. Most were pushed aside by the landing crafts' robust shielding, but one made its way through, and the Navy craft lurched to the side, trailing smoke.

Nika gave a quick prayer that it would manage to land safely.

A moment later, the fighter erupted into a ball of flame, and the twins madly cheered, oblivious to the fact that the depot was still held by Krackles. They couldn't help it.

"But, how . . . I mean who are they? Not the fleet? It's too early," Rika asked.

"The regiment. They were hiding out, waiting to land. They must have started the moment the rescue was launched."

Wave after wave of the landing craft, each carrying up to a dozen Marines or a single AAV, an armored assault vehicle. Not a full tank, but a pretty malicious piece of weaponry.

The incoming waves would be the lead force, clearing the way for the shuttles to come in behind. Nika couldn't see the big shuttles yet, but she knew they were on their way.

Fire erupted from the depot, reaching for the landing craft, but they were robust vehicles, and they could take a pounding.

"Now's our chance," Rika said.

Nika was cheering the fight, but her twin was right. Now that the Krackles were focused on the landing craft, they could get inside. If the fight was going into overdrive now, then they needed to get some cover.

"Everybody up," she said, picking up the little ones and setting them on their feet.

"Which one?" Nika asked.

Rika looked across to the next barracks. It was only 20 yards away, but that was still a consideration.

"Right here. The cafeteria."

The twins hustled the five children, hugging the side wall, to the front of the cafeteria. Ahead of them, not fifty yards away, two Krackles were working some sort of field gun near the body of a dead Marine, but they paid the seven no attention as they ran to the entrance.

For a moment, Nika was afraid that the door would be locked, but it opened, and they ran inside before slamming the door behind them.

"Now what?" Nika asked, her chest heaving with each breath.

Rika looked around, then pointed to the back and the reconstituters, the military commercial versions of the same ones they'd used at the Shrimp 'N Chic just two days ago. They were big and sturdy, and between them and the serving line, would offer them some protection.

"Are we going to eat? I'm hungry," Taylor asked.

"Not just yet, honey. But soon," Nika told him.

They sat the kids on the floor, spacing them where they'd have the most protection. Mei Li's coughing was worse, a rough, hacking cough. Nika knew she needed medical treatment, but that would have to wait.

"Now what?" she asked Rika.

"Now we wait," her twin said to the increased sounds of fighting outside.

Chapter 40
Rika

"Can we eat yet?" Taylor asked.

"Not yet, honey. Just be patient," Nika said.

"But I'm hungry now."

"So am I," Ghist chimed in.

"I know. But we have to wait."

The barracks were empty, and the cafeteria hadn't been stocked in a long time. There was no food inside, so there was nothing Rika could do about getting the little ones some food.

She'd used her father's Kri-Blade to pry open some cupboards, hoping to find some "forever chow," the Marines' term for the emergency rations stored with each unit but had come up empty.

"What time do you think it is?" she asked Nika.

"Maybe noon? I don't know."

The battle outside had been raging for at least an hour. She'd been overjoyed to see the Marines come in, thinking the fight would be over soon, but evidently, the Krackles had a different take on that. They weren't meekly giving up.

She knew that things could still fall apart. Best case was that it would be five or six hours before the Navy arrived in-system, longer for the new Marines to land.

For them to survive, the 109th Marine Regiment had to secure the depot until then. If they fell, it would all be over.

She glanced over at Mace, head in Nika's lap, fast asleep. She envied the little guy, to be able to slip off in the middle of a fight for their lives while she worried about every possible outcome. It was going to drive her crazy.

Her foot where she'd been wanded was still numb. She hoped there wasn't permanent damage to it. She still wondered why the zombie had given up. Tommy and the rest weren't much good at giving her details. Maybe the boy had just been able to drag her far enough that the zombie couldn't reach her and had just left.

She stretched the foot out, hoping to get some more feeling, and in doing so, kicked the glass bits. Shortly after arriving, the front windows had been blown out in an explosion, sending the bits of glass flying. If they hadn't been protected by the heavy kitchen equipment, it could have gotten ugly.

As she massaged her foot, a faint rattle caught her attention.

"I'm still—" Taylor started before Nika slapped a hand over his mouth, cutting him off.

She'd heard it, too.

The door creaked open. Rika gripped the Kri-Blade, all her senses on alert.

"Is it safe?" a voice asked, almost too quiet to hear.

"Looks it. Something blew out the windows, though," a low, gravelly voice said.

"Who knows which side did it."

"Doesn't matter. All I know is we need to hide out and hope for the best," a third voice said, a woman's.

Rika looked at Nika, but her sister, her hand still on Taylor's mouth, shrugged. With their backs to the dining line, they didn't have eyes on the front part of the cafeteria.

"Let's move to the back and wait, the first voice said in a loud whisper.

"And if damned Marines win? What then?" the woman asked.

Rika's eyes went wide, and she gripped the handle of the knife harder.

"No different than if it Masters win. We're on their side, whoever it is," the second man's voice answered.

"Master or Marines. We're screwed," the woman said bitterly.

Rika could hear the crunch, crunch, crunch, of feet walking on broken glass as they got closer. She shifted her weight and rose to a crouch, keeping her head below the top of the serving line.

"Too bad there's no real food here," the first voice said, a little louder and sounding slightly familiar.

Mei Li took that moment to cough again.

"Who's there?" one of them asked as Rika sprang to her feet, brandishing their father's knife.

"Stay the hell back," she yelled into the surprised faces of three zombies.

"Shit!" the woman shouted, jumping back.

"Rika?" one of them asked, and Rika recognized her stalker.

"They're just kids," the older man said, his shoulders relaxing just a bit, even if his eyes were locked on the knife in Rika's hand.

"Ben? Is that you?" Nika asked, coming to her feet.

Ben's eyes widened as he took the two of them in.

"Uh . . ."

"All of you, stay back," Rika yelled again, trying to snarl.

She didn't care if their stalker was there or the President of the Privy Council. They were not getting close to the kids.

"Or you'll what, fresh meat?" the woman asked with an evil grin.

"I'll cut you like the freaking piece of crap you are."

"Pretty big words for such a small package," the woman said, turning to come around the serving line.

Rika rushed to meet her, but her stalker grabbed the woman by the arm and jerked her to a halt.

"Stop it, Alla. You asked what happens if the Marines win. You think they're going to be sympathetic if there're a bunch of dead kids here?"

"You better not!" Tommy said, coming to stand by Rika.

"Get back," she hissed, giving the brave boy's chest a slight push while keeping her eyes locked on the zombie.

"Who's saying anything about dead kids? The Masters don't want dead'uns, either. I'm just going take that damned blade from her, remind her who she is."

"Are you an idiot, Alla?" the older man asked.

"Look," he said, turning to face Rika and the rest. "We don't want any trouble. How about we go and sit back here, and you just sit there while we wait."

"Wait for what?" Nika said.

"To see who wins this mess. Who comes out on top."

Nika looked to the stalker, who had not released the woman's arm yet. "Ben?"

The woman twisted to look at the stalker, then laughed. "Oh, my good god, Ben. Is this your breeder? Out of all the fresh meat in this place?

"She's not my breeder," the stalker fumed. "Stop saying that."

She turned back to the twins, then said, "Which one is it? Or you trying to double your pleasure."

"Shut up!" the stalker shouted.

"Both of you, shut up," the older man yelled before turning back to Rika.

"How about it? We'll just quietly sit over here. If the Masters win, we can help. You two want to be together, right? We can make it happen. And if the Marines win, you can tell them we didn't hurt you."

"God, Lyle. You think that's gonna make any difference? You know the penalty for becoming a servant. It's death."

"If you hurt them, it sure will be."

"OK, OK. You win."

She shook her arm free from the stalker and smiled at Rika. It didn't look authentic.

Rika looked back at Nika, who nodded.

"OK. You go sit over there on that wall. But if any of you moves, so help me, I'll cut you."

The woman stroked the wand at her belt but said nothing.

"And I'm not your breeder," she hissed at her stalker.

At least he had the decency to look embarrassed.

Rika watched them until they sat on the ground. The older man held up his hand in supplication and smiled.

Rika stepped over to Nika and asked, "Can we trust them?"

"Probably not. Ben, maybe. Not the woman."

"Ben? The stalker? We can't trust him."

"I told you, he saved me before, after the first switch. And he gave me the target info that Dad needed."

Rika scowled. "You be his breeder then, if you're so up on him."

"Well, what are you going to do? Take all three with Dad's knife? We don't have much of a choice. Besides, you heard the man, if it's the Krackles."

"Don't even think that."

"I don't want to think of being separated from you again. That's what I don't want to think of."

Rika wasn't happy, but her twin was right. She couldn't take on three zombies, armed with wands. She wasn't going to let them out of her sight, though. If they came after them, she vowed to take out at least one, starting with the woman.

Tensions were high the next hour. No one moved. The older man tried smiling for the first thirty minutes but gave up. The woman smiled too, but it was not a friendly smile.

The ebb and flow of battle was hard to decipher. After almost 45 minutes, a series of heavy explosions rocked the depot, knocking the remaining bits of window out of the frames.

Even the woman lost her sardonic smile after that.

Tommy got up and came to Rika, bending over to whisper in her ear. "Are those zombies going to take us away?"

"Not on my life, little man. Not on my life."

"Thanks, Miss Rika."

He leaned in and kissed her cheek before going back to his place.

A tear formed and slid down her face, to her embarrassment. She quickly wiped it away.

"It's quiet," Nika said.

Rika listened. Her twin was right. The sounds of combat had died off.

"I guess we find out now, huh?" the woman shouted from the far wall.

Five minutes passed. Ten. Twenty. Rika could hear the occasional faint sound, but nothing that gave her a clue as to what had happened. It took a force of will to suppress a tremendous urge to go to the door and look out.

Thirty minutes after the sounds died away, Rika heard movement in front of the cafeteria. Sounds of heavy tread. Like Krackles. Or combat Marines.

The others heard it, too. Slowly, like defendants in court ready to hear the verdict, everyone rose.

Rika wanted to shout out, she was so wound up. All of this, all of their efforts, was it for naught?

The door flew open with a kick, and an armored Marine, weapon raised, ran in and darted to their right, a second one on their butt and darted to their left.

"Freeze, Regency Marines," he yelled through his shoulder speaker.

"I've got kids . . . and zombies!"

The woman stepped forward, arms out as she said, "We're prisoners of—"

The blast hit in her the chest, dropping her in her tracks. The stalker raised his hands, and the older man dove to the ground as the second blast missed him, punching a hole into the wall behind him.

A streak ran past Rika, shouting, "No, no! Cease fire, cease fire. My Dad's Colonel Franklin Ingersoll."

She reached the stalker and threw herself in front of him, turning to face the Marines, hands in the air.

"Do not fire!"

The Marine hesitated as two more ran through the door. "Corporal, what do I do?" he asked, not on the fire team circuit, but still on the speaker. His M87 was locked on the stalker . . . and Nika.

"Are you really the colonel's daughter?" the corporal asked.

"Nika Ingersoll. And that's Rika over there."

"Thank God. The colonel's going to want to hear this. But Miss Ingersoll, you need to step away from that zombie."

"I won't. You're not to hurt him."

"We've got our orders. Until everyone is recovered, we, uh, take out all the traitor scum we find."

"This zombie gave us vital information for the rescue operation. Without him, who knows how many would have died."

"Baba, let it go," Rika said. A wrong twitch by someone, and her twin was collateral damage.

"Oh, crap. Why is it always us? Wait one."

They all stood staring at each other. The Marine's M87 looked huge, and the muzzle was not wavering.

It probably took only twenty seconds, but it seemed like an hour, before the corporal said, "Stand down, Grabowski. Secure the zombies and bring out the kids."

Rika let out a huge sigh of relief.

The Marines clumped forward in their armor. "Stand aside, ma'am," Grabowski said as he pulled out a white tie-tie.

"Arms!" he shouted at the stalker, who looked nervously at Nika before he stuck them out. The tie-ties automatically wrapped around his wrists.

"You, up!" he said to the older man, who was still on the floor.

The man carefully stood, making no sudden moves. He stepped over the dead woman and held out his hands. Five seconds later, he was secured as well.

"You gave them vital information?" he asked the stalker.

"I'm sorry. I didn't mean to."

"Well, thank God you did, son."

"Come with me," the Marine ordered the two zombies.

Rika watched them march off across the cafeteria as her twin came up behind her and took her hand.

"What now? I mean, what's going on? Are we winning?" she asked the corporal.

"Winning? We won, ma'am. The Krackles started withdrawing half-an-hour ago. They're running, trying to get away before the Navy gets here. Not many will, I'm betting."

"We won?" Nika and Rika asked in unison.

"Yes, we won. You're safe now."

Epilogue

Four months later . . .

"Franklin Ingersoll, did you mess up my kitchen drawers?" the twin's mother asked, coming out into the living room holding a whisk and looking ready to kill.

"I didn't mess anything up. I just made things more practical. We call it "Efficiency Engineering" in the Corps. With the large utensils on the top left, you only have to move your hand—"

"I don't care what you called it in the Corps, I call it messing up my kitchen."

"But if you just try it—"

"I don't want to try it! I've been running our home for nineteen years, and things are the way I like it. You don't get to come in here and change things now."

The twins looked at each other. Nika's single raised eyebrow was all the communication they needed.

Colonel Franklin Ingersoll, Regency Marine Corps, (Retired), looked like a scolded five-year-old.

Their mother saw it too. She softened and said, "I know you're trying, honey. But really, I've got things the way I like them. If you want to change something, ask me first."

"It'll get better, son. She needs to adjust, too," Grandma Dellie said from her overstuffed easy chair.

There had been many changes since the invasion, and this was one of the best, as far as the twins were concerned. With the shock of almost losing their family, their parents had invited the old woman to leave St. Regis and come live with them. To everyone's surprise, she had agreed.

"Happy wife, happy life, you know," she added.

Both twins rolled their eyes at that. They loved their grandmother, but she had a rather old-fashioned outlook on life and relationships.

"I think I'll go fishing," their father grumbled, walking over to grab the small rod he kept in the front door closet.

As far as the twins knew, he'd never caught anything in Morales Creek, but that didn't stop him from spending hours, sometimes, trying. Or not really trying, they realized. He just needed space.

The aftermath of the invasion and rescue had been confusing to the twins. The rescue itself had been trumpeted by the Regency as a success. In many ways, it was. Over 900 civilians had died in the initial invasion, but of the prisoners at the depot, none had been taken off-planet. One-hundred-and-nine prisoners had died in the fight at the depot with twenty-three missing, and one-hundred-sixty-four of the one-hundred-fourteen Marines and Navy corpsmen in Golf Company had been killed, but over twenty-thousand people had been saved.

It hadn't gone as well at the other locations. Over four-hundred had died at Riesetown, and on the mainland, several thousand people had been taken as slaves while the Krackles fled.

The press had lauded their father as a hero, but that feeling was not shared by some of the brass. The twins didn't know all the details, but it had to do with his decisions and timing.

With the first Krackle transports coming in to Storyville, it was up to him as the local commander to kick off the entire rescue operation. Across the planet, each other mission had to wait for him. And he delayed it, waiting for the whomper to hit the depot to give the Golf Company Marines better cover. It made tactical sense, but the argument was that it handicapped some of the other missions.

Rika had been incensed when she heard that and had told him that, but he shushed her, saying they were right. He'd let his concern for those at the depot take precedence in his decisions.

Nika wasn't so sure he was right. Maybe he did by his own way of thinking, but all across Arcadia, human prisoners had been outside, waiting to be taken off the planet. So, even if he was focused on the depot, it made no difference to the end results.

Then there was the fact that he was down on the ground with Golf Company, instead of where he could command the entire regiment. The twins had snuck a look at the official letter of censure, and the phrase "ceded command of the regiment to his acting executive officer" was the kiss of death.

With the letter, his chance at a general's star had vanished. But that wasn't why he'd retired. He'd lost too many Marines in the regiment, written too many letters to grieving families. A person could only take so much of that over a career, and he'd reached his tipping point.

But there was another reason, more important to him, that he'd told his wife and twins. He'd come close to losing them, and all he could think of during the operation was all the time he'd lost with them while he was deployed away from them. All those birthdays, holidays, skinned knees, ball games, family dinners. Those were lost forever.

It was time for him to leave the Corps and become a father.

His retirement ceremony had been three weeks ago. He'd received a medal for the rescue, a certificate of appreciation for twenty-eight years of service, and was shown the door. Since then, he'd been home and underfoot, interspaced with visits by his old Marines showing up to pay their respects.

It was obvious he didn't know how to fit in yet, but he was trying. "Fishing" had become his way of stepping back and catching his breath.

Nika caught him before he opened the door and gave him a hug. "Love you."

The scowl left his face for a moment, and he replied, "Love you, too . . ."

"Nika," she reminded him with a tender smile. He still couldn't tell them apart.

"Nika. Love you, too."

He opened the door where Fel stood surprised, hand upraised to knock.

"Fel!" he said, a smile coming across his face. He raised the rod and gave it a little shake. "Want to come with me and catch that trout I know is in the creek?"

Fel looked past their father to catch Rika's eye. "Uh, sorry, sir. I'd love to, but I came to see Rika . . . and Nika before we go to the party. Can I get a rain check?"

"Sure, Fel. But it better be quick. When do you report in?"

"Right after the new year, sir. On the ninth. I'll come see you before then."

"You'd better, son," their father said before he sauntered off.

"The son he never had," Rika said with a laugh.

"It's not like that," Fel protested.

"We know," Nika said. "Your girlfriend is just giving you some grief."

"We're not dating!" Rika and Fel said unison.

"You could have fooled me," Grandma Dellie said from her chair.

Hero heard Fel's voice, and he jumped from his bed, his front paws scrabbling over the tile floor, pulling his paralyzed back legs in their doggie harness as he rushed to him. The vets had done all they could for the dog, but his hind end would never move on its own again. He didn't seem to mind, however, and he was now adept at maneuvering his wheeled harness.

Fel knelt while Hero tried to lick away his hands. "How you're doing, boy?" he asked. "The girls treating you right?"

Rika looked fondly at the big young man. She'd never really cared much for him, but she'd seen another side of him during the invasion. His care for Hero had been touching, and he was smarter than she'd realized. They weren't really dating per se, despite Nika's teasing to the contrary, but yes, they'd gone out a few times, and she enjoyed spending time with him.

She didn't know how far it would go. Fel was off to Marine boot camp after the first, and that didn't synch with her plans, but no one ever knew what the universe had in store for them.

"Thanks for spending time with Dad," Nika said.

"I respect him. And he's helping me prepare for boot camp."

It was more than that, both twins knew. Fel had rejected his own father, and in some ways, the very concept of fatherhood. The colonel now gave him another example of what being a man meant, an example he could embrace. The two of them had spent quite a bit of time together since the invasion, something about which the twins wholeheartedly approved.

"You ready for the party? The last gasp of the Young Guns, huh?" Fel asked them.

The Young Guns had already died. Calder had left the planet in the aftermath of the invasion to go live with relatives on Broadmore. Lonnie and Nick were married and moved to Riesetown. Mark was still under PTSD therapy and was avoiding them. Hiyori was one of the 24 missing from the depot. She'd been spotted at the depot, but there had been no sign of her after the rescue. It was as if she'd vanished.

The twins wondered if she'd been taken by the Krackles, but the official version was that no humans from Yaakov were now Krackle slaves. They knew she could have been caught in one of the major explosions, but they still wondered.

For the rest? There just didn't seem the time. Even the twins, who'd been so keen on keeping all of them together, had given up. They'd left their childhood back at the pool on Morales Creek four months ago.

But now, most of those left had agreed to a small New Years Eve party at the Wild Goose in town. One last hurrah before officially retiring the group.

"So, have you two decided?" Fel asked with a forced air of nonchalance.

The twins looked at each other before Rika said, "We're accepting the appointments."

The twins had initially been minor celebrities after the invasion, each even getting a certificate of appreciation from the governor. But slowly, their part in the rescue was making the rounds, and a week ago, they'd received the president's appointment into the highly competitive Regency Military Academy back on Laramie. Usually, candidates had to undergo multiple interviews and suffer countless tests, but there they were, tickets for their future.

As military brats, the twins had never considered joining the service, this was a little difficult to pass up. Still, they waited for six days before telling their parents, concerned how their father might take it given recent events.

To their surprise, he'd cried—tears of pride. Still, it had taken them until the night before to decide on quitting the uni and accepting the appointments.

"Oh. Well, good for you," Fel said in a neutral voice, leaving more unsaid, however.

Rika knew what he was thinking. With him in boot camp and then off to his first duty station, and the twins accepting the Academy appointments, it might be hard to meet for a long while. But as she'd already known, them as a thing didn't really synch with her immediate plans.

"We're dropping out of Aster Poly this semester. No use paying for classes that we're going to get for free at the Academy," Nika said. "Maybe Rika, I mean, maybe we can come see you graduate from boot camp."

He perked up and said, "Really? That would be great!"

"Dad, too. I think he'd want to come," Rika said.

"I would hope so,' Fel said, rising from Hero, who still wanting attention, scooted closer to his leg.

His eyes fell on the frame on the wall, and he gave a puzzled frown. "I thought you were going to get that knife fixed?"

The Kri-Blade was back in its place, but no longer as shiny, and with several nicks on the cutting edge.

"We were going to do it for Dad's birthday, but he said no. He said those nicks are battle-earned and should never come off," Rika said, beaming with pride.

Fel stepped closer to examine it, Hero following. "Yeah, I think I understand him. It means more this way." Whatever else he was going to say was interrupted when his wristcomp went off, and he gave it a look.

"Gren's got the Dart warmed up, and Lemul's with her. You ready to hit it?" he asked.

"You go-ahead. We'll meet you," Rika said.

Fel looked unsure. "But you're coming, right? You have to be there."

"Don't worry, Fel. We'll be there. We can't miss the last blast of the great Young Guns Pack."

"OK, but don't take too long. We've got a table reserved at four. Hard to get on New Years Eve, you know."

"Don't worry," Rika said, almost pushing him out the door.

"OK, why didn't you go with them?" Nika asked after the door closed behind him.

"You have to ask? You're Gemini Twins. Of course, she's going with you," Grandma Dellie said.

The twins loved having her in the home, but they kept forgetting she was there, listening in.

Nika pulled Rika around so they were face-to-face. "But you don't approve."

"No, I don't."

Nika had a stop to make before going to the party. It was New Year's Eve, and Ben was still in jail, awaiting a decision from the regency as to his fate. She wanted to let him know he wasn't forgotten.

No one in the family approved of her seeing him. To them, and everyone else, he was a traitor to humankind, alive only because Nika had forestalled the executioner's axe.

Nika had let everyone assume that Ben had volunteered the information she'd gotten from him, not that she'd tricked him. She felt a little guilty for that, but she owed Ben. No matter how you looked at it, stepping in and claiming her had saved her life, probably Gren's as well.

He could never really claim her, but he could claim a personal debt, one she was happy to pay by saving him. And now, it was just being human, to have compassion for someone in distress. A quick visit, wishing a Happy New Year.

"If you don't approve, then why?"

"Because you approve, Baba."

"And?"

"Grandma's right, Baba. We're the Gemini Twins. Whether we each approve or disapprove doesn't matter. We started this life together, and that's not changing."

Tears came to Nika's eyes, and Rika tenderly wiped them away with her hand.

"We're Gemini Twins, now and forever. Now, say goodbye to Hero, and let's go see this zombie of yours."

Nika laughed, gave Hero a pat on the head, and took Rika's hand in hers.

"I don't know what the next four years will bring, but I don't care as long as you're with me.

Together, they stepped through the door, hand-in-hand, to face the new year and their future.

Thank you for reading *Gemini Twins*. I hope you enjoyed it. If you liked it, please feel free to leave a review of the book from wherever you bought it.

If you would like updates on new books releases, news, or special offers, please consider signing up for my mailing list. Your email will not be sold, rented, or in any other way disseminated. If you are interested, please sign up at the link below:

http://eepurl.com/bnFSHH

Other Books by Jonathan Brazee

Women of the United Federation Marines
Gladiator
Sniper
Corpsman

High Value Target (A Gracie Medicine Crow Short Story)
BOLO Mission (A Gracie Medicine Crow Short Story)
Weaponized Math (A Gracie Medicine Crow Novelette, Published in
The Expanding Universe 3, a 2017 Nebula Award Finalist)

The United Federation Marine Corps
Recruit
Sergeant
Lieutenant
Captain
Major
Lieutenant Colonel
Colonel
Commandant

Rebel (Set in the UFMC universe.)
Behind Enemy Lines (A UFMC Prequel)
The Accidental War (A Ryck Lysander Short Story Published in
BOB's Bar: Tales from the Multiverse)

The United Federation Marine Corps' Lysander Twins

Legacy Marines
Esther's Story: Recon Marine
Noah's Story: Marine Tanker
Esther's Story: Special Duty
Blood United

Coda

The Navy of Humankind: Wasp Squadron

Fire Ant (2018 Nebula Award Finalist)
Crystals
Ace
Fortitude

Ghost Marines

Integration (2018 Dragon Award Finalist)
Unification
Fusion

Call to Arms: Capernica

Conscientious Objector
POG
Veteran

The Return of the Marines Trilogy

The Few
The Proud
The Marines

The Al Anbar Chronicles: First Marine Expeditionary Force—Iraq

Prisoner of Fallujah
Combat Corpsman
Sniper

Werewolf of Marines

Werewolf of Marines: Semper Lycanus
Werewolf of Marines: Patria Lycanus
Werewolf of Marines: Pax Lycanus

To the Shores of Tripoli

Wererat

Darwin's Quest: The Search for the Ultimate Survivor

Venus: A Paleolithic Short Story

Duty

Semper Fidelis

Checkmate (Originally Published in The Expanding Universe 4)

The BOHICA Warriors
(with Michael Anderle and C. J. Fawcett)
Reprobates
Degenerates
Redeemables
Thor

SEEDS OF WAR
(With Lawrence Schoen)
Invasion
Scorched Earth
Bitter Harvest

Non-Fiction

Exercise for a Longer Life

The Effects of Environmental Activism on the Yellowfin Tuna Industry

Author Website
http://www.jonathanbrazee.com